THE YEAR WE FELL DOWN

by Sarina Bowen

Published by Rennie Road Books

Cover image: ollyy / Shutterstock

Cover design by Tina Anderson

Copyediting by Nancy Smay

ISBN 978-0-9910680-0-5

http://www.SarinaBowen.com

The Year We Fell Down is a work of fiction. Names, places, and incidents are either products of the author's imagination, or used fictitiously.

Chapter One: *Gargoyles and Barbecue*

"Hope" is the thing with feathers —
That perches in the soul —
And sings the tune without the words —
And never stops — at all —
EMILY DICKINSON

— Corey

"This looks promising," my mother said, eyeing the dormitory's ivy-covered facade. I could hear the anticipation in her voice. "Try your key card, Corey."

It was move-in day at Harkness College, and parents of the new frosh were oohing and ahhing all around campus. As the official tour guides will tell you, three of the last six presidents held at least one degree from the 300-year-old college. And twice a day, students from the Carillon Guild climb 144 steps into Beaumont Tower to serenade the campus on bells weighing upwards of a ton each.

Unfortunately, my mother's interest in the dorm was neither historical nor architectural. It was the wheelchair ramp that captivated her.

I rolled up to wave my shiny new Harkness ID in front of the card reader. Then I pushed the blue button with the wheelchair on it. I held my breath until the pretty arched door began to swing slowly open.

After everything I'd been through in the past year, it was hard to believe that this was really happening for me. I was in.

Wheeling up the ramp and into the narrow building, I counted two dorm rooms, one on my left and one on my right. Both had wide doors — the telltale sign of a handicapped-accessible room. Straight ahead, there was a stairway with a pretty oaken banister. Like most of the old dorms at Harkness University, the building had no elevator. I wouldn't be visiting any of the upstairs rooms in my chair.

"The floor is *very* level," my mother observed, approvingly. "When they told us the building was eighty years old, I had my doubts."

That was putting it mildly.

The fact that my parents had begged me not to come to Harkness was just the latest bitter irony in a long string of bitter ironies. While other new Harkness parents were practically throwing confetti for their offspring today, mine were having two heart attacks apiece, because their baby girl had chosen a college a thousand miles from home, where they couldn't check up on her every half hour.

Thank goodness.

After the accident, my parents had pleaded with me to defer for a year. But who could take another year of hovering, with nothing better to fill the time than extra physical therapy sessions? When I'd put my proverbial foot down about heading off to college, my parents had changed tactics. They tried to convince me to stay in Wisconsin. I'd been subjected to a number of anxious lectures entitled "Why Connecticut?" And "You Don't Have to Prove Anything."

But I wanted this. I wanted the chance to attend the same elite school that my brother had. I wanted the independence, I wanted a change in scenery, and I *really* wanted to get the taste of last year out of my mouth.

The door on my left opened suddenly, and a pretty girl with dark curly hair stuck her head out. "Corey!" she beamed. "I'm Dana!"

When my rooming assignment had arrived in our Wisconsin mailbox, I wasn't sure what to expect from Dana. But during the past month we'd traded several emails. She was originally from California, but went to high school in Tokyo, where her father was a businessman. I'd already filled her in on my physical quirks. I'd explained that I couldn't feel my right foot, or any of my left leg. I'd warned her that I was in a wheelchair most of the time. Although, with a set of cumbersome leg braces and forearm crutches, I sometimes did a very poor imitation of walking.

And I'd already apologized for her odd rooming assignment — living with the cripple in a different dorm than the rest of the First Years. When Dana had quickly replied that she didn't mind, a little specter of hope had alighted on my shoulder. And this feathered, winged thing had been buzzing around for weeks, whispering encouragements in my ear.

Now, facing her in the flesh for the first time, my little hope fairy did a cartwheel on my shoulder. I spread my arms, indicating the chair. "How ever did you recognize me?"

Her eyes sparkled, and then she said exactly the right thing. "Facebook. Duh!" She swung the door wide open, and I rolled inside.

"Our room is fabulous," Dana said for the third time. "We have at least twice as much space as everyone else. This will be great for parties."

It was good to know that Dana was a beer-keg-is-half-full kind of roommate.

And in truth, ours was a beautiful room. The door opened into what Harkness students called a "common room," but the rest of the world would call a living room. Off the common room were two separate bedrooms, each one large enough to turn a wheelchair around in. For furnishings, we each had a desk and — this was surprising — a double bed.

"I brought twin sheets," I said, puzzled.

"So did I," Dana laughed. "Maybe accessible rooms have double beds? We'll just have to go shopping. Oh, the hardship!" Her eyes twinkled.

My mom, huffing under the weight of one of my suitcases, came into the room. "Shopping for what?"

"Sheets," I said. "We have double beds."

She clapped her hands together. "We'll drive you girls to Target before we leave."

I would have rather gotten rid of my parents, but Dana took her up on it.

"First, let me have a look around," my mother said. "Maybe there are other things you need." She traipsed into our private bathroom. It was amply proportioned, with a handicapped accessible shower. "This is perfect," she said. "Let's put a few of your things away, and make sure you have somewhere to dry your catheters."

"*Mother*," I hissed. I really did not want to discuss my freakish rituals in front of my roommate.

"If we're going to Target," Dana said from the common room, "we should look at the rugs. It echoes in here."

My mother hurried out of the bathroom to humiliate me further. "Oh, Corey can't have an area rug while she's still working on walking. She could trip. But where do you girls want Hank to install the television?" my mom asked, turning about.

I jumped on the change of topic. "My father is hooking us up with a flat-screen, and a cable subscription," I said to Dana. "If that's okay with you. Not everybody wants a TV."

Dana put a thoughtful hand to her chin. "I'm not much of a TV watcher myself..." Her eyes flashed. "But there may be um, certain sorts of people who will want to gather in our room, say, when sporting events are on?"

My mother laughed. "What sort of people?"

"Well, have you met our neighbor yet? He's a junior." My new roommate's eyes darted towards the hallway.

"Across the hall?" I asked. "In the other accessible room?" It wasn't the first place I'd look for a hot guy.

She nodded. "You'll see. Just wait."

Our shopping trip took far longer than I'd hoped. My mother insisted on paying for Dana's new bedding, with the argument that the peculiar accessible beds were all our fault. Dana chose a comforter with a giant red flower on it. I chose polka dots.

"Very cheery," my mother said approvingly. My mom had always liked the cheery look. But after the year we'd just had, she clung to cheery like a life raft. "Let's get the matching shams, ladies. And..." she went into the next aisle. "An extra pillow for each of you. Those beds won't look right otherwise."

"She doesn't have to do this," Dana whispered.

"Just go with it," I said. "Wait..." I beckoned, and Dana leaned down so I could add something privately. "Take a peek at the rugs. If you see anything good, we'll come back another time."

She frowned at me. "But I thought..."

I gave her an eye roll. "She's insane."

With a wink, Dana ducked into the rug aisle.

When we got back, my father was standing in the center of our empty room, flipping channels on the TV he'd mounted on our wall. "Success!" he called out.

"Thanks, Dad."

His smile was tired. "No problem."

As irritating as I'd found my mother this past year, things were even trickier with my father. He and I used to talk about ice hockey all day long. It was our shared passion, as well as his livelihood. But now an uncomfortable silence hung between us. The fact that I couldn't skate anymore just killed him. He'd aged about ten years since my accident. I hoped that with me out of the house, he would be able to get back into his groove.

It was time to ease my parents into hallway, and send them on their way. "Guys? There's a barbecue for First Years on the lawn. And Dana and I are going to it. *Soon.*"

My mother wrung her hands. "Hold up. I forgot to install your night-light." She darted into my bedroom, while I bit back an angry complaint. Seriously? I hadn't had a night-light since I was seven. And when my brother went off to Harkness four years ago, there wasn't any handholding for him. Damien got only a plane ticket and a clap on the shoulder.

"She can't help herself," my father said, reading my face. He picked his tool kit up off the floor and made his way toward the door.

"I'm going to be fine, you know," I said, wheeling after him.

"I know you are, Corey." He put one hand on my head, and then took it away again.

"Hey, Dad? I hope you have a great season."

His eyes looked heavy. "Thanks, honey." Under other circumstances, he'd be wishing the same for me. He would have inspected my safety pads, and we would have found a corner of the room to accommodate my hockey bag. He would have booked plane tickets to come out and watch one of my games.

But none of that was going to happen.

Instead, we went into the hallway together in silence. But there, my reverie was broken by the sight of a guy hanging up a white board on the wall outside of his door. My first glimpse was of a very tight backside and muscled arms. He was attempting to tap a nail into the wall without letting his crutches fall to the ground. "Damn," he said under his breath as one of them toppled anyway.

And when he turned around, it was as if the sun had come out after a rainy day.

For starters, his face was movie-star handsome, with sparkling brown eyes and thick lashes. His wavy brown hair was a bit unkempt, as if he'd just run his fingers through it. He was tall and strong-looking, but not beefy, exactly. It wasn't a linebacker's body, but he was definitely an athlete.

Definitely.

Wow.

"Hi there," he said, revealing a dimple.

Well hello, hottie, my brain answered. Unfortunately, my mouth said nothing. And after a beat I realized I was staring at his beautiful mouth, frozen like Bambi in the forest. "Hi," I squeaked, with great effort.

My father leaned over to fetch the crutch this handsome creature had dropped. "That's some cast you have there, son."

I looked, and felt my face flush. Because looking at the cast meant allowing my eyes to travel down his body. The end of my slow scan revealed one very muscular leg. The other was encased in white plaster.

"Isn't it a beauty?" His voice had a masculine roughness which put a quiver in my chest. "I broke it in two places." He extended a hand to my father. "I'm Adam Hartley."

"Ouch, Mr. Hartley," my father said, shaking his hand. "Frank Callahan."

Adam Hartley looked down at his own leg. "Well, Mr. Callahan, you should see the other guy." My father's face stiffened. But then my new neighbor's face broke into another giant grin. "Don't worry, sir. Your daughter isn't living next door to a brawler. Actually, I fell."

The look of relief on my dad's face was so priceless that it broke my drooly spell, and I laughed. My gorgeous new neighbor extended a hand to me, which I had to roll forward to shake. "Well played," I said. "I'm Corey Callahan."

"Nice to meet you," he began, his large hand gripping mine. His light brown eyes loomed in front of me, and I noticed that their irises had a darker ring around each one. The way he leaned down to shake my hand made me feel self-conscious. And was it hot in here?

Then the moment was broken by a shrill female voice erupting from inside his room. "Hartleeeey! I need you to hang this photograph, so you won't forget me while I'm in France. But I can't decide which wall!"

Hartley rolled his eyes just a little bit. "So make three more of them, baby," he called. "Then you'll have it covered."

My father grinned, handing Hartley his crutch.

"Honey?" came the voice again. "Have you seen my mascara?"

"You don't need it, gorgeous!" he called, tucking both crutches under his arms.

"Hartley! Help me look."

"Yeah, that never works," he said with a wink. Then he tipped his head toward the open door to his room. "Good to meet you. I have to solve the great makeup crisis."

He disappeared as my mother emerged from my room, her face a tight line. "Are you *sure* there's nothing else we can do for you?" she asked, fear in her eyes.

Be nice, I coached myself. *The baby-proofing is finally over.* "Thanks for all your help," I said. "But I think I'm all set."

My mother's eyes misted. "Take good care of yourself, baby," she said, her voice scratchy. She leaned over and hugged me, crushing my head to her chest.

"I will, Mom," I said, the words muffled.

With a deep breath, she seemed to pull herself together. "Call if you need us." She pushed open the dormitory's outside door.

"...But if you don't call for a few days, we won't panic," my father added. Then he gave me a quick salute before the door fell closed behind him. And then they were gone.

My sigh was nothing but relief.

A half-hour later, Dana and I set off for the barbecue. She bounced across the street, and I wheeled along beside her. At Harkness College, students were split into twelve Houses. It was just like Hogwarts, only bigger, and without the sorting hat. Dana and I were assigned to Beaumont House, where we would live from sophomore year on. But all First Years lived together in the buildings ringing the enormous Freshman Court.

All the First Years except for us.

At least our dormitory was just across the street. My brother had told me that McHerrin was used for a jumble of purposes — it housed students whose houses were undergoing renovation, or foreign students visiting just for a term.

And apparently, McHerrin was where they put gimps like me.

Dana and I passed through a set of marble gates and headed toward the scent of barbecued chicken. This was Freshman Court, where each building was more elegant and antique than the last. They all sported steep stone steps stretching up to carved wooden doors. I couldn't help but ogle their ornate facades like a tourist. This was Harkness College — the stone gargoyles, the three centuries of history. It was gorgeous, if not handicapped-accessible.

"I just wanted to tell you I'm sorry that we're not living in Fresh Court with the rest of our class," I said, using my brother's slang for the first year dorms. "It's kind of unfair that you're stuck in McHerrin with me."

"Corey, stop apologizing!" Dana insisted. "We're going to meet lots of people. And we have such a great room. I'm not worried."

Together, we approached the center of the lawn, where a tent was set up. The strains of someone's guitar floated on the warm September air, while the smell of charcoal wafted past our noses.

I never dreamed I'd show up for college in a wheelchair. Some people say that after a life-threatening event, they learn to enjoy life more. That they stop taking everything for granted.

Sometimes I felt like punching those people.

But today I understood. The September sun was warm, and my roommate was as friendly in person as she was over email. And I was breathing. So I had better learn to appreciate it.

Chapter Two: *Look Mom, No Stairs!*

— *Corey*

The next morning was the first day of classes. Armed with my special copy of the The Harkness Accessible Campus Map, I rolled through the sunshine toward the math department. As advertised, the building had a perfectly adequate wheelchair ramp and wide doors on its western side.

So Calculus 105 was accessible, if not exciting.

After that, it was off to Economics 101, a class my father had suggested. "I always wished I knew more about money," he'd confessed, in a rare moment of regret. "I asked your brother to give econ a try, and he liked it. I'd like you to give it a try, too." This was a powerful negotiating tactic, seeing as I'd played the Big Brother card for my own selfish purposes. My knockout punch in the fraught discussion of where I should go to college this year had been: "Damien went to Harkness, I'm going too." Neither of my parents had been able to look their disabled daughter in the eye and argue with that.

They'd caved, and so to please my father, I signed up for a semester's worth of microeconomics. Whatever that was. The upshot was that my Monday, Wednesday and Friday mornings — with Calculus and then econ — were going to be awfully dull.

The economics lecture hall was big and old, with ancient oak seats in tight rows. There was no obvious wheelchair parking spot, so I reversed myself into position against the back wall, next to a couple of old mismatched chairs.

A minute later, someone dropped heavily into the

chair next to me. A glance to my right revealed a tanned, muscular forearm stowing a pair of wooden crutches.

It seemed that my hot neighbor had arrived.

My little feathered hope fairy woke up and whispered into my ear. *Economics just got better.*

With a groan, Hartley kicked his backpack out in front of him on the wood floor, and then wrestled the heel of his broken leg on top of it. Then he tipped his head back against the paneled wall behind us and said, "Shoot me, Callahan. Why did I sign up for a class so far away from McHerrin?"

"You could always call the gimpmobile," I suggested.

Turning his chin, those chocolaty brown eyes caught me in their tractor beam. "Sorry?"

For a second there, I almost forgot what I'd been saying. The gimpmobile. Right. "There's a van." I handed him my accessible map. "You call this number ahead of time, and they'll pick you up for class."

"Who knew?" Hartley frowned at the map. "Is that what you do?"

"Honestly? I'd rather paste a bright red L to my forehead than call the van." I made the universal sign for "loser" with my fingers, and Hartley snorted with laughter. His dimple appeared, and I had to fight off the urge to reach over and put my thumb over it.

Just then, a skinny girl with straight dark hair and giant glasses slid into the seat on the other side of Hartley.

"Excuse me," he said, turning to her. "This section is reserved for gimps."

She looked up at him, eyes huge, and then bolted from her chair like a frightened rabbit. I watched her run down the aisle and slide into another seat.

"Well, I knew you were kidding," I said.

"Right?" Hartley gave me another smile so warm and devilish that I could not look away. Then he slapped a notebook onto his lap just as a professor began tapping the microphone on the lectern.

Professor Rumpel looked to be about 109 years old, give or take a decade. "Class," he began. "It really is true what they say about economics. The answer to any test question is 'supply and demand.'" The old man let out a breathy gust of air into the microphone.

Hartley leaned closer to me and whispered, "I think that was supposed to be a joke."

The proximity made my face feel hot. "We are in serious trouble," I whispered back.

But really, I was referring to me.

Hartley's cell phone rang as class ended, so I gave him a friendly wave and rolled out of the lecture hall alone. Then, after consulting my trusty gimp map, I headed toward the biggest dining hall on campus. Harkness Commons had been built in the 1930s to accommodate the entire college at once. Slowly, I wheeled into the crowded, cavernous space. Before me stretched over one hundred wooden tables. After swiping my ID at the door, I had to watch the flow of bodies inside to determine where to go next.

Students flowed past me toward one wall of the room. So I wound my wheelchair through the tables toward what looked like a line. Drifting forward while trying to read a chalkboard, I accidentally bumped the person in line in front of me. She spun around quickly, a look of irritation on her face until she looked down and realized what had hit her. "Sorry!" she said quickly.

I felt my face flush. "I'm sorry," I echoed. And why

was she sorry, anyway? I'm the dope who ran into her.

This was one of the strange truths about driving a wheelchair. Nine out of ten times, anyone I bumped — or maybe even flattened — would apologize. It made no sense at all, and somehow it also pissed me off.

I found the end of the line. But then I noticed that everyone else in line had collected a tray already, and silverware. So I steered myself out of line, found the trays and cutlery, and then added myself to the end again. Waiting in line in my chair put me at eye-level with other people's rear ends. It was the same way the world had looked when I was seven years old.

— Hartley

I swear to God, the guy who made my sandwich could not have moved slower if he had both wrists tied together. I stood there, my ankle throbbing, my good leg shaking. It didn't help that I'd skipped breakfast. By the time he handed the plate over, I thought I might pass out.

"Thanks," I said. I took the plate in my right hand, and then jammed my right crutch under my armpit. I tried to walk away like that, without gripping the crutch handle. My balance off, I swayed, and then had to lean against the service counter just to stay vertical. My crutch fell to the floor with a bang.

Fail. The only saving grace was that the sandwich didn't jump ship, too.

"Hey gimp!" a voice called from behind me.

I turned around, but it took me a minute to find Corey, because I was looking for someone my own height. After an awkward second, I looked and spotted her. "Callahan," I said. "Did you see that suave maneuver?"

With a smile, she took the plate out of my hand and set it on her tray. "Don't kill yourself in the name of a..." she looked at the plate. "Turkey club. I'll carry it for you if you can give me a second."

"Thanks," I sighed. I hopped aside, and waited while the same under-motivated sandwich guy made her lunch.

Several hours later (I might be exaggerating), our tray contained two sandwiches, chips, cookies, my glasses of milk and her diet soda. "I think I see a free table over there, in the next zip code," I muttered, crutching forward. Corey wheeled our booty to the table, where I yanked one of the heavy wooden chairs out of the way to make a parking spot for her.

Then I collapsed into a chair. "Jesus, Mary and mother of God." I rested my forehead against the heels of my hands. "That only took about seven times as long as it's supposed to."

Corey handed me my plate. "It's a new injury, isn't it?" she asked, picking up her sandwich.

"Is it that obvious? I did it a week ago at hockey preseason training camp."

"Hockey, huh?" A strange look crossed her face.

"Sort of. See, I didn't break it playing hockey, because that would at least make sense. I broke the leg falling off a climbing wall."

Her jaw dropped. "Did the ropes break?"

Not exactly. "There may not have been ropes. Also, it may have been two in the morning." I winced, because it's no fun telling a pretty girl how big an idiot you are. "Also, I may have been drunk."

"Ouch. So you can't even tell people that you're the victim of a poke check gone wrong?"

I raised an eyebrow at her. "Are you a hockey fan, Callahan?"

"Kind of." She fidgeted with a potato chip. "My father is a high-school hockey coach," she said. "And my brother Damien was the senior wing on your team last year."

"No shit! You're Callahan's little sister?"

She smiled, which made her blue eyes glitter. She had a kick-ass smile, and rosy coloring, as if she'd just run a 5K race. "That's right."

"See, I knew you were cool." I took a gulp of milk.

"So," she picked up her sandwich. "If your break is only a week old, you must be in a lot of pain."

I shrugged while chewing on a bite. "The pain I can handle. But it's just so fucking awkward. Getting dressed takes a half hour. And taking a shower is ridiculous."

"At least temporarily."

I froze mid-bite, dismayed by my own stupidity. "Shit, Callahan. Listen to me bitching about twelve weeks in a cast..." I put down my sandwich. "I'm kind of an asshole."

She flushed. "No, I didn't mean it that way. I swear. Because if you can't complain a little bit, then neither can I."

"Why not?" I think I'd just proved that she had every right to bitch. Especially with assholes like me running around.

Corey toyed with her napkin. "Well, after my accident, my parents sent me to a support group for people with spinal cord injuries, which is how I ended up..." she waved her hands over her lap. "Anyway, the room was full of people who can't move a whole lot more body parts than I can't move. Many of them can't feel their arms. They can't feed themselves, or turn over in bed. They couldn't even get out of a burning building, or send an email, or hug someone."

I rested my face in my hand. "Well that's uplifting."

"Tell me about it. Those people scared the crap out of me, and I never went back. And if *I* can whine — and trust me, I do — you might as well gripe about hopping around like a flamingo." She picked up her sandwich again.

"So..." I didn't have any idea whether this was too personal a question. "When was this?"

"When was what?" Her eyes evaded me.

"The accident."

"January fifteenth."

"Wait...*this* January fifteenth? Like, eight months ago?" She gave me a tiny nod. "So...last week you said, 'fuck it, it's September. I'd better move across the country and get on with it?'"

Corey pounded her soda, quite possibly to escape my scrutiny. "Well...more or less. But seriously, what *is* the proper mourning period over the use of one's legs?" She looked me full in the face then, one eyebrow raised.

Fuck. This girl probably just cured me from whining for the rest of my life, right there. "You are hardcore, Corey Callahan."

She gave me a little shrug. "The college offered me a year's deferral, but I didn't take it. You met my parents. I didn't want to sit home and watch them wring their hands."

My phone rang, and I had to give Corey the universal signal for "just a second" while I picked up Stacia. "Hi, hottie," I answered. "I'm sitting at a table against the back wall. Love you too." I stashed the phone. "Okay...wait. So a little tender loving care drove you into a different time zone?"

"The three of us were half insane last year. This was best for everyone."

That hadn't occurred to me, but it should have. When you have an accident, it doesn't just happen to you. "I can almost see it. My mom drove me batshit crazy last week. But I probably deserved it."

"Your mom was pissed about your broken leg?"

"Sure she was. It's not like I broke it saving babies from a burning building. My mom missed a couple days of work taking care of me, and now there's a whopping E.R. bill, too."

"Your coach must be spitting fire," Corey pointed out.

"You got it. I've heard the 'You Let Everyone Down' lecture several times already." I began to watch the door for Stacia. A couple of minutes and a half a sandwich later, a gorgeous girl appeared in the archway. As she stood there, scanning the tables, I couldn't look away. Stacia had it all. She was tall, and yet somehow curvy, with flowing yellow hair and the bearing of a princess. When she spotted me, her big hazel eyes lit up. Then she pointed those long legs in my direction. And the first thing she did when she arrived beside me was to kiss me full on the mouth.

We'd been dating for most of a year, and it still shocked me every time she did that.

"Stacia," I said after she released my lips. "This is my new neighbor Callahan. She and her roommate Dana are in Beaumont House, too."

"Nice to meet you," Stacia said quickly, with the barest glance at Corey. "Hartley, are you ready to go?"

I laughed. "Babe, you don't *know* how hard we had to work for this food," I said. "So give me a few minutes to finish it." I pulled out a chair for her.

Stacia sat down, but didn't bother to conceal her irritation. She stabbed at her phone while I took my time with my cookies and milk.

Corey had gone quiet, but that was okay, because Stacia was always ready to fill dead air with another of her first-world problems. "My hairdresser says she can't fit me in tomorrow. That's so wrong," my girlfriend complained.

"I'm pretty sure they have salons in Paris," I said, not that she'd listen. Stacia was the pickiest girl on the planet. The food in the dining halls didn't meet her standards — so she bought most of her meals off campus. Her shampoo was mail-ordered, because none of the fifty brands at the drugstore would do. She wasn't exactly warm to new people, either.

And yet Stacia looked at *me* the same way she looked at a shopping bag from Prada. The fancy girl from Greenwich, Connecticut wanted *this* guy. This guy right here, the one in the Bruins cap and the Gold's Gym T-shirt.

I could tell you it didn't make me feel a foot taller, but I'd be lying.

Corey drained her soda, and then began to stack our stuff back on her tray.

"Hey, Stacia?" I put my hand on my girlfriend's wrist to get her attention. "Will you do us a solid and bus this?"

She looked up from her phone, surprised. Then she glanced from the tray to the back of the dining hall, as if calculating the effort. For a long moment, she hesitated. I could tell that Corey was just on the verge of offering to do it when Stacia rose suddenly, grabbed the tray and stomped off.

I shook my head, aiming a sheepish smile at my new

neighbor. "At her house, the staff does that sort of thing."

I could tell by the look on Corey's face that she had no idea whether I was joking or not. Actually, I wasn't.

See, Stacia was a piece of work. But she was *my* piece of work.

Chapter Three: *The Furniture Genie*

— *Corey*

"So how was the first day?" Dana asked when I arrived home that afternoon. She was perched on our window seat, painting her fingernails.

"Good," I said. "I found all three of my classes on the first try. You?"

"Yeah! And I really like my history of art professor."

"Is he hot?" I made a comical wiggle with my eyebrows.

"He is if you're into seventy-five year olds."

"Who says I'm not?" I did a wheelie in my chair, because there was really no furniture in my way. Dana's desk was against one wall, her trunk shoved up next to it. Our room still echoed.

"Whoa! Isn't that dangerous?" she asked.

"Nope." I did it again, popping back onto two wheels and then spinning in a circle. "But it does make me dizzy."

"Isn't there such a thing as wheelchair basketball?" Dana asked, blowing on her nails.

"Probably," I dodged. Given my sporty history, more than a dozen people had asked me the same question already. But before my accident, I'd never been interested in hoops. And I was doubly uninterested in some kind of adaptive bullshit. Why did people think that sounded like fun? Why must all gimps love basketball?

Dana capped her nail polish. "So...I'm going to the jam tonight. Do you want to come?"

"What's a jam?"

"It's a concert, a showcase for the a cappella singing groups. Are you going to rush?"

I shook my head. "I gave up choir in the eighth grade because it conflicted with hockey."

"You don't have to be crazy good," Dana argued. "There are ten groups, and it's social as much as musical."

"Let's go to the jam, then," I said. "We'll check it out."

"Awesome! It's right after dinner. I'll find this auditorium..." She hopped up to dig a campus map out of her bag.

"Nice TV, ladies," a sexy voice said from the open doorway.

I looked up to see Hartley leaning against our doorjamb. "Thanks," I said, my heart rate kicking up a notch.

"What you really need is a sofa right here," he pointed to the empty wall just inside the door. "They're selling used ones on Fresh Court."

"We saw them," Dana said. "But we don't know how to summon a furniture genie to carry it for us."

Hartley scraped a hand along his gorgeous jaw. "I guess two gimps and a chick won't cut it. I'll work on it at dinner." He looked at his watch. "...Which starts now. Takers?"

"Sure," Dana said. "I haven't been to the Beaumont dining hall yet."

"So let's go," Hartley said, turning his crutches toward the outside door.

Dana and I followed Hartley out of McHerrin and down the street. Beaumont House, in all its Gothic glory, had big iron gates. Dana swept her ID in front of the reader and the gate clicked open. She held the door for Hartley and then for me.

The gimp parade was slow going, with Hartley on

crutches, and me driving cautiously. The flagstone pathway was uneven, and I didn't want to catch my wheels on one of the cracks and do a face plant. It was hard enough being The Girl in the Wheelchair. I didn't need to be The Girl Who Ejected From Her Wheelchair.

We made our way through one small stone courtyard and into the larger one, which was on every official Harkness tour. My brother Damien had once complained about dodging tourists and their cameras when he was on the way to class. But if that was the price of living in an historic granite and marble castle, so be it.

On the far side of the courtyard, Hartley stopped our progress. "Shit," he said, looking up at the building. "The dining hall is on the second floor. I forgot about the stairs."

"You know, Beaumont dining hall isn't on the accessible map," I said. "I think I'll try another dining hall." Commons wasn't open for dinner, but I'd already memorized which houses had first-floor dining rooms.

Hartley leaned over the handles of his crutches and shook his head. "I'm not climbing it, either. But…how does the food get up there? I bet they don't carry it up the stairs." He frowned up at the building. "I can't believe I've eaten here for two years and never wondered about that." He turned toward another gate leading out onto the street. "Dana, we'll meet you inside. There must be a service entrance. This way, Callahan."

My face pink, I followed Hartley out onto Pine Alley, which backed up to both Beaumont and Turner House.

"That will be it," Hartley grinned. He limped toward a gray metal door with an intercom beside it. He pushed the button.

"Yeah!" came a voice.

He looked at me, his dimple showing. "Delivery!"

A moment later, the gray door slid open to reveal a dimly lit elevator carriage, which was not even full height. "Classy," Hartley said. "Well, let's do this." There was a slight lip, which almost tripped him up. But he ducked inside, holding the door while I rolled myself backwards into the car. The door slid shut with a grinding sound that scared me. Was this going to become one of *those* moments — the kind you look back on later and wonder why you followed a hot guy into a shaky, unmarked elevator? But Hartley only chuckled as the car seemed to tremble around us. "I hope you have good lungs, in case we need to yell for help."

The car rose so slowly that I didn't relax until the door finally wheezed open. When we emerged into a brightly lit kitchen, a guy in a chef's hat frowned at us, and several busy people in white aprons turned to stare. "Don't tell me you lost our reservation?" Hartley scoffed, looking around. "This way, Callahan." I followed him across a tile floor, around a glass-faced serving bay, and into the melee of students waiting with trays in hand.

"There you are!" Dana said, making room for us. "How'd you get up here?"

"In the service elevator," Hartley said. "It worked like a charm. Dana, can you grab us one more tray?"

"Sure, take this one." She darted off, returning with another tray and two more sets of cutlery.

The line snaked forward, and eventually we were up next. "Can you see over?" Hartley asked.

No, as usual. "What looks good?" I asked.

"Meatball sub. Fish looks a little scary."

"Easy decision, then."

"Two subs, please," Hartley said.

"Can I help you guys carry anything?" Dana asked. Hartley answered, "Callahan and I have a system." When he looked away, Dana gave me a meaningful eyebrow twist. I bit back a grin.

When we had our food, Hartley pointed a crutch toward a half-filled table in the middle of the room. "Over there, ladies."

As we approached the table, a guy with dark red hair waved. "Hartley! Christ, look at you."

"You always know just what to say, Bridge."

The redhead got up and came around the table to see Hartley's enormous cast. "That is *serious*, dude. I'm so fucking sorry."

Hartley waved a hand, like he didn't want to hear it. I recognized that reaction, because I'd felt that way, too. Sometimes even the nicest things that people say only remind you of all that's gone wrong. "Get rid of one of these chairs for Callahan, would you?" Hartley said.

Bridger dismissed one of the heavy wooden chairs with a flick of one finger. He was another hunky athlete, with a broad chest and bulky, freckled biceps emerging from the sleeves of his Harkness Hockey T-shirt. Bridger was *almost* as attractive as Hartley, and had a friendly warmth that I appreciated. When Hartley introduced us as his neighbors, he grinned. "I traded Hartley to you two. We were supposed to be roommates. Come to think of it, I might have pushed him off that wall so I could have a single."

"Nice," Hartley said. "Can you do us a favor after dinner? These ladies need to buy a sofa on Old Campus. It's only about a fifty-yard trip, no stairs. And you can see my fancy handicapped pad."

"Alright. What are you doing tonight, anyway?"

Hartley shook his head. "It's not up to me. Stacia leaves in the morning."

"I see." Bridger's eyebrows went up. "Go easy on that leg, dude. Save the tricky positions for next time." When Hartley threw his balled up napkin at his head, Bridger only laughed. "Did they give you any good painkillers?"

"Yeah, but they made me puke, so I left them at home. It's plain old Advil for me, and I take them by the fistful."

Another guy sat down with us, a preppy blond with a country club haircut. "The leg hurts that much?" he asked.

"Everything hurts," Hartley said. "...My good leg, from working so hard, my hip, from swinging the cast through. My armpits."

"Your crutch handles are set too low," I said, wiping my mouth on my napkin.

"Really?" Hartley perked up.

"Really. Move them up a notch, and never lean on the underarm supports. Trust me."

He pointed a french fry at me. "You are a very useful neighbor, Callahan."

I shook my head. "If there was a game show for physical therapy trivia, I could win big."

The preppy guy gave me a weird look. But I was used to those. So instead of feeling bad about it, I finished my meatball sub. It was delicious.

After dinner, Dana and I paid forty dollars for a used couch in a shade of not-too-ugly blue. Bridger and the preppy, whom they called Fairfax, carried it into our room.

"Thank you, thank you!" Dana said, dancing in

front of them to open up our room. The accessible door was so wide that they didn't even have to tip the sofa to carry it in.

"Nice room," Bridger said, setting down his end of the sofa. "Let's see yours, Hartley."

With both our doors blocked open, I heard Hartley's friends exclaim over his single across the hall. He didn't have a common room like ours, but I'd noticed that his room was also generously sized. "Christ, a double bed? Nice."

"Just in time for your girlfriend to leave the country," Fairfax snickered. "Where is she, anyway?"

Hartley's voice answered. "The mall? A salon? Somewhere expensive. Whatever. Who wants a beer before she gets back?"

After admiring our new furniture, and dragging Dana's trunk over to be our coffee table, we made our way across campus to the singing group jam. Inside the auditorium, we were handed a program on a half-sheet of paper. There were ten groups listed, each one singing two songs. "They have to hand this out," Dana explained as we parked ourselves in the designated handicapped spot, where my chair wouldn't stick out into the aisle. "So that the rushes can remember who sang what."

The groups all had cute names, like the Harkness Harmonics, and the Tony Tones. When the lights dimmed, the first group walked onstage — twelve guys in matching T-shirts and khaki shorts. I checked the program. They were the Minstrel Marauders.

"A cappella is kind of nerdy," Dana leaned over to say. "But in a good way."

After a few minutes, I was inclined to agree with her. One guy on the far end held up a pitch pipe and blew a single note. His eleven friends hummed a chord. And then the leader stashed his pitch pipe, raising both hands. When he brought them down again, the group launched into a rendition of "Up the Ladder to the Roof" in four-part harmony. And somehow they made a song that was on the radio when my parents were little sound cool. I'd always thought that athletes were my type. But I had to admit that a dozen men rocking out to an up-tempo love song was pretty appealing.

"They're great," I whispered.

Dana nodded. "They're supposed to be the best men's group."

The next bunch were the Mixed Masters, a coed chorus. They looked like they were having an awful lot of fun, but they lacked the perfection of the Marauders.

"*Next...*" Dana whispered. But the following group — Something Special — made her squeeze my wrist. "This is my 'reach' group," she said.

The women made a perfect semicircle on stage. They linked arms, and then began to sing a lovely, haunting version of "Desperado" by the Eagles.

When it was over, the applause was furious. "Wow," I said. "They rock."

"I know," Dana sighed. "But did you notice how *blond* they are? I wonder if that's a coincidence. Maybe you should audition, Corey. Your have almost the right coloring."

"No way," I said automatically, putting a hand up to my sun-streaked hair.

I wondered why Dana didn't hear the flaw in her own logic. If Something Special cared so much about appearances, imagine what a wheelchair or crutches would do to the pretty line of smiling faces? Did Dana honestly think that any of the attractive groups onstage would look right with me parked in the center of them?

The jam was fun to watch, but I knew where I stood. So to speak.

Chapter Four: *You Think You're So Sneaky*

— *Corey*

There was a knock on our door the following week, as Dana and I dug into our course reading. "It's open," I called.

The wooden door swung in to reveal Hartley and his crutches. "Evening," he said. "Is everybody working hard? I can come back another time."

Dana snapped her book shut. "I have an audition in a half-hour. What's up?"

"I have a strange and selfish request."

"That sounds interesting," Dana said. "If not promising."

"You're a smart girl, Dana." He flashed his dimple, and I felt myself slip a little further under his spell. That smile could melt glass. "See, I have a QuirkBox. But no TV. Bridger and I were a good team — but the TV was his."

"QuirkBox is a game console?" I asked.

He nodded. "Anyway, if you ever want to play, I would hook it up in here. It only takes a second."

"Well, go ahead," I said. "Give it a shot."

"You're the best," he said, a look of joy on his face. "I'll be right back."

The door fell closed, and we heard the sound of Hartley thumping back across the hall.

"Big fan of gaming?" Dana asked me.

"No," I grinned. "However..."

She laughed. "I think we should call him 'Hartthrob' from now on. I'd better get ready for this audition." She went into her room to have a fashion crisis.

"Video games aren't really my thing. I'll just watch," I told Hartley as he hooked it up. From the couch, I had a nice view of his backside.

"Suit yourself." A minute later, the game lit the big screen, and a team of incredibly realistic hockey players in Bruins jerseys took the ice.

I leaned forward in spite of myself. "That's Anton Khodobin! You can see their *faces*?"

Hartley chuckled. "Yeah, but I know it's not your thing." Balancing on his crutches in front of the TV, he held the controller in his hands. At the sound of the buzzer, there was a face-off, which Hartley's player won. His team was skating against the Islanders, and Hartley passed the puck from his center to his left wing.

A tense moment followed, when the Islanders' defenseman got his stick on the puck. But Hartley snatched it back with a grunt of satisfaction. He skated forward, lining up a shot. The goalie lunged, but before I could see what happened, Hartley moved his shoulders into my line of sight, and the screen disappeared behind his body. Without thinking, I pushed off the sofa to move around him.

And I fell.

In the split second before I hit the floor, I realized my mistake. It still happened once in awhile, and only when I was *very* distracted. I would actually forget that I could no longer stand unassisted, and hurl myself to the ground.

I went down with a thump, my arm making an exaggerated smack onto our makeshift coffee table.

Hartley's head whipped around. "Shit, are you okay?"

"Sure," I said, my face getting hot. "Just, um, clumsy." I rubbed my arm where it had hit the table.

"Look out," I said, nodding toward the screen. The Islanders had stolen the puck and were breaking for Hartley's goal. When he looked away from me, I quickly hoisted my butt back onto the couch.

He paused the game, and then turned around again, studying me.

I looked down at my hands.

"Heads up," Hartley said. And when I looked back at him, he tossed me the controller, which I caught. "What team do you want to be?" He gave me a huge smile, just the kind that made me feel all squishy inside.

"Pittsburgh," I answered, without hesitation.

"Good pick, Callahan," he said, grabbing the other controller and pulling up a menu on the screen. "This will only take a second to set up. And then you will learn from the master."

There were many things I would have liked to learn from "the master." But that night, I settled for a video game called RealStix.

The next time Hartley came over to play hockey, I was ready for him.

"Do you remember how to do this?" Hartley asked, handing me a controller.

"I *think* so."

This time, we sat side by side on the sofa, with Hartley's cast balanced on the coffee table. He pressed "play," and our two players stared one another down for the face-off. The digital ref dropped the puck between us, and I hooked it with my stick. Then, after passing to my wing, I skated toward the goal.

Hartley's goalie came into view. I angled towards him, the puck aiming toward the right hand corner of the net. On the screen, Hartley's guy inched over to cover that side. I faked to the left, and the goalie swerved right on cue. I slammed the puck right again and sent it into the goal.

Then I giggled as the fake crowd went wild.

"What the fuck, Callahan?" Hartley paused the game. "You deked my goalie?" Slowly, his surprised face evolved into a wicked grin. "Hold on, girl. You *practiced*, didn't you!"

I fought against my own smile. "Wouldn't you, if you were me?"

"Jesus Christ, you're going to pay for this..." Then, with some kind of ninja speed, he leaned over and grabbed my arm, raising it up. Before I even knew what was happening, he had his fingers under my armpit, tickling me.

"Hartley!" I shrieked, shoving his hand away and clamping my arm against my side.

"You think you're so sneaky." He reached for my arm again, but it was a fake-out. I had an older brother, and I knew all the tricks. Even as he dove for my waist instead, I wrenched my elbow down, protecting myself. But Hartley only rose up on his good knee and dove for my vulnerable left side. I shrieked again when he pressed my shoulder against the sofa, his free hand finding two tickling places at once.

Above me, his brown eyes laughed. As I looked up into them, I felt a rush of warmth, and then something else too. His expression changed, growing more serious. It looked almost hungry.

A giggle died on my lips as our eyes locked.

"*What* is going on out here?" Dana came out of her room, fastening an earring.

Releasing me, Hartley tossed himself back onto his own side of the sofa and picked up his game controller.

And the moment was broken. Or maybe there was no moment, and I imagined the whole thing. As Dana smiled at us, I looked over at Hartley, but he looked the same as always. "*Somebody* got shelled," I answered Dana to cover my own confusion, "and lost his cool."

"*Somebody* needs to be taught a lesson," Hartley argued, restarting the game.

"Bring it," I said.

Dana put on a jacket. "Should I have called in a babysitter for you two? No fighting, okay?"

But we didn't even answer her, because the game was back on. Hartley won the face-off this time, and I couldn't get possession. But with a stroke of luck, my goalie evaded him, falling on the puck.

"Whew," I said. "That was close." I looked around for Dana, but she had already gone. "So, we're still at one-zip, Pittsburgh's lead."

"Now you're *bragging*?" Hartley asked. "I'm going to wipe that smile off your face."

My fluttery little hope fairy put a word in then. *I can think of a few ways to do that,* she simpered.

RealStix Video Hockey became our thing together. The Bruins vs. Puffins rivalry grew into my favorite obsession. Sometimes we'd play a quick game before dinner on a weeknight. Dana would just shake her head and call us junkies. These games were fun, but we were often interrupted by phone calls for Hartley. He'd pause the game and answer, because at that hour of the day Stacia was just retiring to bed. "Sorry," he said the first time it happened. "But I can't call her back later. It's eleven o'clock over there."

"No problem." Only, it was a problem. Because the phone calls were excruciating.

"Rome for the weekend? That sounds like fun," Hartley would say. The indulgent tone he took with her sounded wrong on him. "I bet you'll give your credit cards a workout. You'd better buy some extra luggage while you're at it. You'll never get all your designer booty home."

I sat through these conversations with gritted teeth. Not only did they interrupt my new favorite hobby, but they drove my mind into alleyways where I didn't wish to go. "Hi, hottie," Hartley often answered his phone. Or, "hi baby." It was hard to say which term of endearment bothered me more. Because nobody had ever called me by either one.

The truth was that my blazing attraction to Hartley made me start to measure out the distance between girls like Stacia and me. Before my accident, I'd always assumed that a passionate romance would eventually come my way. But listening to Hartley butter up his gorgeous girlfriend niggled at me. Was there a guy out there for me, who would refer to his wheelchair-bound girlfriend as a hottie?

I really didn't think there was.

Part of the bargain I'd made with my parents was that I would continue physical therapy at Harkness. My new therapist was a sporty-looking woman in a Patriots cap. "Call me Pat," she said, shaking my hand. "I spent the weekend with your file."

"Sorry," I said. "That sounds like a dull read."

"Not at all," she smiled. I noticed she had freckles everywhere. "Your trainers seem to have found you refreshing."

I laughed. "If 'refreshing' is a euphemism for 'bitchy,' then maybe I'd buy it."

She shook her head. "You've had a very challenging year, Corey. Everyone understands that. So let's get started."

First, Pat stretched me. That's how therapy always began — with the unsettling sensation of someone moving my body around as if I was a rag doll. Pat worked my legs around the hip joints, followed by knees and ankles. Before asking me to sit up, she hesitated. "Can I take a peek at your skin? Nobody will see."

I looked around. The therapy room door was shut, and there were no faces outside its window. "Just quickly," I said.

Pat lifted the back of my yoga pants and took a peek down the back of my underwear. The concern was that I would get pressure sores from sitting in my chair all day. "No problems there."

"I'm not high risk," I said. "My parents asked you to check, didn't they?"

She smiled. "You can't blame them for caring."

I could, actually.

"If we can get you out of that chair," Pat jerked her thumb toward the offending object, "then nobody will worry about it anymore. How many hours a day are you up on your sticks?"

"A few," I hedged. The truth was that I hadn't figured out yet how to blend my crutches into my Harkness schedule. "I'm still working out how far apart all the buildings are."

"I see," she said. "But if you're going to participate in student life, we've got to get you climbing stairs. Otherwise, you should have picked a college built in the seventies. So let's do some leg press."

I tried not to grumble too much. But a year ago, I used to put twice my body weight on the leg press.

Now? Pat put on sixty pounds or so, and still I had to push on my quads with my hands to move the platform. A first-grader could do better.

Really, what was even the point?

But Pat was undeterred by my lousy performance. "Now we'll work your core," she insisted. "Good torso stability is crucial to helping you balance on crutches." It was nothing I hadn't heard before. Pat had learned her lines from the same script as the other therapists I'd seen. And I'd seen plenty.

Unfortunately, nowhere in any script were the words for the things that really bothered me. Pat knew what to do when my hips wobbled in the middle of a plank exercise. But nobody had ever taught me how to handle the odd looks I got when people made eye contact with me in my wheelchair. Sometimes I saw looks of outright pity. Those seemed honest, if not helpful. And then there were the Big Smiles. There can't be many people in the world who walk around grinning like maniacs at random strangers. But I got a lot of Big Smiles from people who thought that they owed it to me. It was like a consolation prize. *You don't have much use of your legs, so have a Big Smile on me.*

Of course, I never complained about these things out loud. It would only sound bitchy. But the last nine months had been humbling. The old me used to be offended when guys stared at my boobs. Now I only wished people would stare at my boobs. When they looked at me now, they only saw the chair.

"Four more crunches, Corey. Then you'll be all set," Pat said.

I looked up into Pat's determined face and crunched. But we both knew I would never be *all set*.

Chapter Five: *Drunk Giraffe on Stilts*

— Corey

September quickly became October, and life was good. I stayed on top of my course-work, and I learned to navigate the campus with increasing ease. Dana was in the throes of the singing group rush process. Her audition song was *Hey There, Delilah,* and with all her practicing, I had started to hear that song in my sleep.

I didn't have much of my own social life yet, but that was probably going to take some time. Hands down, my favorite Friday and Saturday nights so far had been spent playing RealStix with Hartley. As hockey season got going, Hartley's friends were increasingly unavailable. They were either at practice, or headed to parties in corners of the campus Hartley didn't wish to climb to. On those nights, he would flop onto the couch next to me for a few games of hockey. Sometimes we put on a movie afterward.

"You know, you depend too much on your team captain," Hartley said one night, when I was losing.

I wasn't about to tell him, but the reason I was losing that night had very little to do with my center, and everything to do with the fact that Hartley was not wearing a shirt. I'd spent the last half hour trying not to drool over Hartley's six-pack.

He cracked open a bottle of beer and offered it to me, but I waved it away. "Digby is good, but there are other players on the ice."

"But Digby is dreamy," I said, setting down my controller. And it was true — even the digitized version of the Puffins' captain made my heart go pitter-patter. He was *almost* the hottest hockey player I could name. The hottest one was sitting beside me on the sofa.

Hartley snorted into his beer. "Seriously?" He laughed, which meant I got to see more of his smile. "Callahan, I thought you were a real fan. I didn't realize you were a puck bunny."

That made me gasp. "And *I* didn't realize you were an asshole."

He held up two hands defensively, one of them still clutching his beer. "Whoa, just a little joke."

I bit my lip, trying to dial back my irritation. Puck bunny was a derogatory term for women who liked hockey players much more than they liked hockey. Nobody had ever called me that before. The happiest moments of my life had been spent *on* the rink.

Hartley eased his broken leg onto the table and cocked his head, like a golden retriever. "I hit a nerve? I'm sorry."

Reaching across the sofa, I took the beer out of his hand and stole a swig. "I guess I should start painting my face and yelling at the refs. Since I'm such a big *fan*."

I stretched the bottle back in his direction, but he didn't take it back. He just looked at me so intently that I wondered if he could hear my thoughts. "Callahan," he said slowly. "Are you a hockey *player?*"

For a minute, we just blinked at each other. I'd always *been* a player — since I was five years old. And now, at best, I was just a fan. And that really stung.

Swallowing hard, I answered the question. "I was a player. Before, you know... Before I gave it up." I felt a prickle behind my eyes. But I was not going to cry in front of Hartley. I took a deep breath in through my nose.

He licked his lips. "You told me your father was a high-school coach."

"He was *my* high-school coach."

"No shit?" Hartley cracked open a new beer without ever breaking eye contact. "What position do you play?"

Did I play. Past tense.

"Center, of course." I knew what he was really asking. "Captain. All state. Recruited by colleges." It was so hard to tell him this — to show him exactly what I'd lost. Most people didn't want to hear it. They would change the subject, and ask if I'd considered taking up knitting, or chess.

But Hartley only reached over, clinking his beer bottle against the one that I still held. "You know, I knew I liked you, Callahan," he said. At that, my battle against tears became even tougher. But I took a long pull off the beer in my hand and fought them off. There was another moment of silence before Hartley broke it. "So…I guess this means I should teach you how to flip the screen perspective, so you can always see where your defensemen are. Slide over here."

Happy to have that conversation over with, I scooted closer to him on the sofa. Hartley wrapped his arm around me in order to hold the controller in front of my body where I could see it. "If you push these two buttons at the same time," he said, depressing them with his thumbs, and looking up at the screen, "it toggles between the player's view and the coach's." I was tucked snugly against him, where I could feel his breath on my ear when he spoke.

"Right," I breathed. The heat of his bare chest at my back was incredibly distracting. "That's…useful," I stammered.

As he showed me a couple more maneuvers, I inhaled the clean scent of his soap, and admired the sculpted forearms reaching around to encircle mine. There should be poetry written about those arms.

Hartley explained something about body-checking, but I didn't quite catch it. Every time he said "body" all I could think about was his.

"Okay?" he finished, as I struggled to take in oxygen. "Now when I beat you, you won't be able to claim ignorance." Giving my short ponytail a gentle yank, he withdrew his embrace.

With flushed cheeks, I scooted quickly back to my own end of the couch. "Come on, then," I said, mustering up a few brain cells. "I'm ready to mow you down."

"We'll just see about that," he chuckled.

The next Friday night, I bumped into Hartley as we were both coming in the front door of McHerrin. "RealStix later?" I asked. *Please?*

He shook his head. "The hockey team doesn't start their play season for another week, so Bridger's having a party. You should come — there are only six stairs. I made him count them for me. Can you do six stairs?"

I considered the question. "I can do them, as long as I don't mind looking like a drunk giraffe on stilts. Only less graceful."

He grinned. "That's me on a good day. I'm going over at eight, and I'll knock on your door. Bring Dana, and anyone else you feel like." He went into his room.

"Do you want to go to Bridger's party tonight?" I asked Dana when she finally came home.

"I would, but I can't," she said. "There are two rush parties. Will you help me choose an outfit?"

"Sure," I said, feeling even better about my decision not to rush a singing group. If you had to sing well *and* dress well, I was not a good candidate.

We chose a slinky purple sweater for Dana, over jet-black jeans. She looked pretty, but it didn't look like she was trying too hard. "But what are you wearing?" she asked me.

I only shrugged, glancing down at my Harkness T-shirt. "It's a kegger in Bridger's room. Who would dress up for that?"

Dana rolled her eyes at me. "Come on, Corey. The jeans are okay, but you need a cuter top." She strode into my room and began opening dresser drawers. "How does this one fit you?"

"Well, it's pink."

"I can see that. Put it on."

Humoring her, I threw my Harkness tee on the bed and grabbed the top that Dana held out.

— *Hartley*

When I opened the door to the girls' common room, I could hear voices from behind Corey's half-open bedroom door.

"There. Can I go now?" Corey asked.

"That's *so* much cuter," Dana gushed. "It hugs you in just the right places. Now, wait. Put on these hoops."

"Fine," Corey sighed, "because it's quicker than arguing with you."

"And I'm not letting you out of the house without lipstick."

"God, *why?*"

That's when I laughed, and Corey's door opened all the way. "Gotta go," she called to Dana.

"Wait!" her roommate cried, fumbling on Corey's dresser top. "Don't you *own* any mascara?"

"Good luck at the rush parties," Corey called as she crutched toward me in a hurry. "*Run,*" she mouthed, and I opened the door.

Corey managed the six stairs into Bridger's room with little difficulty, which was great since I wouldn't have been any help. But that night, the party itself was the real work. It was exactly what I should have anticipated. Warm beer in plastic cups? Check. Music too loud to talk over? Check. Girls tossing their hair at all of my teammates? Check and check.

Bridger's room was thick with Harkness Hockey jackets and sweatshirts. The puck bunnies fanned out around them, fawning. I followed Corey's stare to find a rather drunk young woman grinding up against Bridger. When I caught Corey's eye, she raised an eyebrow. All I could do was shrug. You might think that there wouldn't be any puck bunnies at an ambitious school like Harkness. But you'd be wrong. At every home game, there was at least one homemade poster reading: "Future Hockey Wives." They weren't even subtle about it.

When Corey and I had battled all the way into the party, Bridger gave us each a warm smile and a warm beer. It was then that I discovered the logistical difficulty of drinking a beer while supporting oneself on crutches. Corey, who was obviously smarter than I was, had wedged herself onto the arm of Bridger's beat up old sofa. Leaning her crutches up against the wall behind her, she had her hands free.

From her perch, Corey surveyed the room that Bridger and I would have shared if not for my broken leg. Beaumont House was a hundred years old, and the university hadn't renovated it in a few decades. So the dark wood moldings were scratched, the walls yellowing. But it was still one of the coolest places I'd ever been. The arched windows were hung with real leaded glass, divided into tiny shimmering rectangles.

An oaken window seat stretched beneath.

Students perched on its edge, cups in hand, the same way they'd been sitting since the 1920s. I'd always thought that was cool, but tonight it just seemed depressingly stagnant.

Bridger even had one of those felt banners hanging above his not-functional-since-the-1960s fireplace, reading *Esse Quam Videri*. The university motto was: To Be, Rather Than to Seem. It was a nice sentiment, but the vibe in Bridger's room that night was more along the lines of: To See, To Be Seen, and To Drink a Lot.

The first beer went down quick. "You need another?" I asked Callahan.

"Not really," she said with a smile.

And good thing, because I probably couldn't carry one back to her without spilling it. With my cup in my teeth, I made my way through the crowd to the keg without crushing anyone's toes with my crutches. Bridger took the cup out of my mouth and refilled it.

"What happened to that octopus I saw hanging on you earlier?" I asked him.

He tipped my cup to avoid too much foam. "Christ. I had to peel her off me. That's Hank's little sister."

"Seriously? I thought she was younger."

"That's the problem. She's sixteen, and just visiting for the weekend. Now she's reattached herself. To Fairfax, of all people."

I scanned the scrum of bodies. Sure enough, on the window-seat I spotted a half-lidded girl wrapped around our teammate. And Fairfax looked pretty deep into his cups himself. "Fuck. Where is Hank, anyway?"

"I really don't know. Haven't seen him for a while. Probably someone offered him a smoke." Bridger handed me my cup, and we both watched a drunken

Fairfax shove his tongue in the girl's mouth. "That's just some kind of wrong," Bridger muttered. "Do you have your phone?"

"Sure. Hold this." I gave Bridger my cup, and shot off a quick text to Hank. "911. Put the bong down and come get your sister."

Bridge and I drank a beer together while watching the door. But Hank didn't appear. I looked back toward the happy couple. "*Dayum.* Did she just grab his junk?"

Bridger winced. "We'll have to stage an intervention. If that was my little sister..." he let the sentence die. "That girl is drunk off her ass."

It had to be done. "Coming through," I called, and Bridge and I wove our way towards the window seat. They were still hot and heavy by the time we got over there.

I tapped the girl on the shoulder. "Excuse me, Hank is looking for you." Their lips made an audible popping sound when they came apart. "Whah?" the girl slurred.

"Your brother," Bridger said, pulling her off Fairfax. "Right now."

"Holy shit, Darcy!"

Hank had appeared, towering over us. The dude was almost seven feet tall. He put one giant hand on his sister's shoulder, and held up his phone with the other. "Thanks, Hartley. I owe you."

I shrugged it off, but not before Fairfax noticed. After Hank dragged his sister away, he fixed me with a wobbly stare. "So you're cock-blocking me now?"

Seriously? "No, man. I'm helping you out. You've got to throw the little ones back. It's the law."

"You are such a bastard, Hartley. Always such a *bastard.*"

I clenched my fists on instinct.

"Oh, *fuck* no," Bridger spat, putting a hand on my chest. "You are not punching Fairfax at my party. No matter how big a douchecanoe he is tonight."

But my blood was boiling already. That fucking word. Why do people have to use that fucking word?

"Dude, no," Bridger pled, both his hands on me now. "Let this one go. If you hurt him, he tells Coach…nothing good comes from that. And the guy is *plowed*, Hartley. He won't even remember this in the morning."

As if to prove the point, Fairfax began to sag onto the window seat.

I shook Bridger off me, but I didn't lunge at Fairfax.

"No good deed goes unpunished," Bridger added, handing me the crutch I'd dropped.

Right. So this had been fun.

I turned away without another word, heading back towards Corey, and her perch on the sofa arm. The sofa proper was taken up by with two couples engaged in varying stages of foreplay. But the wall beside Corey was empty, and so I maneuvered myself into position to lean upon it. With just a third of a beer left, I could dangle the cup from two fingers and still hang onto my crutches.

"Everything okay?" she asked mildly.

"The leg is killing me tonight," I mumbled, staring into the last of my beer.

She tugged her bag off her shoulders. Digging into the bottom, her hand emerged with a tiny bottle of Advil. God bless her, she tapped two of these into my palm.

"You are such a babe," I said, tossing them back into my mouth.

"Uh huh," she said with an eye roll.

I gave her a wink, and the puck bunny standing in front of us gave Corey a dirty look. She was a fluffy-haired cheerleader type wearing some kind of tight, shiny shirt.

"Stacia really left you high and dry, didn't she?" the shiny-shirted girl asked me.

"How do you figure?" I shifted my weight to put more of it against the wall. I was fairly miserable, and it was only ten o'clock.

"She's wandering Paris, and you're stuck here in sunny Harkness Connecticut. How's that fair? A whole semester without any action?" She tossed her hair, and the invitation was unmistakable.

I winked, shaking my phone in one hand. "See, that's what Skype is for." The girl and her friend dissolved in a fit of giggles, while Corey rolled her eyes again. "The only tricky part is getting the whole thing in the picture." I held the camera at arm's length and waist height, as if zooming out on my crotch, and they howled again. I drained my beer, wondering why I came to these things.

A guy we called Kreature pushed through the girls to talk to me, and I was happy for the interruption.

"Hey man. How's it going?" I asked. "Have you met Callahan's little sister?"

"Nice to meet you," Kreature shook Corey's hand. "Practice was just brutal today, Hartley. Lunging sprints on the track, followed by murder drills on the ice. No scrimmage. It was exhausting and boring at the same time."

"Giddyup," I said, crushing my empty cup.

"Trust me, man. It was a day when missing practice meant missing *nothing*."

"No kidding?" I said. But privately, I thought,

bullshit. I'd have done anything to be at practice today, instead of laid up with a giant cast on my leg. I cut my glance over to Corey's for half a second, and found her with a knowing smile.

Yeah. She was the only one in the room who understood.

After Kreature went away, Corey put her bag over her shoulders again, and found her crutches. "I'm going to take off," she said.

"I'll walk you out," I volunteered immediately.

She headed for the doorway, and I managed to follow without clubbing anyone with my cast.

"You don't have to walk me out," she said as we reached the landing outside Bridger's door. "Why do the stairs two extra times?"

The pain in my ankle made me grimace. "I'm not, Callahan. I'm just using you as an excuse to sneak away." With great care, I crutched down the first stair. "Come on, you can say it. That was a totally pointless evening."

"Was it? Honestly, it wasn't as bad as I thought it would be. Nobody puked on me, and I didn't do a face plant on the stairs." Callahan hopped down one stair, and then another. Compared to me, she was practically a gazelle.

"I guess it's all about expectations," I muttered, tackling the second stair.

"Everything is," she agreed quietly.

Chapter Six: *More Fun than Disney World*

— Corey

On my way out of the room on Monday morning, I found a note that had been slid under our door. It was a folded piece of paper reading CALLAHAN on the outside. Inside, it read: *I can't come to econ today because I'm having two screws put in my knee this morning. Share your notes with me, pretty please? H.*

I waited until after lunch to text him. *Got your note. Surgery? So sorry.*

A couple of hours later he replied: *Don't B sorry. Anesthesia rocks. You don't have to visit, but if you do, bring food.*

Me: *What kind of food?*

Hartley: *OMG who cares? Hospital food is vomit.*

I laughed, because it was true.

When I stuck my head into Hartley's hospital room later, the first thing I saw was his bandaged knee, draped over a machine, which bent it and straightened it repeatedly. "That looks like fun." At least his giant cast was gone, and there was a smaller one — a boot cast — on his lower leg.

"More fun than Disney World." He turned his head and offered me a pale smile. He was wearing a hospital gown, and an IV dripped liquids into his arm.

I fought off a shudder at the familiarity of it all. "Sorry," I said. "Why the surgery, anyway?"

He pressed his head back against the pillows. "The hockey coach wanted me to see his favorite ortho guy. And that guy said it would heal faster with screws in it."

"Well...that's good, right?"

He shrugged. "It's good for my knee. But my ankle

will heal at the same speed, no matter what. So I'm trying to figure out what's changed, except for the fact that I now have steel body parts."

"You're going to set off metal detectors." I rolled further into the room. "You don't mind me visiting? I always hated visitors."

Hartley picked his head up. "You hated visitors? What do you have against people who like you?"

"I didn't want to be *seen*, that's all. It was so humiliating to be flat on my back, unshowered, and basically naked except for the little cotton gown."

"That's where we're different," Hartley said with a tip of his head. "I'm cool with not showering. And nudity."

I fished a white paper bag out of my pack.

"What did you bring me?"

"An Italian sub and a bag of chips. And Gatorade."

"Have I ever told you that you're beautiful?"

"Any time I offer you food."

"Exactly. Gimme that." He held out his hands, and I passed him the bag.

I looked up at the IV, and the drugs running into his arm. "Are you supposed to be eating?"

"Who cares? I'm hungry." He unwrapped the sandwich and took a bite. "Mmh," he said. "Beautiful."

"Me or the sandwich?"

"Both." He took another bite. "Callahan? How long were you in the hospital?"

The question made my chest feel tight. The accident wasn't something I liked to talk about. "Six weeks."

His eyes widened. "That is a long time to eat really bad food."

I nodded, even though the bad food wasn't even in my top ten things to hate about the hospital.

"How much school did you miss?"

"Three months. I went back for the last few weeks. Luckily, I'd applied early action to Harkness. So my acceptance letter came before the accident."

"But you graduated on time?"

"The school district sent me a tutor once I got into rehab."

"That's aggressive."

"Is it?" I sighed. "There was nothing else to do with my free time. Better to learn a bunch of calculus equations than to just sit and think all day long." I pointed at his knee. "Tell me you wouldn't rather be at an economics lecture right now."

He thought about it. "Sure, but only if I could keep the sandwich." He opened the bag of chips and offered them to me. I took one and we crunched in silence for a minute. "What was it like going back to school in a wheelchair?"

I sighed. "Really? You're going to make me talk about this?"

He spread his arms wide. "You don't have to. But when in Rome..."

"It was just as dreadful as you'd think. People were very, very nice to me, of course. But that didn't make it any less awful. I was a conversation stopper. When I'd roll by, nobody could stand to talk about the theme for prom, or whatever. They felt like they couldn't."

Hartley was quiet for a moment. "Well that sounds craptastic. Did you have to go back?"

"I didn't *have* to — but being at home was even less fun. My parents were stressed out all the time. I thought if I went back off to school, they could, you know, back away from the ledge a little. I was sick of being under their microscope." And now I was really sick of this topic. "Dana is out on her own ledge right now. Tomorrow is tap night."

Hartley gave me another pale smile. "Yeah? If they spring me from this joint tomorrow, I'll sit and wait up with you guys. We'll have to play a few games of hockey, of course."

"Naturally," I agreed.

When I came in from the library just before nine the next night, Hartley's room door stood open. I put my head in, finding him seated on his bed, his desk chair propped under his leg. "Hey, Callahan," he said, tearing a piece of paper out of his notebook and balling it up.

"Hey yourself." I studied him, taking in the pale face and the weary look in his eyes. "You don't look so good."

"Thanks for the compliment." He shot the wadded paper toward the distant trashcan. It went in, of course. Because Hartley was Hartley.

I crutched further into the room. "Seriously, are you okay?"

"I will be. The second day is always the worst, right? I just need a good night's sleep. You know how hospitals are." He squinted up at me.

"Yeah, I do." I maneuvered over to sit down next to him, careful not to bump him at all. "How many times did they wake you up to check your vitals?"

"Lost count." He leaned down for his water bottle on the floor, and then drained it. "Callahan, would you mind refilling this for me?"

"Of course I wouldn't." I jumped up. Hooking the bottle's strap over my finger, I crutched into Hartley's bathroom and refilled it. "Can you take another dose of ibuprofen yet?" I asked, spotting the bottle on the sink.

"Hell, yes," he said.

I took two tablets out of the bottle and tipped them into my pocket. Then I brought the water back over to him. It scared me to see Hartley in pain and vulnerable. He looked all wrong. Before I could stop myself, I reached up, pressing my palm against his face. Big brown eyes rose up to study me. "You don't feel feverish," I said quickly. "Post surgical infections can be scary."

He closed his eyes, and let the weight of his head tip into my hand. For a long moment, I didn't move. I knew I needed to pull away, even though I wanted to do just the opposite — to wrap my arms around him and hold on tight. If I thought he'd let me, I would have done it.

With a sigh, I slid my hand down to his shoulder and put the water bottle in his hand. When he straightened up, I fished the pills out of my pocket.

"Only two?" he asked, his voice hoarse.

"But that's the dose! How many would you usually take?"

"Three or four, of course."

"The bottle says two, Hartley."

"Tell you what, Callahan. I'll sit on you, and then you can tell me why it makes sense for your dose to be the same as mine." His mouth smiled, but his eyes were too tired to join in.

"You're a pain in the ass, Hartley," I said to cover my concern for him. I made the trip back to his bathroom for one more pill.

"Thank you," he whispered when I came back. And after he'd swallowed all the tablets down, he leaned back on his hands, a grimace on his face. "What time is it?"

I checked my watch. "Just about nine."

"We have to go sit with Dana," he said.

I blinked. For a moment, I'd completely forgotten that it was supposed to be Dana's big night. Very shortly, all the singing groups would begin running across the Freshman Yard, tapping their favorite First Years in a mad dash for the best singers. "Right. Are you sure you want to move?"

He closed his eyes for a moment and then opened them again. "Good thing it's just across the hall."

"Hang on," I said. "Let me set up first."

I crutched back into my room, moved a bunch of books off the sofa, and lined up the coffee table for Hartley's knee. Then, struck by inspiration, I nudged my wheelchair out my door, across the hall, and into Hartley's room. This was perfect, because I'd gone to the Beaumont library (which had only three stairs) on my braces, and didn't need it myself.

He was standing when I found him. "Check this out," I said. "You don't even have to walk."

"Well, thanks," he sighed. I kicked the chair around behind him, and he sat. Quickly, I adjusted the footrest out in front of him, raising his bad leg into the air. He put his hands on the wheels and pushed. "So this is how the world looks to Callahan," he said, heading out the door.

"Dana, we're here!" I said as we entered my common room. "And it's nine. What do we do?"

She came skidding out of her bedroom. "We just wait."

"Can I turn on the football game?" Hartley asked.

My roommate frowned. "On mute. I need to be able to hear them knock."

Hartley was kind enough not to point out that since Dana had cranked our windows all the way open, and the door to the building was right outside, we'd never miss them. He picked up the remote in silence. When he found the football game, he backed my chair up near the couch and began fumbling for a way to transfer.

"Hey guys!" Bridger said, walking in with a bag of ice. "Special delivery. I'm gonna put it in your mini fridge, okay, bro?"

"Thanks, man. I could use some now, actually."

Bridger disappeared, and Hartley turned his attention to the task of getting out of my wheelchair.

"You could just stay there," I offered. "Keeps you from jostling it."

Hartley considered this idea, and then shook his head. He stood up on his good leg and tipped his body onto the couch. "I'm better off here," he said under his breath.

And he didn't look me in the eye.

Without comment, I moved the wheelchair away from the sofa. But the truth was, it bothered me. Hartley obviously couldn't stand the thought of sitting in a wheelchair when a passel of singing group girls entered the room. I'd always felt like the chair made me either pitiful or invisible, and Hartley had basically just agreed with me.

I was distracted from these distressing thoughts by the sound of pounding feet outside the window. Dana's face froze with excitement.

Quickly, I crutched into the hallway and opened the outside door. Twelve girls in red T-shirts ran past me and into our room. They had linked arms and begun to sing Aretha Franklin's *Respect* before I even made it back inside.

The second the song was over, the girls asked Dana if she wanted to become a member of the Merry Mellowtones. I held my breath, because I didn't know what Dana was going to say. I knew this group wasn't her first choice. On the other hand, they'd come for her early on, which meant they really cared.

"Maybe," she said quickly. The allowable answers were "yes," "no" and "maybe." But if a group wanted to, they could give away your spot after ten p.m., which was just forty-five minutes away.

"We hope you'll change that to a yes!" The pitch handed Dana a card with her phone number on it. Then they ran off to tap the next person on their list.

"Crumbs," Dana grumbled when they'd gone. "Should I just have said yes?" She took up her position at the window again. "I really want Something Special," she whispered. "But it's kind of a stretch."

"I want something special too, baby," Hartley grinned, his hands behind his head.

"Hartley!" Dana yelled.

"I guess the pain relievers are kicking in," I muttered.

Bridger came back into the room with a plastic bag full of ice, which Hartley eased onto his knee. But then his phone began to ring. Even the minimal shifting required to ease his phone out of his back pocket made Harley wince in pain. He checked the phone's display and then silenced it.

"Awful late for Stacia to call, isn't it?" Bridger asked.

Hartley gave a one-shouldered shrug. "She's probably drunk dialing me from some club. I can't deal with her and pain at the same time."

Bridger snorted. "Remind me why you stay loyal to someone who doesn't even know how to comfort a man in pain?"

"Leave it alone, Bridge." Hartley's voice was exhausted.

"Okay. But then don't ride me for being a man-whore, when you make commitment look so appealing." He sat down on the sofa.

"I don't want to ride you, Bridge. You're not my type."

"But thanks for the visual," Bridger returned, and I laughed.

Across the room, Dana seemed oblivious to the entire conversation. She worried the card in her hand and paced back and forth. Her own hope fairies were obviously working overtime, whispering words of encouragement, fighting off the dread.

"Hang in there, Dana," Bridger said, pointing at the T.V. screen. "Dude, the volume?"

Hartley just shook his head.

For a long time, nothing happened, except the Patriots scored a touchdown. So at least we had that going for us. While the minutes crawled by, Dana tried alternately to wear a hole in our new rug and tatter the edges of the card the Merry Mellowtones had given her. Meanwhile, Hartley's color improved, and he stopped making weird pain faces every time he moved.

And I was on some kind of emotional overload. It was hard to keep from hugging the both of them. Dana looked stressed out and forsaken. Clearly I'd made the right decision about rushing a singing group. Tap night was a kind of medieval self-torture, whereby the world notified you, within the span of an hour, just how desirable you were.

Who needed that? It was better to receive rejection in bite-sized slivers. I got regular doses every day — in the look on Hartley's face at the idea of sitting in a wheelchair, or the Big Smiles I got from people who didn't know what to say. I watched Dana's crumbling bravado and asked myself, why buy problems when they're giving them away for free?

Just as I began to wonder whether Dana could take any more, there was another pounding of feet outside, and every muscle in my roommate's body tensed. There was a knock on the outside door. And then Bridger leapt up, running out of our room to let them in.

A gaggle of girls in purple T-shirts ran into our room, linked arms and began to sing the school fight song in four-part harmony. Dana's face lit up like the Rockefeller Center Christmas tree.

"Dana, would you like to be the newest member of Something Special?" the pitch asked when the song ended.

"YES!" Dana shrieked.

The guys clapped, and I put my arms around Dana. She was actually shaking with joy.

Suddenly, the evening's lessons tilted in a way that hurt my heart. Dana's big risk had paid off. She'd found her tribe. The big bunch of purple-shirted girls hugging her now was not insubstantial. I smiled a face-cracking smile, and was so happy for her.

At the same time, it cost me.

Chapter Seven: *Your Poster Boy*

— Corey

By the time the leaves finished turning yellow and red, midterms were almost over. I'd aced my Spanish test, and limped through calculus. Economics was my favorite class now, since Mondays, Wednesdays and Fridays always found me seated in the gimp section with Hartley. And after class it was off to our lunch in Commons.

The only dark spot in every week was Physical Therapy.

"How are we doing on the stairs these days?" Pat asked, as she always did.

"Fine. Slow." For some reason, P.T. turned me into someone who spoke only in monosyllables.

"Let's practice," she said.

"Yes, let's," I deadpanned.

Pat led me out into a stairwell that I'd never seen before. "Okay, have at it," she said. "Let's see your technique."

One at a time, I placed my crutches onto the first step, and then hopped my feet up to meet them. Then I did it all again. And again. But when I was seven steps up, I turned to look at Pat.

That was a mistake.

I could see exactly how easy it would be to trip, and fall down those seven concrete steps. I had a vision of my body bouncing over their edges. *Falling backwards.* It was the very thing that terrified me.

I was suddenly stranded there, in the middle of the flight of stairs. I was afraid to keep going up, and I couldn't turn around to go back down.

Then Pat stood behind me. "I'm spotting you," she

said, her hand on my shoulder blade. "Just a few more."

Sweating, I sucked it up. After each step she touched my back, so I'd know she was still there. When I made it to the landing, we stopped.

Pat tapped her chin, making thoughtful faces while I panted. "I know that you were taught to use two crutches," she said. "But I think you might do better with one, plus the railing." She guided me over to the handrail, and took my right crutch away.

The second span of steps was easier, because I had a death grip on the banister.

"We'll take the elevator back down," Pat announced when I'd made it to the top. She gave me back my crutch, and pressed the button.

Grim and perspiring, I followed her back into the therapy room. She had me sit down on the mat and remove my braces. "You know, Corey…"

I hated when people began a sentence that way. It almost always led to nagging.

"…The more we can get you walking, the better you'll feel. You haven't plateaued yet. I know walking feels ungainly to you, but there are some great things we can do to make your stride more natural."

"Like what?" My straight-legged "stride" could hardly be *less* natural.

"There are new braces which bend when you want them to and lock when you need it. I think you're a really good candidate. But the manufacturer requires that you to commit to eight more months of therapy on them."

"If a brace needs eight months of therapy to work, how good could it be?"

Pat smiled the smile of someone who was trying to be patient. "I think they're miraculous. But you have to train your trunk, torso and glutes to help you. Think about it. In the meantime, let's work on crawling."

I gave Pat a weary look, because crawling was one of the more exhausting things we did.

"Hands down on the mat, please," she said.

With a barely cooperative sigh, I turned over, placing my hands on the mat. Then I curved my back like a cat, pulling with my weak quads into something resembling all fours. Pat adjusted my uncooperative legs behind me.

"Let's go," she said. "There's only eight minutes left, anyway."

I stepped one of my hands forward on the mat.

"This is easier if you move the hand and the opposing leg together," she said. "Let me show you." Pat got onto her hands and knees too, demonstrating the proper way to unweight the leg that I wish to move.

The door to the therapy room swung open, and a voice said. "Oh goody. Women on all fours."

"*Mister* Hartley," Pat's voice was frosty. "That is not an appropriate way to speak to me or my patient."

"Don't worry, Pat," Hartley said. "You get to punish me for the next hour, and Callahan will get her chance to punish me over RealStix later."

"Damn straight," I said, sitting my butt down on my useless lower legs, which is a total no-no, for circulatory reasons. At the rehab center, they used to have a fit if I sat on my feet even for a second.

"Let's go, Corey," Pat said. "I need you to do the length of the mat."

But I hesitated. I *really* did not want Hartley to watch me crawl like a drunk, my butt swaying in the air. I met Pat's eye and gave the tiniest shake of my head.

Pat studied me for a second. Then she called out,

"Hartley, I need a favor. Could you please go down to the front desk and collect my mail? I'm expecting something. And there's still a few more minutes until we start."

"O-kay..." he said slowly. "Is there anything else I can get you while I'm out? Coffee? Dry cleaning?"

"That will be all," Pat said.

When he walked out, I lifted my ass in the air and prepared to crawl. "Thank you," I said in a low voice.

"Not a problem," she sighed.

"So, Corey," Dana said, putting on a jacket. "Did you hear about the Screw Your Roommate Dance next week?"

Hartley was setting up our hockey game, but we hadn't started playing yet. "Those are always fun," he said. "I set Bridger up last year. I handcuffed him to a tree in the courtyard, and gave his date the key."

"Sounds...interesting," I said. "Do you want to go, Dana?" Although, since she'd brought it up, I could assume the answer was yes.

She shrugged. "I think it sounds like fun. Don't you? What's your type, Corey? Do you have a type?"

Hartley handed me a game controller. "There's only one man for Callahan, and he's pretty unavailable."

At that, my heart took off galloping like a pony, and I actually tasted bile in my mouth. Because I was sure that Hartley knew how I felt about him, and that he was about to say it out loud.

"The Pittsburgh Puffins probably have a game that night," Hartley continued, "otherwise, I'm sure the captain would fly up if you asked."

My heart rate began to descend back into the normal range.

Dana giggled. "The captain of the Pittsburgh Puffins, huh? Now I have to Google him." She leaned over my laptop computer where it sat on the trunk, tapping on the keyboard. "Ooh!" she said. "I see. Wow."

"Yeah," I agreed, while Hartley snorted.

"Hey, Corey?" Dana said. "You're getting a Skype call. It's Damien. Should I answer?"

"Sure, thanks."

Dana handed me the laptop, and my brother's face materialized on the screen. "Hi shorty," he said. "What's shaking?"

"Not much. I'm just hanging out. Are you still at work?" I could see office furniture behind him.

"Yup, it's a glamorous life." My brother was working as a paralegal for a year before he went to law school.

Beside me, Hartley plopped down on the sofa, a bottle of tequila in one hand, a cocktail shaker in the other. "Whoa! It's Callahan! How are you, man?"

"Dude. *Why* would you be in my sister's room, and not at practice?"

"Well, Captain, the reason would be the giant fucking cast on my leg. These days I can only play hockey on a screen, and your sister has the sweet TV. This is how we party in the gimp ghetto." Hartley looked down at the other supplies he'd brought. "Fuck. I forgot the limes. Be right back." He grabbed his crutches and stood up, ambling toward my door.

Damien waited a moment before crossing his arms and hooking his eyebrows. "Please tell me you're not seeing him."

This made me laugh. "I'm not seeing him. But — God, Damian — why do you care?"

"He's not who I would pick for you."

Well I'm not who he picked, so it looks like you don't need to worry. "That's funny, Damien. Who *would* you pick for me?"

"Nobody, of course. You're my little sister."

"I see."

"Please stay away from the entire hockey team. They're pigs."

"I think you just called yourself a pig."

My brother's smile was wide. "I just call 'em like I see 'em."

"I have a video game to win here, bro. I'll talk to you later."

Damien frowned. "Don't let Hartley get you drunk."

"Really? You'd lecture me about drinking? Ease up, okay? Or I'll tell Mom what really happened to that bottle of cooking sherry that went missing when you were in tenth grade."

He grinned. "Later, shorty."

I won our first game. Afterwards, instead of rubbing Hartley's face in it, I told him that I needed a little advice.

"Yes, you should trade your goalie to another team. He's weak." Hartley was squeezing lime juice into a cocktail shaker. I watched him pour the tequila in, and then add a dollop of honey. He had been told to stop icing his knee, so the plan was to use up the rest of the bag of ice Bridger had brought him on margaritas.

"No, seriously. It's about the Screw Your Roommate dance. Dana wants me to set her up. But since I live under a rock, I don't know who to call."

He shook up our cocktails. "What's her type?"

"I'm not sure. She's not really into sports. I could see her with a theater nerd, or a musician."

"Then you might be asking the wrong guy for help." He uncapped the shaker and strained the results into two dining hall glasses. "I wish I'd thought to snag some salt. Cheers." He handed me a glass.

I took a sip. "You know, I thought the honey was a strange choice. But it's quite good."

"Stick with me, babe."

If only I could.

"Tell me this," Hartley said, bending his knee a few degrees, and grimacing. "If Dana asks me for advice about who to set *you* up with for Screw Your Roommate, what should I tell her? There are a couple of frosh on the hockey team who would like to go. I don't know their game schedule, though."

I shook my head. "I'm not going."

"You don't want to be screwed?"

I felt my face heat. "Gosh, I wonder if that joke has ever been made before?"

"It's a tough crowd here for a Friday night," Hartley grinned. "Look, it's really kind of fun, and a low pressure way to meet people. No offense, Callahan, but you're not exactly getting out there."

I nearly choked on my drink. "Hartley, if I wanted someone to nag me about meeting people, I could always call my mother."

"I'm not nagging you, I just don't understand. I know why I'm sitting here on a Friday night, popping Advil on the couch. My leg is sore and my girlfriend is overseas. I'm on, like, the injured reserve list."

I took a very large gulp of my drink, the lime shimmering on my tongue. "The injured reserve list is a good analogy. I think I'm still on it. It's a *dance*, Hartley. Why would I go?"

He swirled his drink in his glass. "Okay, so maybe

it's not your best event."

"You think? And you'd set me up with an *athlete?* He would say you had a sick sense of humor."

Hartley put his elbow on the back of the couch and turned so that he could see me better. "You think athletes only like other athletes? Some of the women I've dated think that putting on makeup counts as a physical activity."

Of course he was right, but that didn't mean I felt very dateable. Nothing about me was the same as it used to be. My hair was the wrong length, my legs were beginning to thin out from too much time in the chair. Just because Hartley didn't see all that was wrong didn't mean I couldn't.

After my accident, a well-meaning therapist had given me some literature about body image after spinal cord injury. The pamphlet was full of perky suggestions for "learning to love the 'new you.'" But my heart was full of dark questions that weren't answered anywhere on those shiny pages.

Meanwhile, my margarita was disappearing rapidly. "The old me would have loved to be set up with a hockey player," I told him. "But I don't look the same as I used to. I don't *feel* the same." *Also, I'm in love with you. But that's a separate problem.* "Maybe it will just take a while longer."

"You're still trying to get your feet under you." Hartley's brown eyes were soft. "I hope you don't mind a little gallows humor."

"I adore gallows humor."

"See? You're fun, Callahan. It really isn't all that complicated."

"Everything about it is complicated, okay?" The tequila was starting to get to me. "*Everything.* I don't even know what I'm still capable of."

He frowned. "What do you mean?"

"Never mind." I picked up my game controller, but Hartley took it out of my hands.

"Callahan, do you mean sex?"

I shrugged, miserable. "I can't talk about it with you."

"Well, who can you talk about it with? Because that sounds like a pretty big fucking problem."

"So to speak."

"Seriously. When I told my friends that my leg was broken in two places, everybody said, well, at least your dick isn't broken. So life can't be all that bad."

I tried not to aspirate my margarita. "And that's the difference between how guys and girls speak to one another."

He ran a finger around the rim of his glass. "When you say you're not sure what you're capable of, do you mean..."

"Hartley, really. Not an easy topic for me."

"More tequila, then." He reached over to refill my glass. "Okay, so, if a guy is paralyzed, that means he can't get it up anymore, right? Stacia made me watch Downton Abbey."

I let out a bark of laughter. "Something like that. But it depends where the injury occurred, and what sort of injury it was. Some guys in wheelchairs do fine. But some of them can raise the flag, only they can't *feel* it anymore."

His eyes widened with true horror. "Shit."

"Exactly."

"So, for a woman..."

I shook my head. "Next topic, please."

"I guess a woman could always do it. But if she

couldn't feel it, then she might not want to."

I stared up at the ceiling, hoping he would let it go.

He took a sip of his drink. "Callahan, one thing you might not know about me is that I don't embarrass."

"Well, I do," I said.

But he didn't listen. "Now, a guy who wasn't sure if it still worked would just start slapping things around, like, the minute he got home from the hospital," Hartley said. "Actually, before that. He would be yanking on it the first time he was alone in the hospital bathroom. And the mystery would be solved."

Now he was starting to piss me off. "Honestly, you have no idea."

"Then tell me, Callahan. If I have no idea." He pinned me with his gaze, and then we were having one of our stare downs. I'm a fierce competitor, of course, but it was impossible to win against Hartley. It was impossible to win if you're me, anyway. Because staring into Hartley's chocolaty eyes always took me apart, reminding me just how much I wanted to climb inside his gaze and never come back out.

I looked down into my drink and tried to explain. "Okay, your paralyzed boy? For a long time he won't be able to tell what works and what doesn't, because a spinal injury shocks your entire system. He can't feel *anything* below his ribcage for a while, and it's terrifying. Then the doctors start arguing about what he'll get back, and scaring the shit out of his parents."

When I looked up again, Hartley regarded me with a quiet, liquid gaze.

Though I wished it wouldn't, my throat began to feel hot and tight. "And your poster boy? He has a catheter up his weenie, okay? And he doesn't even know — probably for weeks — if he can *poop* like a normal person." I gulped my drink as an excuse to look away. "It takes a long time for everything to settle back down and start working again. And even then, your boy might be psyched out about the whole thing. Even a committed horn dog might take a vacation from jerking off. If only to preserve his own sanity."

Hartley's expression softened. "That really sucks for our hypothetical friend."

"Hypothetically, yes."

There was a silence for a minute, but it was not an uncomfortable one. My shoulders began to relax again. I'd never told Dana any of the gory details about spinal cord injury, because I didn't want her to think pitying thoughts about me. But something about Hartley always loosened my tongue. Hopefully I wouldn't regret it later.

We sipped our drinks for a little while longer, until eventually he set my game controller on my knee. "Let's find out if your goalie's reflexes are still sharp after two margaritas."

"Yes, let's," I agreed.

Chapter Eight: *But You Shouldn't Have*

— *Hartley*

I was looking over my notes from bio lab when someone knocked on my door. "Enter!" I expected to see Corey wheel in to throw me some attitude about the two more RealStix wins she'd pulled off the other night. But it was Dana who came in. "What's up, girl?"

She bounced into the room and shut the door behind her. "I want to have a party."

I tossed my bio notebook onto the desk and gave her my full attention. "Sounds like a plan. What's the occasion?"

"Well, it's Corey's birthday on Friday." She heaved herself onto my bed. "But we're not having a birthday party, because those are for five-year-olds."

"Obviously."

"I want to throw a party anyway, because...why haven't we done this already? Our room is great, so we're totally overdue. So my gift to Corey is that I'm making a giant batch of my famous sangria. And we'll invite everyone we know."

"Awesome. What do you need from me?"

Dana fidgeted. "Well, are you free on Friday? Because you're the person Corey knows best."

"I wouldn't miss it. And the hockey team has a home game at seven. I could bring Bridger and some of our crew over by ten."

She clapped her hands together. "Perfect! And there's one more thing..."

"Now you're going to ask us to buy the alcohol, aren't you?"

Dana grinned. "How did you know?"

"Because your fake ID sucks, and Callahan doesn't

have one." I picked up my phone to text Bridger. "Call your order into the package store on York, and we'll get Bridger to pick it up Friday night."

"You're the best, Hartley." She popped off my bed and scurried out the door.

Same to you, Dana. The game of roommate roulette was not always kind to First Years. But Dana was awesome, and Corey was lucky to have her.

Friday night, when I approached the outer door to McHerrin, there was already music and laughter spilling out into the night. Nice. "This way, guys."

A dozen hockey players followed me into Corey's room. Dana's Something Special pals were already inside, and I recognized some other Beaumont First Years. Mumford and Sons was playing in the background.

"Welcome!" Dana waved a ladle in our direction. "The sangria is over here." She stood over a big plastic tub, a stack of cups beside her.

I accepted a drink. "Awesome, Dana. Where's the birthday girl?"

She pointed, and I spotted Corey propped up against the couch, thanking Bridger for the wine delivery.

"Don't mention it, Callahan," Bridger said. "I'm going to have a sample," he winked. "You know, quality control."

"Sample the heck out of it, Bridge," Corey said as he walked away.

"Happy Birthday, beautiful." Without thinking, I pulled her in for a hug, which felt great. But then I felt her stiffen in my arms. I leaned back, hoping I hadn't somehow offended her. Sure, we didn't usually go full-frontal. But it was only a birthday hug.

"You went to the hockey game," she whispered.

And then I understood. She'd smelled it on my jacket — that icy whiff that was so familiar. I'd had the same strange reaction only hours before, when I'd walked into the rink for the first time in months. Nothing else smelled like that.

I relaxed my arms around her. "Yeah. I took the gimpmobile. Did you want to go?"

"Nah," she said quickly, trying to cover her reaction. "But who won?"

"We did, of course. And now we're ready to celebrate."

Corey looked around. "You brought all these guys? Awesome."

"Sure. It wasn't easy dragging them into a room full of singing group girls for a cold drink. But I managed. Hey — I'll be right back, okay? I'm going to drop my jacket." I let go of Callahan and crutched into her bedroom. I took off my jacket, and was just reaching into the breast pocket when Bridger came in, startling me.

"Hey, man." Bridger chucked his jacket onto Corey's bed.

"Good game tonight," I said, even though it really wasn't. But the unhelpful injured shouldn't be too critical.

"Eh," he said. "At least we won. Could have been worse. And now there's a redhead showing me the 'fuck me' eyes."

"You'd better get out there, then." I needed him to leave so that I could sneak Corey's birthday present out of my jacket.

"Yeah," he said, but he didn't move. "So what's the deal with you and Callahan, anyway?"

That was a question I hadn't really been expecting. "We're tight, that's all." I gave the most casual shrug I could muster. Bridger wouldn't understand. He didn't have any girl friends, or even any girlfriends. His M.O. with women was simply to exchange body fluids and then move on.

"You two look awfully cozy," Bridger crossed his arms. "She'd be a really big improvement over Stacia."

"That's real nice, asshole. I'll give Stacia your love next time she calls." But it was no secret that Bridger wasn't the president of my girlfriend's fan club. And the feeling was unfortunately mutual.

Bridger raised his hands defensively. "It's just an observation. Corey is more your type than Stacia ever was."

It was hard to argue that point. Before dating Princess Stacia, I'd always gone for the jock girls. Not just *any* jock. But there was something really sexy about a pretty girl who could also throw a football, and who didn't mind watching the Bruins. But that was beside the point. "Stacia's not going anywhere, Bridge." He'd better get used to it.

"Too bad." He turned and left Corey's room.

Alone again, I pulled my gift out of my jacket and dropped it onto Corey's pillow. Shit, if Bridger knew what was in this box, he would never believe that we were only friends. The birthday girl was going to blush like a tomato when she opened it. It was sort of a gag gift, but sort of not. Given the intense discussion we'd had a week ago, I hoped she'd understand.

"Good party," I told her when I came back out into the common room. And it was. Tonight they were *that* room — the one bursting with energy and conversation.

Unfortunately, I was in no mood for a party. I had

just spent the past two hours trying not to scream with frustration. It had cost me five dollars to buy a ticket in the student section to watch my own team play Rensselaer. And they'd barely eked out the win, breaking the 1-1 tie fifteen seconds before the buzzer. There was no less powerful feeling than watching your teammates struggle without you. And all the while, the cold air of the ice rink had slowly frozen my leg into a painsicle.

I felt selfish just thinking it, but what I really needed that second was a couple of hours alone with Corey, shooting the shit on the sofa. I needed the warm glance I always got from her when I walked into the room.

Whatever Bridger might make of it, I needed my Corey fix.

I flopped down on Corey's empty couch, and patted the cushion next to me. She looked down, calculating the effort required to grab her crutches and relocate from the arm of the couch to the seat. It was Crutches Math 101. I did it all day long, too.

Saving her the trouble, I reached up and grabbed her by the hips. A half second later she landed next to me, her face startled. "Good thing this drink wasn't full," she said, staring into her cup.

"Good thing." I arranged my aching leg on the coffee table. "Talk to me, Callahan. What's the gossip?"

"Wow," she said. "Check out Bridger. He sure works fast."

I looked up. And sure enough, Bridger was already making time in the corner of the room, lip-locked to one of Dana's singing group friends. I rubbed my aching leg and grinned. "The dude *does* work fast, and not just with the ladies. Bridge gets more done in a day than most people do in a week. Did you know he's in that program where you get a masters degree at the same time as your bachelor's?"

"Really?" Corey cocked an eyebrow toward the corner, where Bridger seemed to be eating the girls' face. "Where does he find the time?"

"Unlike us normal people, Bridger never sleeps. After hockey season ends, he drives a forklift three nights a week in a warehouse."

"Seriously? You've known each other a long time, haven't you?" She propped an elbow on the back of the sofa and turned her face so she could see me. Corey always gave me her full attention, like there was nobody else in the room.

"Yeah. Bridge and I played on the same league in high school. And we're both members of another club."

"Which one?"

My smile was probably more like a grimace. "The Poor Club. Hartley grew up about ten miles from here, on the wrong side of the industrial wasteland." While Harkness College had a beautiful campus, the city around it was actually kind of a shithole. "And my town isn't much better. When I first came to Harkness, all the money here was a shock."

Corey took a thoughtful sip of her sangria. "But at Harkness, everybody lives in the dorms and eats in the dining hall. I love that about this place. It doesn't matter who's rich."

I shook my head. "Wait until spring, when people start arguing about which Caribbean island to spend break on."

"I'll be spending it in sunny Wisconsin."

"Your girl Dana will probably head down to St. Croix or St. John. I'd put money on it."

Corey's eyes darted to her roommate on the other

end of the room. "Well, her family has a house in Hawaii."

"See what I mean? My frosh year, the first time someone told me they had a second home at Lake Tahoe, I thought, 'That's weird. Who needs two houses?' I had no fucking clue. This place gives you a great education in more ways than one."

"Dude." Bridger appeared beside me, leaning down to ask a question into my ear. "Where do you keep your goalies? I'm all out."

I chuckled, giving him a shove on the shoulder. "They're in the logical drawer. Help yourself."

"I'll pay you back." Bridger straightened up.

Whatever. I didn't have any near-term need for condoms, anyway. "But, dude? Take the party elsewhere, okay?" I didn't need to find Bridger fucking some girl on my bed. When we were roommates that had happened more than once.

"You got it." Bridger walked out of Corey's common room, reappearing less than a minute later. Then he collected his girlfriend for the evening. They swapped spit for a moment in the middle of the room. And then the two of them left together.

Corey watched them go. "Wait...goalies?" I watched the understanding break on her face, and then she snorted with laughter. Embarrassed, she clamped a hand over her mouth. But her eyes danced with glee. "Okay," she said when she could breathe again "I *thought* my brother had taught me every hockey slang term. But apparently not."

"Yeah?" I tipped my head back onto the sofa. "He left out a good one."

Corey grinned. "If you had a little sister, you'd understand. Or so I'm told."

Right. I felt a familiar little kick to the gut at the very idea. If life had worked out differently, I *would* have a little sister. And two brothers besides. But I pushed that thought away. "I get it. Your big brother thinks his baby sister shouldn't think about those things."

Her smile got sly. "Hang on...tell me the truth. How much of a dog was my brother?"

"Well, if the scale is from priest to Bridger..." I held my hands far apart, and Corey giggled. "I'd say he was right in the middle."

"Here's to mediocrity," she said, holding up her glass.

"Cheers."

Corey drained her drink and then pointed at the darkened TV screen. "Do you think anyone would disapprove if we checked the hockey score? I don't think I can make it through the evening without knowing whether my Puffins are smacking your Bruins."

She turned her blue eyes onto mine, and for some reason I felt an unwelcome pang in my chest. "Go for it, birthday girl. That said, I wouldn't want you to get depressed on your big day. Because there's no way you're winning this thing."

"Says you." With a big smile, she began to look around for the remote.

— *Corey*

The Puffins *flattened* the Bruins, 4 to 1. For a while there, I thought Hartley might start crying into his drink.

So at least I had that going for me. Of all the things on my birthday list, though, a Puffins victory wouldn't have been at the top. The gift I really wanted was the Bruins fan on the sofa next to me.

Hartley stayed until the party was over. Then he

gave me a kiss on top of the head, and another "happy birthday." And then Dana and I were alone again.

"Let's leave the cleanup for tomorrow," she yawned.

"Absolutely," I said, privately vowing to do it all myself.

I let her have the bathroom first. When I finally got to bed, I found a small red box on my pillow. In black marker, the words *MR. DIGBY* had been inked onto the cover.

What?

I lifted the lid. Inside I found a purple plastic object measuring about six inches long, shaped like a fat cigar. It took me several long seconds to figure out what I was looking at.

It was a vibrator.

"Oh my God," I said aloud, the words echoing in my empty room. I could only guess that Hartley had this strange gift idea after our uncomfortable talk about sex after paralysis. Even though I was all alone in my room, I felt heat creep up my neck and over my cheeks.

Hell and damn. When someone gives you a gift, you have to at least acknowledge it. Ugh! He had to know how embarrassing I'd find this. Maybe that was the point?

There was no way I could mention this in person. So I took the cheesy way out. I texted him. And it was just my luck, but he texted right back.

Corey: *Uh, Hartley?*

Hartley: *Yes, beautiful? ;-)*

Corey: *Um…you shouldn't have?*

Hartley: *Since U liked RealStix I thought my other favorite hobby might appeal to U too.*

If possible, I began blushing even harder. A bolder girl would have replied "thanks for the visual." But I wasn't that girl.

Corey: *How…thoughtful?*

Hartley: *Too bad I can't see your face right now.*

Corey: ****face palm****

Hartley: *Did I mention that I don't embarrass?*

Corey: *You weren't kidding about that.*

Hartley: *Goodnight Callahan. Nice party.*

Corey: *Goodnight Hartley.*

Chapter Nine: *Peace in the Kingdom*

— *Corey*

"What's the matter, Callahan?" Hartley asked as we made our way slowly toward Commons for lunch.

I stuffed my phone into my bag and caught up with him. "Nothing. My mom is having a cow because I told her I didn't want to fly home for Thanksgiving."

"Why not?"

I shrugged. "It's too many planes, trains and automobiles for only for a couple of days." Flying with a wheelchair in tow was a drag, especially because Harkness students had to catch a bus to the airport. I just didn't want the hassle.

"This place really empties out over Thanksgiving. You don't want to stay here alone."

"I'm not. Dana isn't going all the way back to Japan for Thanksgiving. So we're going to hang out together. The medical school cafeteria stays open that day."

Hartley stopped crutching toward Commons. "You are *not* eating in the med school caf on Thanksgiving." He pulled his phone out of his pocket and tapped it. Then he put it to his ear.

I waited, of course, because a guy can't crutch and talk on the phone at the same time.

"Hey Mom? I need to bring two more friends home for Thanksgiving."

"Hartley! Don't…"

He waved a hand to silence me. "No, don't worry. She's still safely out of the country. These are perfectly normal friends. Nobody will be expecting caviar and fois gras." He paused. "Awesome. Love you." He hung up, stuffed the phone into his pocket and put his hands back on the crutch handles.

"Hartley," I protested. "Your mom doesn't need two extra guests."

"Sure she does. I was already bringing Bridger and his sister. I always bring people, because I live close by. The only guest my mom did not enjoy was Stacia." We waited for the light to change so that we could cross the street. "You and I will have to stay on the first floor, of course. If you don't mind sharing a room with me."

I didn't know what to say. Did I want to go to Hartley's house with him? Heck yes. But I could imagine the pitfalls — me looking ridiculous, mostly. "That's really nice of you," I said, thinking. "Did you say Bridger has a sister?"

Hartley laughed. "Wait until you meet her."

A week later, I watched the streets of sleepy Etna, Connecticut, roll by from the backseat of Bridger's car. Hartley rode shotgun, on the phone again with his mother. "We're just off the highway," he was saying. "Do you need us to pick anything up?"

In the back seat, between Dana and I, Bridger's sister Lucy bounced in her seat. "Over the river and through the woods, to Hartley's house we go..." she sang. "Are we there yet?"

Bridger's sister was nothing like what I expected — mainly because she was seven years old, and in the second grade.

"If you kick the front seat one more time," Bridger threatened from behind the wheel, "I will tickle you until you pee yourself."

"Icky," Lucy agreed, stilling her feet. Her ponytail was a gorgeous russet color, the exact same shade as Bridger's.

"And you'd better not be kicking Callahan," Bridger

added.

"I'm fine," I said quickly.

Hartley was still on the phone with his mom. "That inflatable mattress has a hole in it," he said. "But we're good, because Bridger and Lucy can have the guest room, and Dana will take my old room. Callahan is going to bunk with me, because neither one of us is any good on the stairs." He listened for a moment. "You need to relax, mom. Stop ironing napkins and have a glass of wine. We'll be there in five minutes."

When Bridger pulled into the driveway, Hartley's mom was waiting for us on the porch swing of an old wooden house. When Hartley opened his door, she bounced down three steps and ran over to kiss him and ruffle his hair.

She was pretty, and younger than I expected her to be, with shiny black hair and rosy skin. Her eyes were just as beautiful as Hartley's, only darker. "Welcome! Welcome," she said as Dana hopped out of the car, her smile wide. "I'm Theresa."

"Hi Aunt Theresa!" Lucy yelled, hugging her around the waist.

"Oh! You've gotten so *tall*," Hartley's mom said. "You big girl. The dog is upstairs, Lucy. She'll be happy to see you."

Without another word, the little girl ran up the steps and inside.

"Mom, this is Callahan and Dana."

"I hope we're not imposing," I couldn't help but say. "Hartley wouldn't let us stay on campus for some reason."

"You can't stay there!" she laughed. "Not on Thanksgiving."

Dana pressed a bottle of wine into her hands. "Thanks so much for having us."

"You're always welcome. But hang on, Adam. I didn't realize Miss Callahan was a girl. She won't want to bunk with you."

"Mom, all the ladies want to share my bed."

"Hartley!" I punched him in the arm, and his mother laughed.

He turned to me. "The bed is the size of Massachusetts. I'm not kidding." To his mom he said, "You're not talking me onto that evil couch." Hartley kissed her on the cheek. "How are you?"

"Good," she said.

"Is there anything Bridger and I can help you with while we're here?"

She cocked her head to the side. "The car could use an oil change," she said. "You could do that this weekend. Save me the forty bucks."

"Done," he said.

Theresa had already done most of the work on the Thanksgiving meal. The turkey was almost done, and two pies cooled on the counter.

Even so, Hartley tied an apron around his waist and then poured a quart of heavy cream into a bowl. He took a whisk from a drawer and began whipping quick ovals through the bowl. "What's the matter, Callahan? You've never seen a guy whip cream before?"

I shook off my surprise. "I just wouldn't expect you to cook, Hartley."

"I'm only the assistant." He sped up the motion, the whisk a blur through the white surface. He picked up a cup of sugar and shook some of it into the mixture. Then he began whipping again.

I dragged my eyes away from the mouthwatering sight of Hartley's upper body hard at work. "So what can I do to help?" I asked. "I'm not, um, a cook. But I take direction well enough."

"We've got it covered," Theresa said, although it seemed categorically impossible that at two p.m. on Thanksgiving there wasn't something I could do.

"Mom," Hartley said, "Callahan gets cranky if she thinks you're babying her. If you want peace in the kingdom, give her a job."

His mother laughed. "Sorry, Corey. It's just that I'm not used to it. Not all of Hartley's friends have such a positive attitude toward kitchen work."

"Nice, mom," Hartley said. "Take a couple of shots at her even though she's on another continent."

I pointed to a bag of potatoes on the counter. "Do these need peeling?"

"They sure do," Theresa said, opening a drawer to produce a peeler.

I tucked the bag under my arm, and crutched over to the kitchen table. I heaved myself into a chair. Theresa watched as I unlocked my knees and swiveled to face the table. She brought me a newspaper for the peels, and a bowl for the finished spuds. The peeling was slow work, but I didn't mind.

"Adam, how's the therapy going?" Theresa asked.

"Tedious," he said, still whisking. "Callahan and I have the same trainer. Pat the drill sergeant."

"I think therapists are like dentists," I said. "Nobody is ever excited to see them. Or maybe you and I are just jerks."

"Or maybe it's Pat," Theresa suggested.

"Nope!" I argued cheerfully. "I've pretty much disliked every therapist I've met. And there have been many." I tossed another potato into the bowl. "Although, I might be mellowing with age. I'm not as ornery with Pat as I was with the others."

"Why?" Hartley asked.

"Well, the first therapists I saw were teaching me to do things like put on my own socks, and transfer from the wheelchair to a bed. And I was so pissed off that I needed someone to teach me that, I couldn't see straight."

"I can understand that," Theresa said.

"They know a lot of cool tricks, though. Once they show you something — like how to get from the floor back into your wheelchair without tipping over — it's just so obvious how much you need their help. And that just makes it worse. You hate learning it, but you can't afford not to."

"Sounds like a blast," Hartley said.

"You'd think, since I'd spent so many hours training for sports, that I would have been a model patient, but you'd be wrong," I told them. "Okay, I'm going to stop whining now," I said, tossing a potato into the bowl.

"You're not a whiner, Callahan," Hartley said sweetly. "Except when you lose to me at RealStix."

"But that so rarely happens," I said, and Theresa laughed.

The house began to smell wonderful. Dana and Bridger set the table, swearing that they couldn't use my help at just at that moment. So I sat on the living room couch, flipping pages in my economics textbook. Exams were coming up fast.

Lucy appeared in front of me, a deck of cards in her hands. "Do you know how to play Uno?"

"Well, sure," I closed the book. "Want to play?"

"Yeah! Do you know how to shuffle? I suck at shuffling." She threw herself down on the living room floor and cut the deck in two.

I unstrapped my braces and dropped them on the floor. Then, with no grace whatsoever, I slid off the sofa and butt-scooted over to Lucy. Using my hands, I arranged my legs in a straddle position and took the cards from her. As I shuffled and dealt, Lucy stretched out a hand and cautiously touched my toe.

"Um, Callahan?" she looked at me with a question in her eyes. "Can you really not feel this?"

I shook my head. "Can't. Swear to God." I watched as her finger traced the top of my sock. She might as well have been touching someone else's foot, for all I could tell.

"What does it feel like not to feel?" Lucy had a high little voice, clear and sweet. If someone else had asked me the question, I might have bristled. But there was a guileless curiosity shining in her face, and it was impossible to feel self-conscious.

"Well, I can only say that it feels like nothing. If I were to reach over and pinch your ponytail, you might not notice. Or you might feel a little tug, but not in the place I'm pinching. Like that."

Lucy considered this explanation. "That's a little creepy."

I laughed. "It *is*, honestly. Sometimes I stare at my feet and try to convince them to move. When I was in the hospital I did that all day long. I just couldn't wrap my head around it. I'd say, 'come on feet! Everyone else is doing it.'"

Lucy giggled. "Do you miss walking normal?"

"Well, sure. But mostly I can get where I need to go. Stairs are a big problem, though. And what I really miss is skating."

Lucy frowned, her elfin face tilted up toward mine. "Skating is okay," she said. "But I fall down a lot. Not like Bridger. He skates fast."

"Keep skating, and you'll go fast too. Fast is amazing," I told her. "It feels like flying. I still dream about skating. I think I dream about it every night." I'd never admitted that out loud before. And Lucy's mouth didn't fall open with distress the way my parents' would, if I'd said it to them.

"I dream about riding horses," Lucy said, fiddling with her cards. Then the little girl turned her chin toward the doorway. "What, Hartley? Did you want to play too?"

I looked up quickly, but Hartley was already turning away. I had no idea how long he'd been standing there. "Dinner in fifteen minutes," he said in a gruff voice as he walked away.

There were six of us around the table, and Theresa lit candles as we passed around the dishes.

"No green beans," Lucy argued as her brother filled her plate.

"Just eat three," Bridger countered. "Hartley, guess what they outlawed from the training camp for next year?"

"Let me think," Hartley said, flipping a dollop of mashed potatoes onto his plate. "The climbing wall?"

"Bingo," Bridger said. "Isn't that stupid? The insurance company is making them take it down."

Hartley passed the platter of turkey to his mother. "As long as they don't outlaw hockey, we should be okay."

"Actually, I heard they're talking about jacking the

penalties again," Bridger complained. "Which is stupid. You almost never see anyone get seriously hurt at the rink."

At that, I almost choked on the piece of turkey in my mouth.

"Didn't somebody break both his wrists last year?" Theresa asked.

"That was really a freak accident," Bridger said. "But seriously — look at football. Brain damage, anyone?"

Dana cleared her throat. "This is just lovely, Theresa. Thank you so much for having us." I felt my roommate's eyes on me.

"My pleasure, sweetie."

"I mean, a few broken bones is pretty tame by comparison," Bridger continued, oblivious.

The tension on Dana's face drew Hartley's attention. He looked from Dana to me to Bridger. And then understanding dawned on his face. "Bridge?" Hartley said, his voice edgy. "Can you grab the wine off the kitchen counter?"

Lucy hopped out of her chair. "I'll get it!"

"I get so sick of people saying hockey is only for bruisers," Bridger continued. "It's just not true."

"*Dude,*" Hartley said, exasperated. "Shut up already."

Bridger looked up at the faces around him. When his gaze landed on me, his mouth fell open. "Oh, Jesus Christ."

Next to him, Hartley's mom wore a look of undisguised horror.

"I'm sorry..." Bridger shook his head, speechless. "No idea..."

"There's no need," I said quickly. I *really* wasn't

going to talk about my accident on Thanksgiving.

Just at that second, Lucy came bounding back into the room. "Here," she said, handing Hartley a bottle of vinegar.

He stared at it in his hand. "Um, thanks?" he set it down on the table.

"Hey," Lucy said. "We have to say what we're thankful for." She climbed back in her chair and looked at all of us expectantly.

Theresa swallowed hard, and then her eyes went soft. "You're right, Lucy. Do you want to start?"

"Sure! I'm thankful for…" her little brow wrinkled in thought. "Ice cream, and no homework over Thanksgiving. And mom and Bridger. Oh — and all the Christmas specials start this weekend."

Bridger leaned back in his chair, his eyes made darker by the candlelight. "That's a good list, kid," he said gently. I got a lump in my throat as he put his big hand on her little shoulder. "If I'm next…" he looked around the table again. "Then I'm thankful for the whole crew here. Because you all put up with me," his smile was shy.

"Well you took mine," Dana said. "So I'll say how awesome it is to be back in America. This year so far has been just as great as I'd hoped it would be."

Then it was Hartley's turn. "Well, I'm grateful for Advil, and beer, and elevators, and my mom putting up with me. And for good friends who drink beer and ride elevators and drive me places. And put up with me."

Theresa was next, holding her glass of wine in the candlelight. "I'm just happy to see all of your shining faces around my table tonight." She beamed at each of us in turn. "Thank you for coming."

That left only me. And while I'd been enjoying

hearing what nice things my friends had to say, the truth was that I couldn't think of anything to add. Because I hadn't been a very thankful person lately. "I'd like to say thanks to whichever computer makes the roommate assignment selections. And for getting to sit here with all of you tonight."

And that's the best I could do. At least for right then.

Chapter Ten: *There's Always Custom*

— *Corey*

"I'm no good at clearing the table," I said, balancing my weight against the countertop. "But I can wash or dry."

Hartley tossed me a dish-towel, and Theresa handed me a wet serving bowl.

Bridger walked past the doorway of the kitchen carrying Lucy piggyback style. "I read two chapters already," he said. "Now you're going to sleep." I heard his footsteps on the stairs.

"Why aren't *you* going to sleep?" Lucy argued.

"I will," he said. "After I have a beer with Hartley."

"I'll wait up for you," she said.

"If you wait with your eyes closed, that's okay," he said, chuckling. A half hour later, he came into the living room alone, bringing two six-packs with him.

"You know why I invited you two?" Hartley asked Dana and I, taking a deck of cards out of a drawer in the coffee table.

"Why?" Dana asked.

"So that we could play euchre, of course."

I clapped my hands together. "Yes! Girls against the boys."

"Bring it." Bridger cracked open a beer, offering it to Dana.

"But I don't know what euchre is," she said, reaching for the bottle.

"Fuck, really? And here I thought Japanese schools were superior." He cupped his hands to his mouth. "Hey, mom?"

Teresa stuck her head in the room. "You rang?"

"We need a fourth for euchre. Dana doesn't know

how."

"Ah," she said, coming in. "The best game ever. Do you know anything about bridge? Euchre is like bridge for idiots. Once you watch a couple of hands, you'll be good to go." She took a seat, and the beer that Bridger offered her.

Hartley ran through the rules for Dana. "And there's one kind of cheating that's legal."

"Wait," Dana said. "If it's legal, how is it cheating?"

"Just go with it, Dana," he said. "In euchre, you can steal the deal. If the dealer doesn't realize it's his turn, and you step in, you keep the advantage."

"This is so complicated," Dana complained.

Hartley shook his head. "It isn't, not really. Because there's only six cards in the game. You'll see."

Theresa played a hand with us, and she and I quickly euchred Bridger and Hartley.

"So that was, like, a practice hand," Hartley said.

"What?" I yelped. "No way. Two points for the women."

"Competitive, much?" Hartley asked.

Theresa laughed. "Pot, I'd like to introduce you to the kettle."

"You should see them in front of that video game," Dana said. "I have to leave the room."

"I can only imagine." Theresa picked up the deck and began to shuffle. "Bridger, how's your mom?" she asked.

He shook his head. "Not great. But as long as she keeps her job, things will be okay. The work-week holds her together."

"It must be so hard for her," Theresa said, shaking her head.

"I used to say that too," Bridger picked up his cards.

"But at some point you just have to pull yourself together, and I don't see that happening. Long weekends are the worst. That's why I brought Lucy down here with me."

Theresa winced. "Bring her anytime." Then she looked at her watch. "I'm going to go close my eyes for an hour before I have to go to work."

"*Tonight?*" I asked, incredulous.

Hartley nodded. "It's Black Friday. If mom doesn't go in to work, then the people waiting in the parking lot outside Mega-Mart can't get a hundred bucks off the latest cell phone."

"Ugh," Dana said. "All night long?"

Theresa just shrugged. "It's no big deal. But, Corey? Before I go, I just want to say that my dear son would be happy to sleep on the sofa."

"Bullshit," Hartley said.

"It will be fine, Theresa," I said. "I have crutches, and I'm not afraid to use them."

"She isn't, Mom," Hartley said, taking a swig of beer. "Trust me."

Hartley's mom just shook her head as she left the room.

Dana was a quick study, and our euchre game was soon tied at seven to seven. I dealt the next hand.

"So, Hartley, what's the countdown?" Bridger asked.

"The countdown?"

"When does the horniest man in the Ivy League get his girlfriend back?"

I flipped over a jack, and Dana gasped at our good fortune. But I was distracted by the conversation.

"Pass," Hartley muttered at the card. Then he looked at Bridger. "Two weeks or so, I think. She mentioned coming back before the Christmas Ball."

Before the Christmas Ball? That was December tenth — the same day as our economics final. Suddenly, I saw the demise of our evenings playing RealStix together. I'd always known that Hartley's girlfriend would reappear next term. But that had always seemed so far off. And now she was two weeks away?

At Dana's bidding, I picked up the jack, and tried to look happy about it. But inside I was crushed by the news I was getting.

"How is that fair?" Bridger said. "Her term started after ours and ends earlier? What a scam."

"Totally. And they only had classes Tuesday through Thursday," Hartley added, throwing away a nine. "That left long weekends to travel around Europe. There are pictures on Stacia's Facebook page from Lisbon to Prague."

"I saw those," Bridger said, swigging his beer. "The architecture was not the most interesting thing in them."

Hartley shook his head. "Don't go there, man."

"Does it really not interest you that the same skinny Italian guy is in every shot?"

Across from me, Dana lifted her eyes to mine.

"Like I said, there *is* such a thing as legalized cheating. We have an arrangement," Hartley said, his voice dropped low. "Stacia thinks there's no point in standing on the bridges of Paris without someone to kiss at sunset."

"I don't see you taking advantage of this," Bridger shot back.

Hartley shrugged. "Not my style."

"And that," Bridger said, laying down an ace to win the last trick, "is the reason I don't do relationships."

"That's your call," Hartley said. "But I don't see how

it concerns me."

Quietly, Dana scooped up the cards and began to shuffle them together. I saw what she was doing, and busied myself with worrying the label on my beer.

"How does it *not* concern you?" Bridger asked. "She could at least be subtle about it."

"Stacia is far too high-maintenance to have a long distance relationship," Hartley said. "She needs somebody local to carry all those shopping bags. But it cuts both ways, you know? The minute her little European vacation is over, he's forgotten."

"He lives in New York."

Hartley just rolled his eyes. "To Stacia, that's long distance. And I can't believe you're stalking my girlfriend's... friend."

"She's a piece of work," Bridger said.

"And this is news?" Hartley asked.

Dana flipped over an ace, put the cards on the table and smiled like a kitty cat.

"Christ," Bridger swore. "You just stole the deal, didn't you?"

"Hartley gave me the idea," Dana grinned, "when he said *legalized cheating*." She winked at me, and I made sure to smile. But everything Hartley had just said was eating me alive. His girlfriend was fooling around, and he didn't even care?

My little hope fairy made an appearance then. I hadn't heard from her lately, but there she was, whispering in my ear. *Maybe they'll break up*, she said, her tiny wings tickling my ear.

Right. Not likely.

Bedtime might have been awkward. But it wasn't, because Hartley was incapable of awkward. No matter what, he was always just Hartley, with the lopsided smile and the "fuck it all" attitude.

"Why is there an enormous bed in your den, anyway?" I asked, digging my PJs out of my bag.

"After I broke my leg, I couldn't get up the stairs to my room. My aunt was moving, and her new apartment wasn't big enough for this thing. It's a California king. So she brought it here to get me off the living room couch."

"That was nice of her," I said.

"It sure was. You want the bathroom first?"

"You go ahead," I said. "I take forever."

"Suit yourself."

By the time that I took my turn and got back to our room, he was already snoring.

I shucked off my braces and tucked myself in. He hadn't been kidding. There was a vast expanse of mattress between Hartley's sleeping body and my own. I lay there, listening to the comfortable sounds of his sleep. Drifting off, I wondered how Stacia would feel about the rooming assignments. I knew I wasn't really competition for her. But a girl could dream.

Sometime later, I woke up to the sound of a gasp. Disoriented, my eyes flew open in the dark. Hartley was standing next to the bed, his head bent forward, his arms on the mattress.

"What's the matter?" I croaked.

"Calf. Cramp," he bit out.

"Which leg?"

"Good one. Can't put enough weight on the other one to...argh."

"Give it to me," I said, sitting up. I knew a thing or two about leg cramps.

With a grimace, Hartley sat on the bed and spun his

good leg toward me.

"Press your heel here," I said, patting my blanketed hip. When he'd anchored his bare foot against me, I grabbed his toes with both hands and flexed the ball of his foot back toward him. He let out his breath in a great tumble. After a minute, I slid my hand under his calf and probed with my fingers. "Ouch," I said, finding the knot.

"Happens all the time," he said.

"Overcompensating for your bad leg is straining your good one," I said. I made a fist with my hand and tried to knuckle into it.

"Agh," Hartley said.

"Sorry. I have superhuman strength." He grimaced as I flexed his foot. "What do you do when you're alone?"

"Suffer. And yearn for the competent hands of Pat the Therapist. Although you're no slouch."

"My father taught me. He's good with things like this," I said. "Wait — now I've got it." The knot in Hartley's muscle relaxed under my hand.

He exhaled. "Jeez. Thanks."

"Keep that flexed," I cautioned as he pulled his leg back onto his side of the bed.

"Don't worry, I will." He settled himself onto his back, his extra pillow under his knee. "Sorry for the midnight drama."

"No worries." We were quiet for a couple of minutes, but I could tell that neither of us was sleeping.

Another minute of silence passed, and then Hartley rolled to face me. "You never told me it was a hockey injury. You said 'accident,' and so I thought it was a car."

"Yeah," I sighed, rolling to mirror him. We stared at each other for a second. "The thing is, Bridger was right. Hockey is only the seventh most dangerous sport.

Cheerleading and baseball have greater injury rates. So do football, soccer, and lacrosse."

"So you're saying that you have to be spectacularly unlucky to have a bad hockey injury?"

"Exactly."

"Unfuckingbelievable," Hartley said. We lapsed into silence, and I found myself wishing the bed weren't so large.

There's a mere two feet between us and that luscious mouth, my hope fairy whispered.

"I love your mom," I blurted, dragging my mind out of the gutter.

"She's great," Hartley smiled. "And she likes having the house full of people. I'm not just saying that."

"I can tell. And Bridger's little sister is a cutie. She loves your mom, too."

Hartley propped his head on his hand. "Yeah. But she's Bridger's biggest problem."

"Really? Why?"

"Well, their dad died about two years ago. And his mom isn't holding it together."

"She's depressed?"

"She's a drug addict."

I sucked in a breath. "That's dark."

"Tell me about it. Bridger is worried that his mom will lose her job and fall apart. He might have to drop out if things get too ugly."

"He can't drop out! In a year and a half he'll be a Harkness grad."

"Bridger's only a sophomore, actually. He took a year off before college, and now he's kicking himself."

"You know…" The house was so quiet that even our whispered conversation seemed loud. "I get stuck inside my head too often. I forget that other people have problems."

Hartley was quiet a moment, watching me. Then he reached slowly across the expanse between us and covered my hand with his. Even that small touch made me stop breathing. "Everybody has their shit to shovel, Callahan. Everybody." He gave my hand a squeeze, and then took his back. "Now, yours is right up front where everybody can see it. I don't envy you that. But everybody has some, whether you can see it or not."

I had to stop and think about that. To look at Bridger, you wouldn't know that he was dragging around such troubles. But I suspected there were others who had no shit at all to shovel, or else had an entire team of minions to shovel it for them. Stacia sprang to mind.

"Are you sure?" I challenged him. "Because it seems like some people's biggest problem is that the leather upholstery in their Beemer doesn't come in the perfect color."

Hartley's face broke into the most beautiful smile. "For that, there's always custom, Callahan." He rolled onto his back, putting his hands behind his head. "Thanks for the calf massage."

"Anytime."

He chuckled. "Don't say that, or I'll wake you up every night next week."

Sadly, I was so deep into him, I would probably look forward to it.

Hartley began to breathe deeply as I lay there listening. He was a warm shape in the dark, and just a few feet away. I would have given anything for the privilege of sliding over, closing the distance between us, and wrapping an arm across his chest. It was difficult to even imagine the luxury of belonging with him. I wanted to roll over in the night and curl up against his body. I wanted to feel his breath on my neck while I slept.

This is torture, my hope fairy grumbled, curling up on the pillow beside me.

She wasn't wrong. But it was a sweet kind of torture.

Chapter Eleven: *I'm Good With Gore*

— Corey

Friday, we watched football, ate leftovers and played a lot of cards. Lucy made sure that there was at least one hand of Uno to every game of euchre.

On Saturday, we took Theresa out to dinner at a Chinese restaurant, which offered fifty different varieties of dumplings. Hartley's mom looked worn out from two nine-hour shifts in holiday retail hell. But her tired brown eyes were happy nonetheless. Hartley sat next to his mother, and from time to time she reached over to muss his hair. Dana tried to teach Lucy how to use chopsticks, and I ate my weight in chicken cabbage dumplings.

But later, after both Theresa and Lucy had gone to bed, and the guys had gone out to the garage to drink beer and change the oil in Theresa's car, I had to admit that I was feeling off. There was a vague pain in my stomach, and my body felt hot and weary. Even though it was only ten o'clock, I took a couple of pain relievers and went to sleep.

That night, I didn't even hear Hartley come in and lie down next to me. That should have been a clue that something was wrong. The American Medical Association should add *Indifference to Hartley* as a symptom in their compendium.

Even my hope fairy slept through it. I should have known.

The next morning, I hid my increasing discomfort. I took more Advil and drank two glasses of water. Still, I felt dizzy and hot.

"You're quiet today, Corey," Theresa observed,

proving that you can never get anything past a mom.

"I'm just been thinking about exams," I lied. I refilled my orange juice glass and forced a smile on my face. I needed fluids, and I needed to get home.

Luckily, Bridger had to get the car back to his mother, and so our weekend at Hartley's drew to a close by late afternoon.

By the time we got back to McHerrin, I felt feverish and increasingly ornery. With a heavy heart, I phoned the Nazi police. "Mom, don't freak out," I said. "But I think I might have a bladder infection."

She freaked out.

Ten minutes later — after listening to my mother rant about all the nasty things that can happen if a UTI is left to fester — I told Dana that I was under orders to roll myself to the hospital E.R.

"Crumbs!" she said, jumping off the couch. "I'll come with you."

"You really don't have to," I argued. "It's going to be hours of waiting around for someone to hand me a prescription."

"I'll bring a book. Let me get my coat."

When we went out in the hallway, I held up a finger to my lips. The fewer people who knew I was a wimp, the better. I could hear Hartley's music through the door of his room as we snuck out.

By the time we got to the E.R., I felt shaky and exhausted. The fluorescent lighting made even the employees look ill. The hospital was the very last place in the world I wanted to be. The only saving grace was that the place seemed deserted. "Thanksgiving Day is always nuts," the triage nurse told us. "People visiting with family tend to injure themselves. Go figure. But tonight they're all in their cars on the way home. If most of them aren't drunk, we might have a quiet night."

She took my forms. "Callahan? I pulled your file already. Your parents called ahead."

Of course they did.

"Don't *admit* me," I begged about a half hour later, after peeing into a cup. (By the way, that's no easy feat when you can't squat over the toilet.) "I'll take the medicine, I promise. I *hate* the hospital."

The young E.R. doctor nodded thoughtfully. "I'm sure you do. But your fever is something we want to watch, and there's a risk that the infection could spread to your kidneys."

"But it *hasn't*. I don't have much pain."

He smiled, but we both knew that it didn't matter what I reported, because decreased sensitivity *down there* made me an unreliable witness. "We have to stomp it out, Corey. Spinal cord patients have to be careful. There have been cases when UTIs permanently impaired patients' bladder control."

That made me cringe.

"I believe you that this is probably a fluke," he went on. "But it isn't worth the risk, okay? I just need to ask you a few more questions. Have you been drinking enough fluids?"

I nodded.

"And voiding your bladder regularly?"

Here's where I had to fess up. "Yes. The only thing that changed is that I didn't self-cath for a couple of days." Each morning and evening, I was supposed to use a catheter to fully empty my bladder. But I hadn't brought catheters to Hartley's house, because I didn't want anyone to see them. "I've gone without it a few days before, and I didn't have any problems."

He frowned. "When this is over, you're going to need to be vigilant again, I'm sure you realize that."

I nodded, embarrassed.

"Another trigger is sexual activity, both touching and intercourse," he said. "Try to urinate before and after. Especially after."

"That's *really* not the issue here," I said, turning red.

He actually laughed. "File that advice away for later, then. For now, you'll get one night of intravenous antibiotics, Okay? You'll conk out in a room upstairs, and in the morning we'll release you. You'll be gone before you know it."

Liars.

Dana went home. I put on the stupid gown — open in the back, of course — and watched some bad TV while a nurse stuck a needle in my arm. Overnight, I was interrupted no fewer than four times, as nurses clocked my vital signs and swapped out my IV bag.

I peed about fifty times in the chilly hospital room toilet.

When morning came, I began to ask every human who wandered into my room when I could leave, from nurses' assistants to the bringer of breakfast cereal. Unfortunately, the human I saw most often was a large, surly nurse with garishly hennaed hair. And Big Red was not helpful. "The resident will start rounds at ten," was all she said.

I put on my underwear, jeans and socks. I transferred to my chair, but I couldn't change my top until my IV was removed. Ten o'clock came and went. I stared at the clock, fuming.

Hartley texted me from econ class. *Yoo hoo! Did U oversleep? U R missing a stimulating lecture on international trade.*

Me: *Sounds better than my day. Having a little snafu. C U back at the ranch.*

Around noon, a doctor came in. Naturally it wasn't the youngster from last night, because that would have been too efficient. This doctor had plenty of gray hair and a hasty demeanor. He yanked my chart out of the holder and squinted at the notes. "Okay," he said finally. "Fever's down. I'll leave a prescription with the nurse, and you can be on your way."

He left.

I still had an IV in my arm. Someone brought me a plate of gray mystery meat and rice, which I did not eat.

When Big Red came back, I told her what the doctor had said. "So let's remove this IV?"

"He didn't leave that prescription," she frowned. "I'll check." She turned to walk out.

"Wait!" I called as her wide bottom retreated.

Another hour passed, and when she came back in with my prescription, I could barely be civil. "Would you please take this out?" I begged. "And then I can go?"

She looked at my wrist as if she'd never seen an IV before. "The assistant does that. And I can't release you without someone over eighteen to accompany you."

"What?"

She nodded. "Students need to be picked up after a procedure."

"But..." I felt my blood pressure double. "An IV is not a procedure!"

Big Red shrugged. "That's the rule." She left.

"Fuck!" I yelled, sounding like Hartley. I looked at my watch. He had his Monday afternoons free, because that's when he should have been at Hockey.

No. Sitting there half-dressed, I was not going to call Hartley. Anyone but Hartley. He was the last person who I wanted to see me with unwashed hair in this awful hospital gown.

Unfortunately, Dana had Italian class until two every single day. I texted her, asking me to call when she had a second. Pretty please.

Two o'clock came and went, with no call. I texted again, and she didn't reply. If her phone was dead, I'd never reach her. I couldn't think of what to do. If the E.R. doc who had admitted me was working today, I could try to find him and explain my problem. But that involved wandering the hospital half-dressed, with an IV tower at my side.

I dialed Dana again, putting my phone to my ear. It went right to voice-mail.

"Damn it!" I hollered. I would have stamped my feet, if only they worked.

— *Hartley*

"Is there a problem in here?" I asked, fighting a smile.

Corey's head whipped around to find me in the doorway to her hospital room, leaning on my crutches. "Arrrrgh!" she cried, curling over herself. "I just want *out* of here, but they won't let me go."

"Because you don't have someone over eighteen to escort you off the premises?" I crutched into the room.

Her mouth fell open. "How did you know?"

"I ran into Dana after lunch, and she told me you were here. So I thought that might happen. And Bridger had to spring me after my knee surgery. So why didn't you call?"

Something passed across her face that I couldn't read. "Because it's a long crutch from McHerrin."

"It wasn't too bad. So let's get out of here. Didn't

you ask them to remove that IV?"

The look on her face threatened an imminent explosion. "ONLY TEN TIMES!"

I held up both hands. "Easy, Callahan. Watch that blood pressure, or you might end up in the *hospital*."

At that, Corey deflated. "Would you *please* come here a second?"

"What do you need?" I made my way over to her.

She held out her left hand. "Press down on the IV tube."

Uh oh. "Why?"

"So I can take it *out*, Hartley. And change my shirt. And leave. And get on with my life."

"You are a piece of work, Callahan."

"Just press here," she instructed. Trying not to notice the way the little tube poked right through her skin, I trapped the plastic under my thumb. Then Corey removed all the tape. "Okay, you can let go. Thanks," she said.

Before I could look away, she yanked the little catheter out from under her skin. *Gross.* "Now you're bleeding from the wrist. Isn't that, like, dangerous?"

She looked at me with suspicion on her face. "Seriously, Hartley? You're squeamish?"

I turned around and grabbed a tissue off of the counter, handing it to her, keeping my eyes trained on the wall in front of me.

"*Wow.* Tough hockey star faints at the sight of blood." I heard her giggle as she dabbed at the blood.

"Hey, I haven't fainted since the fifth grade."

The giggle bloomed into a belly laugh. "What did you do after your knee surgery? Weren't there bandages?"

There were, and it wasn't pretty. "I changed them

myself. With my eyes half-closed."

For what it was worth, embarrassing myself had one benefit. At least Corey was smiling again. "And you say *I'm* a piece of work. Turn around so I can change my shirt."

"What, I can't watch? I just saw blood for you." Chuckling, I faced the wall.

I heard her wrestling with her clothes. "I'm good with gore. You can always ask me to change a bandage. Not that we're *ever* coming back to this godforsaken place."

"Sing it to me, sister."

"All done," Corey said.

A nurse with unnaturally red hair walked in then. "*This* is your escort?" she asked, eyeing my cast and crutches, a sneer curling her lip.

Corey whirled on her. "Don't tell me you're *discriminating* against him," she snapped. "We're leaving now." Corey wheeled around the end of the bed and bore down on the nurse. The poor woman lumbered out of the way, and Corey sailed out the door. If a wheelchair could squeal its tires, hers would have.

The nurse stuck a clipboard in my hands. "Sign here, sir."

"Don't mind if I do."

By the time I found her, Corey was holding the elevator door open for me.

Because my leg was aching, we called for the gimpmobile, but they told us it would be a thirty-minute wait.

"Fuck it," I said. "Let's walk."

For Callahan, it was an easy roll towards campus. But for me, it was slow going. When we were about halfway back, I needed a break. Crutching over to a bench outside the medical school, I sat down. "So how did you end up in the hospital, anyway?"

She bit down on her lip. "It was just a stupid little infection. I was a little careless, and everyone overreacted."

"Careless? This weekend?" I massaged my aching leg.

Corey's face went stony. "I'd rather not talk about it, okay? I know you just did me a huge favor, but..." she shook her head.

"Alright. I'm just saying that we could have come back a day early. You only had to say..."

She cut me off. "I didn't *want* to, Hartley. I'm not *fragile!*" The look on her face just cut me. She looked vulnerable, and miserable about it.

"That's not the way it is, Callahan." I grabbed her hands and rolled her closer to me, until our knees touched. "The thing is, we're *all* fragile. It's just that most of our friends are lucky enough not to know it yet."

Her eyes blinked against exhaustion, and I wondered if she might cry. But not Corey. Not my blue-eyed fighter, the girl who dreamed of skating every night, but always had something positive to say. She humbled me every fucking day.

I tugged on her hands again, leaning forward until I could get her into an awkward hug. I don't know if she needed one, but I sure did.

With her chin on my shoulder, she swallowed hard. "Thanks for springing me from jail, Hartley."

"Any time, beautiful. Now let's go home."

Chapter Twelve: *First-Rate Hooch*

— *Corey*

On the first day of December, snow fell past the windows as I crutched through the dining hall. I'd been trying to spend more time on my feet, but it made everything harder. Dana waited for me at the end of a long table, where Hartley, Bridger, Fairfax, and a few others were tucking into hamburgers. When I sat down, she passed me my plate.

"Thanks," I said.

"No biggie." She ate a French fry. "How's the studying going?" Classes had ended, and exams were about to begin.

"Not bad," I said. "I have three take-home exams and then econ. I think I'm getting off easy."

"I'm worried about Japanese," Dana said, her cute nose wrinkling.

"But Dana, you *speak* Japanese."

"Not as well as the professor thinks I should. And he's such a tool. He makes everything more stressful than it should be."

Down the table, Bridger poked Harley in the arm. "Did you tell Fairfax about the birthday present you got today?"

"Is it this week?" Fairfax asked. "Where's the party? Are we making you do twenty-one shots?"

I raised my head. Hartley's birthday was this week? I would need to find a gift. Of course, there was no way to top the gag gift he'd given me. Mine would have to be something more conventional.

"I don't think any of us are invited to Hartley's birthday," Bridger answered. "Tell 'em, dude."

Hartley shook his head. "The package store

delivered a bottle of champagne to me. You know, the kind that costs the GDP of a developing nation?"

"So, Stacia's back in town," Fairfax said.

Hartley pointed his finger like a gun at him. "Bingo. The note said: *Dear Hartley, put this on ice, I'll be there for your big day.*"

My stomach dropped.

"Big day," Bridger grinned. "Dude, you're going to get spectacularly laid."

Hartley shrugged. "The bookies should be careful with their odds. She's been even flakier than usual lately."

"She'll turn up," Bridger theorized. "She sent the bubbly."

"Tell her you're drinking it whether she shows up or not," Fairfax suggested.

"Of *course* I'm drinking it," Hartley said. "That goes without saying."

As it happened, Hartley's birthday fell on the Saturday before exams began. Dana and I spent the day studying in the cozy little Beaumont library. Harkness College had a seemingly infinite number of places to study. You could visit a different library every day, and not repeat for more than a month.

But even I wasn't geeky enough to hit the books again after dinner.

"What are you up to tonight?" Dana asked carefully, fishing earrings out of her jewelry box.

"Um, watching TV?" I didn't need to point out that my pal Hartley was unavailable for video games. But it wasn't like there was anything else to do. During exams, the social activities ground to a halt.

"You could come with me," Dana offered.

I laughed at the suggestion. Dana was on her way out to hear a portion of the English department's all night reading of James Joyce's *Ulysses*. If that didn't showcase the nerdiness that was Harkness College during exam week, then nothing did. "But I'm not even taking that course! Do they hand out big L-shaped stickers at the door, to paste on your foreheads?"

She gave me an eye roll. "That's not nice, Corey. I just don't like to think of you sitting here alone tonight."

"I know," I sulked. "I'm sorry." Obviously, there was no hiding my broken heart from Dana. It wasn't that I'd planned an evening of sitting across the hall while the love of my life got "spectacularly laid." It just worked out that way.

After she left, I turned up the volume of the TV, hoping to blot out any sounds of reunion joy that might filter through the hallway. For a restless couple of hours I flipped channels. At last, I was rewarded with a showing of *The Princess Bride*. It was exactly the right movie for such a crappy night. I lay down on the sofa, braces and chair cast away, and let the familiar story suck me in.

— *Hartley*

When my phone rang, I knew it would be my mom. She always called at 8:30 on my birthday. I was born in the evening, right during an episode of *Melrose Place*. Before I was born, my mom never missed an episode of that cheesy show about West Hollywood brats.

She had me when she was younger than any of the cast members.

"Hi Mom," I answered my phone.

"Happy Birthday, sweetie. Please don't do twenty-one shots tonight."

I laughed. "I promise not to do twenty-one shots. Or even twenty. Maybe I'll stick to nineteen."

"That's not funny, Hartley. You could die."

"I won't drink much. I promise." Just half a bottle of champagne.

"Be careful, sweetie. I was young once."

"You still are, mom." She wouldn't even turn forty until the springtime.

She laughed. "I love you, Adam Hartley."

"I love you too, Mom."

We hung up, and I checked the clock again. I was starting to feel impatient. Stacia had given me only a vague itinerary. She'd flown into JFK that afternoon, but was sticking around the city for farewell drinks with some of her other coursemates. I'd asked, but she didn't say when she thought she'd arrive.

She often pulled stunts like this, and I knew it was intentional. She was the type of girl who understood the value of playing hard to get. Hell, she practically invented it. Worse — it *worked*. Waiting for her always made me wonder if she was done with me. Part of wanting Stacia was knowing that she ought to be unattainable. I wanted her in the same way that she wanted her designer shit — because it was *only* sold in Italy, and nowhere else. Therefore, she *must* have it, and parade it around in front of others.

Fuck. Forget what it said about *her*. What did that say about *me*?

I got up and began to pace around my room, which is not an easy thing to do in a boot cast. Clunk. Clunk. Clunk. Everything about me tonight was ridiculous.

It was going to be strange seeing Stacia for the first time in months. Of course I was looking forward to it, because long-distance Stacia had not been nearly as appealing as the real thing. Truthfully, I was a little worried about getting back into the swing of things with her. She was like song I'd forgotten how to sing. I needed to hear it again to remember why I liked it the first time.

Except songs didn't really do that, did they? Even if you forgot the words, the tune was stuck deep in your soul.

Gah. I was thinking too much. Way too much. And there was nobody around to stop me. The evening marched on, and my anticipation began to fade into disappointment. Stacia wasn't going to show, and in my heart, I wasn't all that shocked. The weirdest thing was that it left *me* feeling like an asshole. As if I ought to be more surprised. As if I should care more than I did.

So when the text from Stacia finally came, it was pretty much anticlimactic. *Sorry, Hartley. I'm stuck here tonight...*

Blah blah blah.

It took me about three seconds to throw down the phone and stand up. There was someone just across the hall that I wanted to see — someone who was always easy to be with. Before I could overthink it, I had the bottle in hand, and was headed for the door.

— *Corey*

Just as The Man in Black was sitting down to poisoned wine with Vizzini, I heard our room door open. Expecting Dana to call out her usual greeting, I didn't sit up or turn around. But it wasn't her that I heard. Instead, there was the distinctive sound of crutches on the wood floor. And its pace was slow — the stuttering thump of someone crutching clumsily, possibly because his hands were overburdened. My heart began to thump in my chest. My hope fairy buzzed to life and began dancing with ticklish feet on my belly.

"Jesus, Callahan, could you take something?"

I kept my eyes on the screen a half-second longer, as if I hadn't seen the film a good two dozen times before. When I sat up, it was just in time to reach over, catching the two glasses dangling from Hartley's fingers. In his other arm, he cradled a fancy looking bottle of champagne.

Hartley didn't say anything more. He simply limped in as if it were the most ordinary thing in the world to walk into my room when he was supposed to be having I-missed-you-so-much sex with Stacia. He slipped the bottle into my corner of the sofa. Then he crutched around the coffee table to the other end. He bent over me, lifting first one of my legs and then the other, then slid in underneath me, my legs in his lap. He hiked his broken leg onto the table and reached all the way over my body for the bottle.

As I watched the Man in Black charge off in search of his princess, Hartley began twisting the wire holder off the bottle of champagne. A moment later I heard the satisfying pop of a cork expertly ejected, and then the glug and fizz as he poured it into glasses.

"Callahan," he said, his voice a masculine rumble. I sat up to accept a glass, shoving my legs onto the coffee table beside his. "Stash this?" he said, handing me the bottle. Without comment, I bent down to find a place for it on the floor.

When I leaned back again, my shoulders collided with his arm, which was draped behind me on the sofa. The arm didn't move. So, gingerly, I rested against it. Hartley gave an enormous sigh, the sound of defeat and frustration. "Cheers, Callahan," he said.

We touched glasses, and some instinct made me avoid his eyes. I wasn't about to grill him on his sudden change of fortune. He was supposed to be getting sweaty with his gorgeous girlfriend, and now here he was, sitting in front of another movie with me.

But this is so snuggly! my hope fairy cried, clapping her tiny hands with glee.

I took a sip of my bubbly. "Wow," I blurted out. It was smooth and tangy and delicious. If expensive had a taste, this was it.

"Smooth, right?" his voice sounded tired.

"It's amazing Hartley. But maybe you find it...bitter?" I looked him in the eye for the first time then, giving him a wink.

He rolled his eyes. "The wine is good, Callahan. It is empirically good. In my family we'd call it first-rate hooch. In Stacia's family, there's an entire dictionary of words for it. You should hear her father go on about wine." Hartley snorted.

"Sounds riveting." But then I felt guilty, since I'd never met them in my life. "If nothing else, she has very good taste." But that was a fraught comment too, because it revealed too much of how I felt about Hartley. "Sorry she was a no-show."

He shook his head with obvious disgust. "She'll turn up tomorrow, full of apologies. She always does." He took another sip and turned toward the movie. Together, we watched Wesley rolling down the hill, yelling "AS...YOU...WISH!" up to Buttercup.

God, it was the perfect moment in a perfect film. Hope fairies everywhere probably sipped from that scene like nectar. Leaning back against Hartley's warm body, I sipped my champagne rather more quickly than I meant to. But it was so good I couldn't help myself.

"Time for a refill?" he asked after awhile.

I bent down for the bottle, and then refilled both our glasses, emptying the bottle. "Happy birthday," I said then. "I don't think I said it before."

He clinked his glass into mine. "Thank you, Callahan."

"I got you a present," I told him. "Is it terrible that I'm too lazy to get up and get it right now?"

In answer, he pulled me a little closer to him on the sofa. The contact with him was making me completely crazy. Behind me, he absently fingered the ends of my ponytail as we watched the film. "I love this part," he said, a smile in his voice. "The Rodents of Unusual Size."

While Buttercup shrieked her way through the fire swamp, Hartley's hand came to cradle the back of my head. His fingers and thumb rubbed slowly along my neck and hairline.

Oh, hell and damn.

In spite of the frantic scene on screen, I closed my eyes, sinking into the sensation of his touch. It should have been relaxing, but his scalp massage had entirely the opposite effect. It was as if the skin at my nape had developed an unparalleled number of nerve endings. Wherever his fingers moved, an electric charge crackled down my spine and deep into my body. I became overly conscious of my own breathing. My second glass of champagne slid down my throat while I tried to convince my heart rate to decline to a more normal pace.

Then, even as I contemplated my own stupidity, Hartley removed his thumb from a very sensitive spot below my ear. And to my slightly drunken disbelief, he leaned closer to me, pressing his lips to the place where his thumb had just been. The feel of his mouth on my neck was almost enough to shoot me through the ceiling.

His moist lips pressed firmly against my body. Slowly, his kiss meandered down toward my collarbone, his tongue singeing me everywhere along its path.

No matter how cool I would have liked to play it, all I could do was to melt back against his chest, my breath escaping as a shaky sigh.

That's when I heard him chuckle, and knew that Hartley understood exactly the effect he was having on me. And even though my breasts had begun to tingle with desire, I found the strength to speak up. "What the hell are you doing, Hartley?"

"Seemed like a good idea at the time," he said without removing his lips from my neck. "Still does."

I took the last sip of my champagne, playing for time while my brain and body had a messy little argument about how to proceed.

Hartley took the glass out of my hand and set it on the trunk. "Look," he whispered. "You can slap me right now, and tell me I'm a prick for coming on to you when my girlfriend blew me off. And then we can watch Billy Crystal bring Wesley back to life." He downed the last of his own glass. "Or you can kiss me, Callahan."

His voice was husky and warm. The sound of it made me turn my head to face him. There was humor in his eyes, but also a depth that I always saw there. He was my friend, maybe my dearest friend, and it was impossible to be afraid of him.

"Why would you complicate our friendship?" I whispered.

"Like it's so simple now?" he countered.

I didn't even know what that meant. But my brain was too scrambled just then to figure it out. Hartley and I regarded each other for a long moment, not speaking. Then he cupped my face with two hands, his touch so gentle that my heart ached just to feel it. And then the months of wishing for his kiss were too much for me. I closed my eyes, and then his lips were on mine. They were just as soft as I'd always imagined them to be — his perfect mouth pressing sweetly against me. His lips opened, parting my own, and I gasped with happiness.

I'd been kissed before, or so I thought. But Hartley's kisses were an entirely new genre. His lips were soft and demanding in equal measure. The slow slide of his tongue against mine destroyed all conscious thought. Soon enough, Hartley grasped my melting body under the arms and pulled me up and over him. He swiveled his good leg onto the couch, his head reclining on the upholstered arm. I could feel his body under me — solid and warm — and it was divine. His big hands curved around my head, controlling the kiss. He took his time, his teeth teasing my lower lip, his tongue sweeping mine in long strokes. I didn't want it to stop.

Ever.

In the background, the Princess Bride hurtled towards its exciting conclusion, but I could barely hear it. Hartley tasted like champagne and pure man. And the kisses were nothing like the sloppy, hurried ones I'd received in high school.

"Callahan," he said finally, while I panted, short of oxygen.

"Mmm?"

"You're kind of…rubbing yourself against me."

Mortified, I pulled back. "Sorry."

He adjusted his neck on the sofa's arm. "Actually, I'm kind of loving it. But I don't think you'd do that, unless you could *feel* it."

"Oh," I said.

Oh.

He grinned up at me. And then he ran one of his hands down my chest, between our bodies and into the waistband of my yoga pants.

"Hartley!" I yelped, grabbing his wrist.

His eyes locked on mine. "Don't you want to know?"

"I just..." My breaths were coming too fast, and my chest suddenly felt tight. I pushed his hand away and took a deep breath.

"Callahan," his voice was low and serious. "Have you done any...research on the topic?"

I shook my head.

His eyes widened. "But you've been worried about it. Maybe for nothing, right?"

I dropped my head to his shoulder and buried my face in his neck. And it killed me how good he smelled — like Hartley. But at very close range.

His hands stroked my hair, and even that made me unbearably happy. "No research at all?" he asked, and I heard the words echo through his chest. "No love for our friend Digby?"

I smiled then, hiding my face in the neckline of his tee. Because there was nobody else I'd spoken to about this. And it was the most embarrassing topic in the world.

"Really, Callahan?" he asked, not letting up. "You're fearless about everything else. You take your P.T. like a Marine, you tell the hospital nurses where to shove it. You call me on my own bullshit all day long. And here's one small thing you can figure out..."

I raised my head. "It's not a small thing," I corrected.

He turned his chin a few degrees in my direction, and once again our faces were a hair's breadth apart. "I beg your pardon," he rumbled. And then he pressed his lips against mine and moved his tongue into my mouth. The kiss was long and slow, and if I could have felt my knees properly, they would have been absolutely liquefied.

But then the sound of voices in the hallway ruined it for me. Stiffening, I felt suddenly vulnerable, lying here in Hartley's arms, my fragile ego laid bare for all the world to see. "Anyone could walk in," I whispered.

"Good point," he said. Hartley stretched an arm toward the floor, where he found one of his crutches. He swung his legs onto the floor. As I began to slide off of him, his other arm caught me under my butt. "Hang on," he said. And then, as his torso rose into the air, I realized that he'd meant it literally. I wrapped my arms around his neck as he stood, holding all my weight in one arm. Before I knew what was happening, Hartley was carrying me, using just one crutch and one leg, hopping towards my bedroom.

The bed was only about fifteen feet away, but even so, it was an outrageous risk. "Oh my God," I squeaked. "We're going to die."

Hartley paused to hitch me up even higher on his body. "That makes you the first girl ever to say that to me on our way into the bedroom."

Chapter Thirteen: *You Say That Like It's a Bad Thing*

— *Corey*

Oh, HELL yes, my hope fairy yelled as Hartley deposited me on my bed and shut the door. Then, even though I could still hear him puffing from exertion, he wrapped his powerful arms around me and picked up where he'd left off, his kiss deep and urgent.

My heart skated around my chest as he curled his hands in my T-shirt and pulled it up, over my head. Then, with exactly the sort of dexterity I'd expect from Hartley, he removed my bra with one hand.

I pulled back. "What are you doing?" I breathed.

"You have a question that needs answering," he said. "And there will never be a better time to answer it."

While I considered this idea, he leaned me gently back onto the bed. *There will never be a better time,* he'd said. Was that because we'd just drunk an entire bottle of champagne? Or because Stacia was coming back?

I was afraid I knew the answer.

"Also..." Hartley's thumbs grazed my breasts, and I sucked in my breath. "I'm a specialist on this topic," he mumbled. Then his tongue landed on my nipple. He circled it once, before putting his warm mouth over my breast and sucking gently.

Oh my God.

I heard a groan escape my own lips, and all reason went out the window.

"That's a girl," he said.

This time, when his hand slipped down my body and into my pants, I forgot to freak out. He kissed me deeply while his fingers slid toward places that had rarely been touched before. When you spend much of your senior year in a hospital, there isn't a lot of time for dating and fooling around. His hand curved, fitting between my legs. I registered the sensation of his fingers there.

He chuckled against my lips. "Callahan," he whispered. "Give me your hand."

He dragged my hand down my torso and into my panties. They were wet, and so was my own body where his hand led my fingers.

"Game on," he whispered.

Then he pulled our hands back into the air, and I exhaled the breath I'd been holding. "That's..." my brain didn't seem to function.

"That's encouraging," he finished for me. "But that's not all you need to know, is it?" He didn't wait for me to answer. Instead, he gave my yoga pants a good yank.

"Whoa," I said. "Not so fast." I rolled onto my side, moving away from him.

He dropped his hands immediately. But then he said, "Chicken much?"

I pushed myself up on an elbow. "*What*? Just because I don't want you groping me makes me a *chicken*? That's bullshit, Harley. Just because nobody *else* ever said no to you doesn't make it impossible."

His eyes flashed with amusement, and something else that I couldn't read. "Fine. If you can tell me to my face that you don't want my talented hands on you," he dragged the pads of two of his fingers across my breast, "then I won't call you a chicken." He scooted closer to me, giving me a tiny kiss, with soft lips. "I'll take it back." Another kiss. "I will say, '*Callahan is not a chicken.*'" He punctuated the statement with a slow kiss. He teased my nipple with his thumb, and I felt lightheaded. "Say it," he whispered between kisses. "Tell me you don't want just a little more of this. In the name of research."

I dropped my head onto the pillow, taking a shaky breath. "This is the weirdest night ever."

He chuckled, and then there was a tug. I saw my panties in his hand. "You say that like it's a bad thing." He threw them on the floor, which is pretty much exactly what I'd been fantasizing about since September. But in my fantasies, we were making passionate love — it wasn't just a random hookup, and it sure wasn't a science experiment.

I felt his hand cup my hip. "Can you feel this, Callahan?"

I nodded, my mouth dry.

He slid a hand down my quad, which I felt, until it dipped below my knees. "How about this?"

I shook my head.

"Interesting," he said, as if he might whip out a clipboard and begin taking notes. In fact, he sounded exactly like the doctors I saw at every visit. *Can you feel this? How about this?*

And suddenly it was all wrong. I pushed his hand away. "You're making me feel like a lab rat."

He withdrew his hand. "Sorry. Wrong approach." He reached for me then, cupping my face in his hands and kissing me. That was better. But things were still off balance. I was sinking under the weight of my own vulnerability. If this were a championship hockey game, I'd know what to do. I'd lash out with some bold maneuver to win back the moment.

Feeling cornered, I reached for the zipper on the hip of Hartley's breakaway pants. I reeled it downward, as far as I could reach.

He broke our kiss to look down, watching me. "What's that for, Callahan?"

"Why am I the only one naked?"

"Well..." he hesitated. "I wasn't going there, you know, to demonstrate my honorable intentions."

"Hartley," I looked into his eyes. "Who could mistake you for someone with honorable intentions?"

An unreadable emotion flashed across his handsome face. But he quickly replaced it with a smile. "Good point, Callahan. And I'm not a guy who needs much convincing to get naked." He unzipped the pants on the broken leg side, and then he sat up and shucked them off, along with his boxers.

And that left me trying not to stare at his erection. He was thick and beautiful, and I'd had at least a little something to do with that.

I dragged my eyes to his face. "Lose the T-shirt."

He smiled, wrestling it off. "Callahan never does anything halfway."

And...*holy cow.*

The room was lit only by the night-light my parents had so stubbornly installed. But its dim rays managed to accentuate the shadows of his muscular pecs, and the flex of his bicep where he propped himself up. His sculpted chest tapered to a trim waist and hips. I'd meant to even the score a little, to spread the self-consciousness around. But it utterly backfired. I now had the most gorgeous naked guy spread out in front of me in my bed, looking as comfortable as he always was. "Is that better?" His dimple quirked at me.

I couldn't even answer.

He was amazing, and I wanted to dive into him and never come up for air. There was no way I could feel any more vulnerable than I did that second. Because I *wanted* him — I wanted this — more than anything else in the world, and I couldn't even let him know. To Hartley, this was an experiment, or just another evening's diversion with his neighbor Callahan. This time without clothing. But to me it was everything, and terrifying, too. I hoped he couldn't read it on my face. My heart thumped spastically.

Whoa! Maybe you are a chicken. My hope fairy reappeared, wearing black lace lingerie, and a pout on her face. *Don't panic now*, she insisted. *This was just getting good.*

The old Corey had always been a risk-taker, a team captain, a fearless girl. I never panicked, even with one minute on the clock and a tied game. I needed that Corey back, and right away.

Before I could think better of my impulse, I pushed up on two hands and bent over Hartley's waist. And then I did something he wasn't expecting, and something I'd never done to a guy before.

I licked him.

It was a single, playful sweep of my tongue. But it had exactly the intended effect. His stomach muscles contracted, and his hands gripped the bed in surprise. I heard him suck in his breath.

I swung back up and pinned him with my gaze. "That's for calling me a chicken."

His startled eyes looked into mine as he exhaled gustily. "*Jesus*, Callahan. Punish me more."

I gave him a catty little shake of my head. For a second longer, we just stared at each other. Then he grabbed for me with both arms, hauling me onto his chest, his tongue slicking my lower lip. The next few minutes were lost to me, as I drank in his kisses and sank into all of his beautiful skin. It was delicious, even though I knew I was a goner. I would never get this night out of my head. The kissing we'd done on the sofa had already ruined me. I didn't even care.

"Where is it, Callahan?"

Hartley was asking me a question, but I was too drunk with lust to focus. "What?"

"Where is it? Where did you stash Digby?"

When enough oxygen reached my brain that I could understand the question, I shook my head. "No way."

"Yes way," Hartley said. He leaned over me and opened the drawer of my bedside table. "Is it in here?"

"Hartley!" I grabbed his arm. But it was too late. He already held the little box in his hand. "Put that back," I said. "That's just too weird."

He shook his head. "No, it isn't. These are fun." He'd dropped the box and pulled off the top. Now he picked it up and showed it to me. "I guess you've never tried one before?"

I shook my head. "Why would I?"

"Why *wouldn't* you? Women love these. But..." his smile faded, and he looked into my eyes. "You especially should give it a shot. I read this article..."

My mouth fell open. "You *Googled* my problem?"

He looked a little sheepish. "I always study to get an A, Callahan. There was this paper about paraplegic women..."

I closed my eyes. "I read that too." A pair of doctors had discovered that paralyzed women often had more sensation *inside* than outside. And guess what the test subjects had used to discover it?

"So you should be willing to try it. And why not on the Weirdest Night Ever?"

"Oh my God," I breathed as the device began to whir quietly in his hand.

"Maybe we can make you yell that," he said, his eyebrows wiggling.

"It's a *machine*," I protested.

"It's a *toy*," he argued. "See?" He pressed it gently against my breast, and I felt a gentle hum which was not unpleasant.

I grabbed it out of his hands, and touched it to *his* chest. Then, as he watched, I dragged it down his body, inch by inch. I studied his face as I went along. When I approached his waist, his smile faded. And when I touched it to the head of his penis, his eyes fell shut and he shifted his hips. I aligned the vibrator with his erection, and he blew out a breath.

But a moment later he broke into a smile, moaning "Ohh... Mr. Digby."

I dropped the vibrator, hooting with laughter. His eyes flew open and he grabbed it off the bed, shutting it off with a twist. I couldn't stop laughing. It loosened something inside my chest, breaking apart a knot of anxiety I'd brought into the bedroom with me. I rolled onto my back, giggling at the ceiling.

Hartley hitched himself closer to me then, his shoulder covering mine. His smiling mouth closed over my lips, and I stopped laughing. There would never be enough of his kisses. The best I could do would be to memorize the shape of his lips on mine, and the way he sucked gently on my tongue. It was hard to worry about much of anything while he kissed me. So this time, I didn't panic when his hand slid down my body. I felt his fingers spread between my legs. I *really* felt them. And that fact made me want to shout with joy. "Okay," I said shakily.

The next sound I heard was the quiet whir of the toy. And then he placed it against my body. It was different from anything I'd felt before. Like a shimmer of pleasure. "Oh," I said, my stomach muscles tightening.

"That's it…" he breathed, leaning closer to me.

His erection brushed my hand, so I closed my fingers around it. This earned me a grunt of satisfaction from Hartley. So I began to stroke him. His breath caught in his chest, and he made a noise in the back of his throat. A very sexy little noise.

Hartley was not too distracted, however, to continue his mission. The little vibrator slid downward. I held my breath.

"Okay?" he breathed.

I nodded because it was. A current of sensation began to gather down there, spreading throughout my core. I sank into the darkness of my eyelids. As Hartley touched me, the world shrank down to the size of our two bodies. I teased Hartley with my fingertips, and our kisses became sloppy and distracted. There was a tiny click, a small adjustment of the toy, and then the sweet shimmer between my legs gathered steam. "Oh," I gasped.

"That's not too much?"

I couldn't even answer him. I could only arch my back off the bed, angling my body closer to his hands. "Oh…" I said again, beginning to see dots before my eyes. And then a tingle in my belly seemed to bloom, and I felt a starburst between my legs. Whatever sounds I made then, I couldn't even hear.

"*Fuck*, yes," I heard Hartley pant, and it made me remember to curve my lazy fingers more tightly around his shaft. I stroked him hard, and he made a strangled sound. And then, "Callahan, I…" The next thing I felt was a spurt of warm liquid against my hip, and in my hand. I slicked my wet hand down him one more time, and his hips jerked with satisfaction.

A moment later, the noise of the vibrator died as

Hartley turned it off, leaving only the sound of two people breathing hard. Hartley put one beautifully muscled arm over his eyes. And since I wouldn't be caught staring, I took a long look at his body, the rise and fall of his broad chest, and the now half-sagging member dipping towards my sheets.

Wow. The full impact of what we'd just done began to sink in. With shaking fingers, I took a tissue off the bedside table and wiped off my hip.

"Sorry for the mess," he said, his voice tight. His eyes were still covered.

"No problem," I whispered. He still wasn't looking at me, and I was starting to wonder why. I pushed his arm off his face, but he only turned his chin away, toward the wall. "What the hell? *Now* you feel guilty?"

He gave half of a laugh. "No way, Callahan."

"Then what's the matter?"

With a sigh, he reached for me, pulling my body across his, gathering me up on his chest. And when I looked down at his face, I was startled to find that his eyes were shining. When he caught me looking, he closed them. "It's just... I wanted that for you," he whispered. "A little less shit to shovel."

My heart was fit to burst, for a dozen conflicting reasons. Fooling around with Hartley had been amazing, and God knows I'd wondered. But lying in his arms was the best thing ever, and I couldn't say so. *I love you, Hartley.* Those words were on the tip of my tongue, but I swallowed them down. Instead, I said: "Thank you for that selfless act of research on my behalf."

He cleared his throat. "You're welcome. And my dick thanks you for letting him play along."

My heart gave a squeeze, because those were not the words of love I craved. So I made a little joke, because that's what I do when things get tense. "Do all guys refer to their dicks in the third person?"

Hartley stared up at the ceiling, his gorgeous face thoughtful. "Pretty much."

We lay there quietly, our heart rates returning to normal. Hartley stroked my hair against his chest, and I tried not to worry about what would happen next.

"I need to ask you a question," I said. Hearing my words, his face took on a wary expression, so I hurried on. "Hartley, what is *your* shit to shovel? Because you never say."

He chuckled. "You noticed that, huh?"

"I did."

He shifted then, turning carefully onto his stomach, folding his arms underneath his chin. We were no longer touching. "Thing is, Callahan, I don't think I can talk about that tonight."

"*Really*," I said, flipping over onto my stomach too. "So all *my* shit is on the table, but not yours?" That didn't seem fair. "You're all up in my business..." Then I clapped a hand in front of my mouth. Even so, a bark of laughter escaped.

"What?"

I put both hands in front of my face. "I can't believe I just said you were *all up in my business*."

Hartley snorted. And then the two of us were shaking with laughter, side by side. And it was just like any other night's joke, except naked.

Then, from the common room, I heard Dana open the outside door, arriving home. Hartley and I glanced at each other, clapping our hands in front of our mouths. As Dana moved about the common room, switching the television off, we shook with silent laughter. We didn't stop until finally I heard the sound of water running in the bathroom. Even then, we were still gasping for air, and fighting off the rippled aftershocks of uncontrollable mirth.

Soon it became very quiet in my suite. Dana had gone to bed.

Hartley took a deep breath. "I think that's my cue to sneak out," he said. Slowly, he sat up, found his boxers and wiggled into them.

No! I wanted to shout. But I held my tongue, and found his T-shirt, passing it to him. I pulled my own over my head. I didn't want him to watch me putting on my other clothes, because it was such an awkward, hopping process. So I pulled the blanket at the foot of my bed up over me instead.

"Before you go, could you, um, push my chair into my room? I'm kind of stranded here."

His eyes opened wide. "Shit, I'm sorry."

I smiled, and hopefully it was convincingly untroubled. "No biggie. I didn't need to go anywhere for a little while there."

He blew out a breath, and I could feel it — that was the moment things got weird.

Hartley hopped into the living room, retrieved his second crutch, and then shoved my chair at intervals into the bedroom. When he made it all the way back to me, he sat down on the edge of the bed. "Goodnight, Callahan," he said, one hand dropping to my knee where it lay under the blanket.

I couldn't feel his touch, but I wanted to.

"Goodnight, Hartley," I whispered.

He leaned back then, giving me a quick kiss on the nose. His face was serious, almost sad. "See you at brunch tomorrow?"

"Yeah," I said as he rose to go. *Because that won't be*

weird at all.

After the door closed again, I lay there for a long time, missing him.

Chapter Fourteen: *Give Us a Kiss*

— *Corey*

There was a polite knock on my door the next morning. Dana's voice said, "Um, Corey? Can I come in?"

"Sure," I said, yawning. It was getting late, but I couldn't make myself face the day.

She walked into my room, looking around as if she expected to see something different. "So...what the hell happened?"

Uh oh.

"Happened?" I asked, my face twitching into an unavoidable guilty smile.

She rolled her eyes. "Spill it, you. Because you are so busted." Dana flounced over to my bed and sat down at the foot of it. "When I came home last night, one of Hart-throb's crutches was on the living room floor, and now it's gone. Was he in *here*?"

I put my face in my hands. "For a little while."

Dana grabbed my hands and pulled them down. "Seriously? His girlfriend blew him off, and so he came across the hall to fool around with you? And where is he now?"

I exhaled. It all sounded so wrong coming out of her mouth. "That's one way to put it."

"Is there another way? Is he breaking up with her, or does he expect you to be his fuck buddy?"

"Dana! It isn't quite as bad as that. You like Hartley."

She looked sad. "I do like him. And I think he..." she flopped back onto my bed. "I don't know what to think. The way he looks at you sometimes..." she shook her head. "I just don't trust him. It's like there's a good

Hartley and an evil one, and they're always at war. I don't want you to get caught in the crossfire."

"Yeah," I said. "But there's a layer to the story that you don't know."

She sat up quickly. "What?"

"Well," I swallowed. "I confessed something to him a few weeks ago, and…"

She stared at me, her dark eyes searching mine. "What is it?"

I took a deep breath, and I told her. Most of it, anyway.

"So…" she rubbed her temples. "That's the weirdest, most romantic story I've ever heard. He talked you into fooling around, so you could find out if you can…?"

I nodded.

"…and it worked?"

My face was getting hot. "Did it *ever*."

Dana hooted with laughter. "Oh my God. And then what?"

I took a deep breath. "Then he teared up. And then he left."

Her eyes were the size of saucers. "I don't even know what to make of that. But I do know you're in trouble."

"Why?" I whined, although I already knew the answer.

"Because you've just exchanged one heartache for another. Now you know how good it can be, but you want it with *him*. Do you have any idea what will happen now?"

It was the question I'd been avoiding since I opened my eyes that morning. "I think nothing happens now. Stacia will come back, and Hartley and I will pretend it never happened." I swallowed. "It's going to be awful, isn't it?"

Dana nodded. "A hundred kinds of awful." She looked at the ceiling. "You know, his mother asked me about you two."

"*Seriously?*" I leaned forward. "What did she say?"

"We were doing a few dishes, and she wanted to know if you two were," Dana made her fingers into quotation marks, "'a couple.' When I said no, she looked really disappointed. Then she said, 'for a smart boy, he can be such an idiot.' It's not just me who thinks there's something there."

I shook my head. "His mother really hates Stacia, that's all. It doesn't mean anything."

"If you say so." Dana stood up. "Let's go to brunch."

"Only if you promise not to smile at Hartley. I'll *die* if he thinks I spilled my guts already."

"It will not be easy. But for you, I will try."

Nervously, I followed Dana to the Beaumont dining hall forty minutes later. I'd stalled, hoping that he wouldn't still be there. So we got there quite late, and Dana grumbled when she learned that there wasn't any more smoked salmon for our bagels.

Wouldn't you know, I spotted Hartley right away. Only one of the big tables was still occupied, and it was packed with hockey players, Hartley at the center of it all. Before I could look away, he gave me a quick wink.

"I saw that," Dana whispered.

"Stop," I muttered. "Let's sit over by the window."

Dana slid our tray onto a banquet, and I set down the newspaper crossword I'd been smart enough to bring with me. "One across is 'half pint,'" I said. "I'd say a cup, but it's four letters."

"I grew up with the metric system," Dana complained. "What's the next one?" She bit into her bagel.

"A modern resident of Elba," I said. "Six letters."

"Syria!" Dana announced.

"Syrian," I corrected. "Now we're cooking with gas." I scribbled in the clue. When I looked up at Dana, I could tell that she was eavesdropping. "What?" I whispered.

She shook her head. "I wonder what he told all of them?" she nudged her chin toward Hartley's table. "When they asked how his birthday night was? You don't think he'd tell them about..."

I shook my head. "He wouldn't brag."

Dana nodded slowly. "You're right. I don't quite understand what it is between you two, but I can't see him gossiping like that." She sipped her coffee. "He cares too much."

Not necessarily, I thought, picturing the way he'd snuck out. "Dana," I dropped my voice. "He won't tell because nobody brags about hooking up with the girl in the wheelchair."

She set down her mug. "Corey! You don't really mean that."

Of course I meant it, one hundred percent. Guys bragged about bedding trophy girls. Girls like Stacia. Even as I formed this thought, Stacia's face appeared under the arched doorway to the hall. The dismay must have shown in my expression, because Dana turned around to look over her shoulder.

If possible, the girl was even more stunning than I'd remembered her. Her long, honey-colored hair fell in curtains down her shoulders. Her model-perfect face was made up in a way that was just not seen in the dining hall on a Saturday morning during finals. She wore a clingy black turtleneck sweater over a plaid wool skirt cut to mid thigh. Her high-heeled black suede boots reached way up, over her knees. Between the boots and the skirt stretched a good six inches of smooth, creamy leg.

Her perfect fucking legs.

The moment that Stacia found Hartley, her face lit up, and she began to prance across the dining hall toward him. His table fell silent, and I couldn't look away. Beaming, she walked around behind his chair. "Well, give us a kiss, Hartley," she said in an affected voice, which proved she knew she was the center of attention.

Into the silence, Hartley mimicked, *"Give us a kiss, Hartley. What, there's more than one of you to service now?"* His friends laughed.

Then, as everyone watched, he pushed back his chair and stood. Stacia took his face in her hands and kissed him full on the mouth.

And he kissed her back.

While his friends hooted, he cupped his hands on her face and closed his eyes. It went on and on.

The world went a little fuzzy at the edges until Dana pinched my hand. "Corey," she said, her voice low. *"Breathe."*

But it was difficult, because I felt as if a vice was squeezing my chest.

"Should we just go?" she asked me.

I forced myself to look only at Dana. "No." It would be too obvious if I got up and bolted from the room. I wished I could sink into the floor instead.

Dana took the newspaper and studied it. "We need an eight letter word for a boat trip. Starts with a C."

"Um," I forced a deep breath into my lungs. "Cruise. Cruising? No — *crossing*."

"That's it," she said. "And the G at the end starts a Greek food."

"Gyros," I said automatically.

"You're on a roll."

I gripped my coffee cup. "I didn't think." What I meant was, *I didn't think it would hurt this much.*

"Oh, sweetie," she said. "Deep breaths."

Over at Hartley's table, they'd found Stacia a chair. I could hear her whiny voice. "But Hartley, you said you'd take me to the Christmas Ball."

"And *you* said you were coming on my birthday," he returned, humor in his voice.

"Interesting choice of words," Bridger put in.

"You don't have to dance," she said. "You are only there to look good in a suit."

"Well, in that case," he said, his voice humming out the same patient, half-amused smirk I'd heard on move-in day as he dealt with her. He spoke to her the way an indulgent father speaks to his little girl.

It was not at all the way he sounded talking to me.

"So where were you, anyway?" he asked her.

"I would have come up from New York," she said, "but Marco had theater tickets."

"*Who* did?" Bridger cut in.

"My ride."

"Interesting choice of words," Hartley said. "But you know, they've invented these things called trains…"

"I thought of that," she sighed. "But I had *so* much luggage."

"Now *that* I believe," Hartley chuckled.

Across from me, Dana just shook her head. "The evil one wins."

"Okay," I said, pressing my palms against the ancient wood of the table. "I'm ready to go now."

Chapter Fifteen: *The Ass Crack of the Year*

— *Corey*

When I told Dana that I was ready to leave, I wasn't kidding around. I needed to put a meaningful distance between Hartley and my crumbling heart. Fortunately, Christmas vacation was about to hand me the perfect excuse.

But first, exams. I hadn't wheedled and begged my way to Harkness to blow it during the first semester.

For the next two days, I worked my butt off in the main library. From a study carrel deep in the stacks, it was impossible to listen for Hartley's voice in the hallway, or wonder whether he'd turn up to play RealStix. I ate take-out salads from the coffee shop and studied like a maniac.

Even my hope fairy took up the cause, fluttering between chapters of my calculus textbook, spouting theorems. She put on a tiny pair of glasses and perched on the lid of my travel coffee mug. Even better, she didn't mention Hart-throb's name. Not even once.

I turned in my take-home exams early, and then turned my attention to economics. When I sat for the exam on the morning of the tenth, I was so well prepared that having Hartley seated beside me wasn't too much of a distraction. I finished before the time allotted. When I wheeled out of the exam, he looked up.

I gave him a quick wave, because it hurt to look at him directly. And then I was gone.

He texted me fifteen minutes later. *Celebratory lunch at Commons? On my way over there.* But I didn't even reply to the text, because I was already on the phone with my mother.

"Is everything okay?" she asked, her voice

breathless.

It wasn't. Not really. But I would never admit it. "I'm fine. But I'm done early, so I changed my ticket."

"But what about the Christmas Ball? Your brother always loved that."

"Well," I said, "it turns out that not everybody sticks around for it."

"Okay, Sweetie." Her voice was uneasy. She wrote down my new flight number and time. And I went back to my room and packed.

By the time the Christmas Ball got underway, I was in the air over the Great Lakes.

Being home for three weeks was boring, but boring was just what my broken heart needed.

Thankfully, my mother didn't dote on me as much as she had the summer before. Not only was I used to doing things for myself again, but she'd had more than three months in an empty nest.

I was careful to smile and tell my parents how well everything at Harkness was going. And I was careful not to brood. I even volunteered to make Christmas cookies with my mom, finally making use of all the handicap accessible changes my folks had made to their kitchen after my accident.

But when I was alone — lying in my new main floor bedroom, or staring out the passenger-side window of our car — my mind always went back to Hartley's birthday. I would relive the sensuous slide of his lips against mine, and the stroke of his tongue. When he touched me, I'd felt it everywhere. How was it possible for him to kiss me like that, and not want to do it again?

Obviously, he'd felt nothing, and I tried hard to make sense of that. I forced myself to replay Stacia's reappearance in my mind, remembering how avidly he'd kissed her. I even made myself calculate how many hours had elapsed between the moment he had gasped with pleasure in my bed and then stuck his tongue in her mouth.

It was fourteen hours. Give or take.

The word *paralysis* kept running through my mind. His heart was like my unfeeling toes. I felt Hartley's touch all the way through, but he hadn't felt mine at all.

For Christmas, my parents gave me a new laptop — a smaller, lighter model — and I had a good time setting it up. Of course, it came with a lecture from my mother.

"The therapist says you need more time in your braces. We thought this would be easier to carry around when you're walking."

"Thanks," I sighed.

"While you're home, I booked seven sessions at the River Center."

"Mom! Don't I even get a vacation?"

"Not from physical therapy," she said. "But if you want, you can do all of them in the pool instead of the gym. To mix it up a bit."

I put my proverbial foot down. "No! Just...no."

"Corey, you're being unreasonable."

I didn't want to argue with her. I just rolled out of the room.

Unfortunately, it wasn't much easier talking to my father. He was in the midst of his hockey season, which I'd been following online. The girls were doing really well this year, but he did not want to talk about it with me. When I tried to make conversation, I received only monosyllabic responses.

"Dad," I said one night when we were all watching

TV in a semi-comfortable silence. "Have you ever played RealStix?"

"The video game? No," he said, surprised. "Have you?"

"It's a lot of fun, actually. My neighbor — the guy with the broken leg — he taught me."

"Adam Hartley?" my mother asked. "I remember him. He's quite a looker."

"Marion!" my father said, laughing.

"I call 'em as I see 'em," my mother said, which made me laugh. And then I noticed something important. For the first time since my accident, my mother didn't look tense.

"Anyway, we're friends," I said. "And we play a lot of hockey on the screen. Since neither one of us can play the real thing."

There. I'd said it out loud.

My father picked up the remote and shut the TV off. There was silence as he turned to study me. "And that's fun for you?"

I nodded.

He hesitated, deciding. "Well, where can we get one?"

We bought RealStix at Best Buy that very night. That was one clue that things were still weird at my house. My very thrifty parents had been spending money like water since my accident. They renovated the house, they bought me every device and distraction I pointed to. So even though Christmas had just come and gone, my father handed over his credit card for a video game console.

Coach Callahan quickly became a RealStix fan, too. And when my brother Damien came home for a long weekend over New Years, he played as well.

But I could easily beat them both. After all, I'd learned from the master.

Hell and damn it. I was thinking about Hartley *again*. That had to stop.

— *Hartley*

I woke up on New Years Eve lying naked in what felt like a cloud. In reality, it was a big guest bedroom in the east wing of Stacia's mansion. I was alone, because whenever I stayed in Greenwich they put me in a room by myself. Her parents weren't idiots — they probably knew that we had sex. But they wanted plausible deniability.

I didn't take it personally. If they wanted to pretend that their baby girl would never fill the jacuzzi tub in her private bathroom and then perform a strip tease for me, that was their prerogative. Good thing they'd been out to a lengthy dinner party the night before.

In my guest room, the sheets were made out of some kind of ridiculously soft cotton. I'd heard Stacia and her mom yammering about thread count once. Seeing as I was twenty-one years old and in possession of a dick, there was no way I paid attention to a conversation like that. But whenever I slept at chez Beacon, I had to admit that their obsession with European bed linens had its merits.

Since my boot cast had finally been removed the day after Christmas, I woke up truly naked, my morning wood brushing the sheets, my feet free to tangle in them.

Delicious.

My mind wandered. I was mostly healed from my injury now. The leg was always sore at the end of the day, and my range of motion wasn't perfect yet. But it was progress. I'd just gotten a note from the Harkness College housing office informing me that they weren't going to bother reassigning me to a room in Beaumont until next year. So I'd be keeping my oversized single, with the private bathroom and the double bed.

Thinking about McHerrin made me think about Corey. Which meant that I was suddenly thinking about her while lying buck-ass naked with a big boner. Unfortunately, it wasn't the first time. For the past two weeks, I kept flashing back to that night in her bed, to the way she felt against my body. When I touched her, she'd made the most erotic sigh I'd heard *in my life*. It was hard to forget a detail like that.

Truthfully, it was just plain *hard*.

And when I really felt like torturing myself, I thought of that intense moment earlier on that night, when she bent over me and... Damn, I'd felt a jolt like never before. *That's for calling me chicken*, she'd said. The fire in her eyes when she'd said it made me want to lose my mind.

Why couldn't I stop thinking about it?

Seriously, we really hadn't done all that much. It was just a little hook up. People did that all the time, right? Admittedly, it wasn't just a drunk and horny flailing. I cared a lot for Corey, but that was only partly why I started it. The things she'd told me about her troubles had really weighed on my mind. More than anything, I wanted her to know that she was one hundred percent sexy. I thought I could prove it to her, and then I did.

The trouble was, I proved it to both of us.

So now I was lying in my girlfriend's house, hard as a freaking board, and thinking about another girl touching me. And then — because I have never gotten away with anything in my life — the bedroom door opened, and Stacia waltzed in. She was already dressed in tight black pants and a soft, expensive-looking sweater.

I cleared my throat. "Hi, hottie."

"Hi." She closed the door behind her and turned to me with a silky smile. And there it was. Whenever I was here, in the lap of sick luxury, and the princess from Greenwich looked at me like I was the tastiest thing she'd ever seen, it just made my year. She was feasting those hazel eyes on *me*, the punk from the ass end of the state, with no father on my birth certificate, and a bank balance that would barely fund the next five months of pizza and beer.

Stacia's attention meant something to me that I didn't like to talk about.

So it was just as well that talking wasn't what Stacia wanted from me. She flung herself onto the bed, and then looked right down at the tent I was raising in the sheet. "Well, hello there," she whispered, her eyes flashing with mischief. "I didn't know you'd already be...*up*." She pressed a kiss onto my shoulder, and then immediately began working her way downward, dragging the sheet with her.

My body did not fail to notice.

About ten seconds later, after sweeping her long hair down my bare chest and abs, she reached the goods. With no preamble, she opened her mouth and sucked me deep inside. *Whoa*. All I could do was take a gasp of oxygen and sink into the mattress.

I closed my eyes, but that was a mistake. Because my brain went right back to where it had been before Stacia opened the bedroom door. And so I found myself picturing someone else's face even as my girlfriend worked me over.

Fuck! That was no good. I wasn't *that* big of an asshole. I opened my eyes again and sat up on my elbows. It was quite the visual, my girlfriend bent over me; her hair splayed everywhere, her mouth busy. Or rather, it should have been. But from this angle it was easy to see that Stacia would soon be making another trip to her colorist. The roots of her hair were a shade she'd never cop to. And then Stacia began to moan, which should have got me back into the groove. But the sound of it was exaggerated, like a porn film.

They were the same noises she always made, so it shouldn't have rankled. It's just that so many things about Stacia were carefully calibrated to reflect an image — her hair color, her lingerie, her voice. She'd once told me that she was taught to always smile while saying "goodbye" at the end of a phone call, because the other person could hear the smile, and they'd feel validated.

And this is what I was thinking about while my dick was in her mouth. Distracted now, I could tell that it was going to take awhile. The urgency was gone, and Stacia was going to need to use some Division One jaw action to get this done. God, I really was an asshole.

But then her phone rang, trilling out the theme to Beethoven's ninth, the ringtone which Stacia used for her mother. For a moment, I thought she was going to ignore it. So I reached down and gently cupped her head, her silky hair falling through my fingers. "You'd better get that," I whispered.

"Sorry," she said, straightening up, then whipping out her phone. "Hello? I'm upstairs, just waking Hartley up." She shot me a look full of innuendo. (And yes, Stacia's house was really that large. Her mother didn't bother looking around for her. It was easier to call her cell.)

The mood was officially broken, and it wasn't even my fault. Giddyup. With Stacia still on the phone, I hopped out of bed and into the bathroom, closed the door and started the shower.

A minute later, as the hot water rained down on my back, Stacia came into the bathroom. "The caterers are downstairs already, and my mom wants my help deciding where to put everything. There's breakfast in the dining room today, because the sun room furniture has to be moved for the party."

I stuck my head out of the shower and smiled at her. "I'll see you down there?" Reaching out, I tagged one of her hands and pulled her in for a quick kiss. She gave me a Stacia grin, and then left the bathroom in a hurry, before her hair could be kinked by the steam. (Say what you will about me, but I paid attention to my girl's little habits. Much more than she ever paid to mine.)

After the world's fastest shower, I dressed. Stacia had bought me clothes for Christmas. Since clothes and jewelry were about the only things she was interested in, she was awfully good at picking them out. The shirt I threw on now was a shamelessly expensive thing from Thomas Pink. I turned up the cuffs to keep it casual, because that's how I roll. But the girl had really good taste. The jeans were some brand I'd never heard of, and could only be purchased in France. Whatever.

Wearing my Stacia-approved threads, I went downstairs to the dining room. Henry — Stacia's father — sat alone at the head of a giant table. "Good morning, Mr. Beacon," I said when he looked up. There were three newspapers stacked in front of him. Someone had taken the time to line the edges up perfectly.

"Morning, son," he said. It always gave me a weird

jolt to hear Mr. B. Call me that. No other man ever did. "The coffee's hot, and I just asked Anna to make me an omelet. If you catch her now, she'd be happy to make one for you." He slid the top newspaper across the gleaming wood surface.

"That sounds like a plan." I passed through the room and walked into the commercial-sized kitchen beyond. There, amid more burnished wood and stainless steel, the personal chef stood swirling butter into a pan.

"Hola, Hartley!" Anna chirped. "Qué quieres para el desayuno?"

If I tried to answer her in Spanish, I'd disgrace myself. "I'd love an omelet, if you're doing those today."

She switched to English, pointing a finger at my chest. "Cheese, onions and ham, well-browned?"

"You always remember." Anna was awesome. I hoped the Beacons paid her a big fat salary, because she sure as hell deserved it.

"El café está allí," she added.

"Gracias. Did Stacia get hers yet?" I asked.

"Haven't seen her." Anna leaned over the cutting board and began to dice chunks of onions into a tidy pile.

"That's not good," I said, heading for the coffee service. "We can't have Stacia under-caffeinated."

"You know what to do." Anna punctuated that sentence with the sizzle of my onions hitting the pan.

I poured two cups of coffee and then went to find my girlfriend. She and her mother were in deep conversation with a woman in a *Katie's Catering* apron. I've noticed that the big, fancy outfits the Beacons hired to work at their home always had homey little names. *Tommy's Taxi. Frankie's Forestry.* But it was such a ruse. There were probably seventeen *Katie's Catering* vans driving around Fairfield County right now, sucking money out of the mansions with a fire hose.

"God, thank you," Stacia breathed into my ear when I handed her the mug. She put a warm hand on my back. And while her mother and the caterer went on and on about passed hors d'oeuvres, Stacia gave me a honeyed smile over the rim of her cup. It was a smile that belonged in a Victoria's secret catalog, and it was aimed at me and me alone.

And yet I felt... *Hell.* I didn't know how I felt. Her perfect body was so familiar in my hands. She had all the right curves in all the best places, and creamy skin, and pretty hair. But somehow I was seeing it from a distance that hadn't ever been there before.

Maybe it was the fact that she'd been half-way around the world for a few months, and I wasn't used to her. But suddenly, I felt a lack that hadn't been there before. The craving I'd always had — to have a big life with the most beautiful girl — she'd always satisfied it. But for some reason, there was an unfamiliar hunger in my gut now, and I didn't really know what to make of it.

Maybe I just needed an omelet.

I gave Stacia a kiss on the cheek and left the women to their party planning. It was time to eat my omelet, and to let Mr. Beacon chat me up about my econ class. And that would probably remind me of Corey. Which would make me think about...

Fuck.

— *Corey*

On New Year's Eve, my parents always drove over to the Friedberg's house in Madison to ring in the New Year with champagne. "Come with us, guys," my mom said.

Champagne was not my friend. "I think I'll skip it," I said.

"I'm going to hang with Corey," Damien said.

After they left the house, Damien and I made ice cream sundaes and flipped channels on the television. Watching the ball drop in Times Square was too lame, so I picked out an old movie.

"So," my brother said after he'd finished his ice cream. "How come you're not hanging out with high-school friends?"

Uh oh. If my brother was quizzing me, it was probably because my parents put him up to it. "You weren't here last year, but it was rough. A lot of my friends dumped me, especially hockey friends. Except for Kristin, and she's in Fiji with her parents."

"Shit, I'm sorry."

"I'm over it." That was mostly true. "But I don't feel like working for it, you know? I'm going back to school in a couple of days, anyway."

"Fair enough." My brother took my empty bowl from my hands. "But Mom and Dad think you're depressed. Like, clinically."

Crap. That meant my mood had been more transparent than I'd hoped. "I'm not, honestly. School is good. I like it there."

"Your roommate seems great."

"She is!"

He measured me with a blue-eyed stare. "I told them they were overreacting. But you're acting really quiet, so it's hard to sell your side of it."

"I'm sure they think school is too hard on me, or something. But really, it's much less interesting than that. It's just boy trouble."

At that, Damien looked startled. "Um, I don't know

if I should hear this part. Sex is, like, the only thing I can't discuss with you."

I smiled for the first time all night. My whole life, I'd tried to stock up on things that made Damien squeamish. There weren't many. "You don't want to hear all the dirty details?" It was a total bluff — I'd never spill.

But it worked. He looked more uncomfortable by the second. "Please tell me you're not sleeping with Hartley."

My reply was quick and easy. "I'm not sleeping with Hartley." *And that's the problem.* But brother still looked a little tense. "Or anyone else," I added.

Relief washed across his face. "So what's the trouble?"

Clearly I wouldn't explain. But I did have a question. "Damien, do you think that you would ever find a woman in a wheelchair sexy?"

His forehead creased. "Well, sure. But I haven't met any women in wheelchairs. Present company excepted. And you can never be sexy. Because you're my little sister."

I snorted. "Unfortunately, the rest of the world agrees with you. When guys look at me, I think they just see the chair. Like I'm not a full-on member of the opposite sex."

"Look, Corey," he put his chin in his hand. "If Sofia Vergara passes me on the street in a wheelchair, I'm still going to chase her down the sidewalk."

"So if I had giant boobs and a role on a hit TV show..."

He laughed. "Don't forget the hot accent. She really rocks it."

Yeah. There was really no hope for me.

When our movie ended, Damien and I played

another game of RealStix. My brother made the unfortunate decision to play as the Red Wings, and I had no trouble crushing him. "Thanks for taking it easy on me," I teased afterwards. He gave me an eye roll and went into the kitchen for a beer.

That's when my phone rang. I plucked it off the coffee table and saw Hartley's number on the display. My heart gave a squeeze of surprise, and out of nowhere, my hope fairy appeared. *Pick it up!* She was wearing a sparkly dress for New Year's.

A smarter girl would not have listened. A smarter girl would have let it go to voice-mail.

I answered it, of course. Then his husky voice was right there in my ear. "Happy New Year, Callahan."

"Hi," I said, my voice breathy. I swallowed and tried to get a grip. "Where are you?" I asked. Wherever he was, it was loud.

"I am at a very stuffy party in Greenwich, Connecticut. But I was thinking about you."

"You were?" I didn't intend it to sound like a challenge. But the question of what Hartley thought about me was a heavy topic on my mind.

"Of course," he said, his voice a warm rumble. "I thought you, of all people, probably couldn't wait to see the ass crack of last year."

I had to pause and think about that for a moment. The year of my accident was officially over. Celebrating was a perfectly sane idea, and just the sort of thing that one friend would consider for another on New Year's Eve. "Good point," I said. "Thanks, Hartley."

"I just hope the next one treats you better. You deserve it."

His words just hung there. They were nice words, but somehow they sounded like a dismissal. "Thanks," my voice was quiet. "I'm sure it will be better. Yours too."

"You never know," he said. His voice sounded lost, somehow. "Look at the clock, Callahan. Happy New Year."

I looked at the time on our cable box just as it rolled over from 11:59 to 12:00. "Happy New Year, Hartley," I swallowed. And then I couldn't stop myself from saying the thing that popped into my head next. "Don't you have someone you need to go and kiss?"

He chuckled. "You Midwesterner, you. My New Year's was an hour ago."

Hell and damn. My little time zone blunder made me feel low. Because I was Hartley's afterthought, the person he called when the real event was over. "I'd better go."

"Take care of yourself, Callahan. I'll see you next week."

Ugh. Even those two minutes on the phone with Hartley worked their way under my skin. Even though I knew it was foolish, I spent the next day analyzing what I should or shouldn't have said, and what I might have done differently.

Damien flew back to New York, and so I didn't even have him around to distract me. I needed to stop thinking about Hartley, but my brain would not quit conjuring up his dimpled smile.

In my daydreams, Hartley snuck into my bedroom at night, pulling back the covers and slipping into my bed. There were very few words between us in my fantasies. In fact, there were only two. "I'm sorry," Hartley whispered. And after that, there was only kissing and the hasty removal of clothing. And then...

Hell and damn.

Everything that happened in my dreams was something he did with Stacia and not with me. And when I tried to make sense of why, my heart broke into ever-smaller pieces.

The math just didn't add up for me, because she was so awful. Beautiful and awful. It wasn't that I didn't understand why he'd want to undress the equivalent of a swimsuit model. But the investment seemed strange. Even during our brief New Year's call he'd confessed to being at a very boring party with her. Why do that? The only logical conclusion was that the allure of her gorgeous body more than made up for the pain of spending time with her.

I just couldn't wrap my head around it. Hartley was hot. But it wasn't just his body that I wanted. We had fun together — lots of it. We sparred and we joked. I knew he enjoyed my company. There wasn't any doubt in my mind.

But obviously it wasn't enough. *I* wasn't enough. And I couldn't help blaming my disability. A *whole* Corey Callahan — with two working legs, and none of the baggage that comes with being broken — might have been enough to shift me from the kind of girl that he wanted for a friend, into the sort of girl he wanted in his bed.

But I was stuck this way. He was with her, and I was alone. Very, very alone. I needed to get a life, and I needed to do it fast. All the time I'd spent hanging out with Hartley had been wonderful, but it meant that I didn't have other friends.

And now that felt like a big error.

When I'd departed for Harkness in September, I'd left the Student Activity Guidebook on my desk. Last summer, I'd only found the listings depressing. Nothing could replace hockey in my life, and I hadn't imagined that anything else in that book was worth considering.

But now I read it avidly. I needed a new hobby, and a new set of faces in my life. It was the only way to get over Hartley. There would be no more Friday nights spent smiling across the sofa at him. Instead, Stacia would march him around to dances and parties, and he'd let her. Soon enough his leg would be completely healed, and he wouldn't even have to ask which floor the party was on. He wouldn't be a gimp anymore, not even a little. Even that little link between us would be severed.

It depressed the living hell out of me.

As I searched for my new passion, my copy of the student activities booklet became as dog-eared as an old lady's bible. Needless to say, things like the debate club and student politics held no appeal. Music wasn't my thing, and those groups were already formed. Drama? Right. The next big production at the student theater was going to be *A Midsummer Night's Dream*. It was hard to imagine Titania or the fairies on crutches.

I almost didn't bother to read the Intramural Sports section. At Harkness, the houses competed against one another, accumulating points. It was just like in *Harry Potter*. Instead of Quidditch, there were the usual muggle offerings: soccer, basketball, and squash. There was nothing for me there. I paused on "billiards," but my chair wouldn't really sit up high enough for me to reach the table. And anyway, I sucked at billiards, even as a whole person.

When I finally spotted it at the bottom of the last page, I laughed. There it was — a sport for me. It wasn't perfect. In fact, it was a little bit ridiculous. But I thought it might be a winner.

"Mom?" I found her in the laundry room, folding my father's underwear.

"Yes, honey?"

"I will do those sessions in the therapy pool. Not the gym."

Her face brightened. "Great! Let's find your bathing suit."

"Do you think I could start tomorrow?"

She ran for the telephone.

The pool therapist was a blond Amazon named Heather. She was a few years older than me, and almost certainly a favorite among the male rehab patients. They must be lining up for sessions with Heather and her bright red one-piece.

After a half an hour with her, I was clinging to the side of the pool, panting. As it turns out, swimming with only your arms is exhausting.

"Really, Corey," Heather said. "Most patients use the float belt, at least at the beginning. It doesn't make you a wimp."

"But we don't have a lot of time," I said.

"What, exactly, are your training goals for our sessions together?" Heather asked, tipping her perfect chin towards me.

"Swimming as hard as I can. And one extra thing. I need to figure out how to climb into an inner tube, with my butt in the center."

"Because you want to…go river tubing?" she guessed.

"Not exactly," I said.

When I told her my plan, she laughed. "I'll find an inner tube, then. This will be fun."

Chapter Sixteen: *It's What I Do*

— *Corey*

I didn't see Hartley at all the night I got back. Sticking to my new plan, I ate dinner with Dana and one of her singing group buddies in the Trindle House dining hall. When we came home, his door was dark underneath. *This is going to be fine*, I told myself. Hartley would probably divide his time between his own room and wherever Stacia lived — probably in Beaumont House. I would get a little distance from him, and work on moving on.

Operation Forget About Hartley was underway. O.F.A.H., for short.

From my bedroom I made an important phone call. There were two students listed as contacts for the intramural team that I wanted to join: the team captain, and a manager. The manager's name sounded friendlier, so I looked up her number in the campus directory, dialing before I could lose my nerve. Allison Li answered on the first ring.

"Hi, Allison?" I said, my voice barely shaking. "I'm Corey, a First Year, and I was reading over break about the co-ed inner tube water polo team?"

"Hi Corey!" she said. "We'd love to have you. And you have good timing. We're having a practice tomorrow night."

"Well..." I squeaked. "I need to make sure that you're serious when you say that there's no experience necessary."

"Corey, if I can be blunt, anyone with a *pulse* is welcome. Especially girls. The rules are that we have to have three women in the water at all times. Last year we had to forfeit a couple of games because we couldn't fill out our team. There are a total of eleven games — one against each house."

That sounded promising.

"Great," I said. "My next question is something you probably don't hear too often. Do you happen to know if the practice pool is wheelchair accessible?" Crutches on a slippery pool deck sounded like a bad idea.

To her credit, she paused only slightly. "I think so. Yeah — sure it is. I've seen therapy sessions in there."

"Allison," I said. "I promise I swim a lot better than I walk."

She laughed, which made me happy. "Okay, Corey. I'll see you tomorrow night? We start at seven."

"I'll be there."

I hung up feeling all kinds of victorious.

"Callahan."

I woke up slowly to the sound of someone whispering in my ear.

"Callahan, check it out."

My eyes opened, and then I jerked awake. Because Hartley was standing over my bed in shorts and a T-shirt. And my heart seized up at the sight of him. Those brown eyes and that lopsided smile were even more affecting than I'd remembered.

Get a grip, I ordered myself.

"Look." He grinned down at me, pointing at his leg.

And then I saw what he meant. Hartley was standing there with no cast on his leg, and no air boot. Not even a brace. "Wow," I said. I raised myself onto my elbows, in preparation for sitting up. Then I raised myself all the way, holding up a hand for a high five. "Nice going."

He smacked it. "Thanks. I'll see you in economics."

He walked out, limping a bit, and leaning on a cane I'd never seen before.

When the door shut on him, I let out a breath of air. Operation Forget About Hartley was going to be tough. But I would fight the good fight.

After my first lecture of the new semester — a Renaissance art history course — I made my way to Economics 102, reversing my chair against the wall as I always did. A minute later, Hartley came walking in. I felt him more than saw him. He slid his cane under his seat and folded into the chair next to me.

"S'up?" he asked, his voice warm.

I looked up, and was instantly trapped in his brown-eyed gaze. My stomach lurched, and I felt my neck begin to heat. My heart rate kicked up.

Hell and damn.

He was still waiting for me to say something. "Not much," I finally stammered. Why was this suddenly so hard?

Tell him about water polo! My hope fairy was back, circling my head like a quivering halo.

No.

I was not going to tell him. The old me would have blurted out how anxious it made me — how fearful I was of embarrassing myself. If I did, Hartley would listen. He'd stare into my eyes and say just the right thing. But I was done confiding in him. Because it only led to heartbreak.

"So, the professor for econ 102 is supposed to be more fun," Hartley said. "But I've heard the material is drier."

With a deep breath, I opened my notebook on my lap. "It does sound pretty dry," I agreed. "Trade balances and currency exchange? I can't say I'm very excited about it."

Just then, the professor came in, tapping the microphone on the lectern. And I was saved. I fixed my attention up front. Soon, I was drifting on the professor's words as he began to explain the concept of deficit spending.

Why was I even here? At this very moment, Dana was sitting in another lecture hall, listening to the first lecture of a Shakespeare course. She'd invited me to take it with her, but I'd said no. Now I realized that Econ 102 was a feeble attempt to hold on to one little part of Hartley, and to our time together. With a class that I didn't even like.

It was pathetic, truly.

After class, Hartley and I left the room, heading for Commons, as always.

"How's Dana?" Hartley asked. "I haven't seen her."

"She bought herself a half-pound of chocolate covered espresso beans as a jet lag remedy. Apparently vacation was just long enough to put her back on Japanese time. And then she had to fly back here again."

"Brutal," Hartley sympathized.

And that's when I spotted Stacia. "Hey!" she called. Her wave from across the street could have been said to include me or not, depending on your perspective.

When we crossed to her side, the first thing she did was to lip-lock Hartley. It was no quick peck, either. She stepped into him, put her hands on those sculpted shoulders and gave it to him. For a long minute I stopped there, awkwardly wondering what I was supposed to do while they kissed.

Just when I was sure I'd combust with discomfort,

she said, "Let's go to Katie's Deli for lunch."

"What?" Hartley asked, lifting his sore leg off the sidewalk, like a flamingo. "That's an extra two blocks. Besides, Callahan and I always go to Commons after econ. Not only is it nearby, it's already paid for."

"But..." she whined, "I've been pining for an eggplant wrap for four months."

I held up a hand. "Actually, you two can duke it out. I need to try to make it to the dean's office between classes. So I'll catch you guys later." I pointed my wheels down College Street, back towards Beaumont. As I began to roll away, I looked over my shoulder and waved.

Hartley actually gave me a bit of a dirty look, and somehow it made me feel giddy. O.F.A.H. was back on track.

I headed for the Beaumont House dean's office, just as I'd said I would. Unfortunately, I discovered that it was up three marble steps and through a narrow, hundred-year-old doorway under one of Beaumont's gorgeous granite archways. On my crutches, it would have been entirely manageable. But I hadn't gone home to switch. So I parked myself outside the door and called the office on my cell. I could hear the phone ringing inside, and the secretary answering. "Hello?"

"Hi," I said. "This is Corey Callahan, and I'm right outside, but in a wheelchair..."

"Sure, Corey," the woman's voice was friendly. "Do you need to speak to the dean? I'll send him right out."

Only thirty seconds later he emerged, pad and paper in hand. Dean Darling wore a beard and a corduroy blazer, complete with collegiate elbow patches. He looked like he'd been born right here, amid the musty libraries and granite facades. "So sorry, my dear," he said, his British accent thick and proper. "These old buildings…"

"I love these old buildings," I cut in.

He sat right down on the office stoop. "Well, now. Is it something you can speak about in the open? Or shall we find a conference room somewhere…"

I shook my head. "It's a little thing. I just want to swap one course for another, but I already turned in my schedule."

"Not a problem," he beamed, uncapping his gold pen. "What will it be, Miss Callahan?"

"Monday, Wednesdays and Fridays at ten-thirty," I began. "Let's drop the Economics and add a Shakespeare lecture, the Histories and Tragedies."

"Ah, a fine course, I know it well," he said, scribbling. "I'm sure you will find it delightful."

"I'm sure I will too."

"How are you getting on, Corey?" the dean asked, cocking his head. "Your preliminary grades looked wonderful."

"Did they?" I couldn't help grinning. Grades weren't due to come out for another week, but I was hoping I'd done well.

He nodded. "Well done," he said. "But how is the rest of it? We have you living over in McHerrin, I believe? I looked at the suite myself after speaking with your parents this summer."

"It's perfect," I said. "And my roommate is terrific."

His head bobbed happily. "Good, good. Now, I'm sure you're off to lunch." He looked up, in the direction of the dining hall. And then he grimaced. "The stairs! Oh, dear God." He scrambled to his feet. "I was so focused on your living quarters…how did they assign you to Beaumont?"

"I *asked* for Beaumont. My brother was in Beaumont."

His face was still creased with dismay. "But...where do you dine every evening, when Commons is closed?"

"Here." I pointed toward the courtyard. "Adam Hartley and I discovered the freight elevator early on."

"Oh!" the dean was flustered. "Into the kitchen?"

I nodded. "They're used to me now."

His color deepened. "I feel terrible about this. You could be reassigned to an accessible house, with a first-floor dining room."

That wasn't happening, because I didn't want to lose Dana as a roommate. "It's fine, I promise. Please don't reassign me. I'm used to the place. Besides — I'm supposed to be learning to do the stairs on my crutches. I've been a bit lazy."

He hesitated. "If you're sure, Miss Callahan." He cleared his throat. "If you are met with any other thoughtlessness on our part, will you please tell me? Any little thing."

"I will."

"Corey," He held out a hand, and I shook it. "I always say that I learn from students every single day. And now you've wizened me even before tea time."

"My pleasure," I smiled.

That evening, I put on my bathing suit under a pair of tear-away exercise pants, and made it to the gym a good fifteen minutes before water tube practice was set to begin. I wanted to transfer from my chair to the pool without my teammates watching. Locking my chair, I removed my pants and then did a twist maneuver to slip to the floor. I took off my T-shirt and stowed my clothes in my pack. Then I unlocked the chair's brakes and gave it a gentle shove toward the wall.

I was scooting my butt to the edge of the pool when I heard a voice behind me. "You must be Corey?"

I looked up to see a friendly face smiling at me. "Allison?" She extended her hand, and I shook it.

She knelt down on the pool deck just beside me. "Have you played before?" she asked.

I shook my head. "But I did a lot of swimming over break." I cleared my throat. "I used to play a lot of ice hockey, actually. So, getting past the goalie is fun for me."

Her eyes widened. "Awesome!"

"Is it okay if I get wet?"

"Sure," she grinned. "We'll get started in about five minutes."

"Good to know," I said. And then I aimed my shoulders toward the open water, tucked my head under and rolled forward, into the blue.

When I came up for air, I saw the rest of the Beaumont water polo team — a half dozen others — converging on the pool. Allison and another guy I recognized from the Beaumont House dining hall stretched a float rope across the pool, dividing it.

"We're going to take this end," the guy said in a very chipper British accent. I swam under the rope and over to the side near where he stood. "For anyone who doesn't know me, I'm Daniel. And since we're such a bloody well-organized team," people chuckled at this. "I'm going to go over the rules for at least one or two minutes. And then we're going to scrimmage. So everyone grab a tube..." he pointed at a pile in the corner. "And let's get wet."

Everyone walked toward the pile of tubes, and my

pulse began to race. The tubes were about eight feet from the corner of the pool. It was going to be one of *those* moments, when I had to ask someone for help.

I hated that.

Stuck, I clung there to the side, watching everyone else get a tube and then wander toward the pool edge. Nobody seemed aware of me, which would usually suit me just fine. Allison and Daniel were the last two on the pool deck, and I fixed my eyes on her, hoping she'd look my way.

It worked. She stopped on her way back toward the pool and smiled at me. She pointed at the tube in her hands, and then at me. I nodded gratefully, and she tossed it. But just as I caught it, I saw Daniel's gaze land on me. And then his brow furrowed, and he looked around, his glance landing on my wheelchair across the way.

Daniel scratched his ear, frowning. He knelt down by the side of the pool. "You know, this gets a little rough sometimes. It's hard to stay in the tube."

My face began to heat. "It's fine," I told him. "I'm a strong swimmer."

But then, because there is always enough time each day for a moment of pure mortification, I had trouble getting into the tube. It was larger than the ones that aqua trainer Heather had found to practice with. So it took three tries to hoist myself up and over the edge. The rules — which Daniel began reading aloud — required that each player's "derriere" be seated in the middle of the tube before taking possession of the ball. Furthermore, it was legal to tip any player holding the ball out of his or her tube, forcing that player to give up the ball.

"So now let's mix it up," Daniel called. "We'll

scrimmage, seven minutes a period." He dug into a sack of pinny vests, tossing them to four players.

I didn't have a pinny, so that put me on Daniel's team. Allison was on the other. I recognized most of my teammates from the dining hall, but I didn't know all their names. Daniel blew his whistle, and play began.

The other team got the ball and began passing. I figured out how to propel myself around with my hands as flippers. I noticed that only a couple of people managed to use their feet as well. You had to be pretty tall — with long legs dangling over the tube — to kick effectively. For once, having useless legs was not going to be much of a disadvantage. We were all flopping about like flounders, trying to maneuver. And more than one person began to laugh at the effort.

Inner tube water polo was not a game that took itself too seriously.

A lanky guy named Mike intercepted the ball, passing it to Daniel. I spun quickly, positioning myself in front of the net. "Open!" I called, lifting my arms. But Daniel passed it to another of our teammates, this one further from the goal. She shot and missed.

And then, that scenario repeated itself a dozen more times.

By the time Daniel blew the whistle, I was hopping mad. I knew the problem wasn't that my teammates thought I'd drop the ball. There was plenty of that happening anyway. The trouble was that my Beaumont teammates — all of whom had seen me crutching and wheeling around the dining hall — thought I was fragile. They were afraid to put me in the position of being tube tackled. It was ridiculous. And I was so frustrated I wanted to spit.

"Hey, Daniel!" a voice called from the other end of

the pool, where another team was having their own practice. "Wanna rumble?"

Daniel looked over his crew. "If *rumble* is a crass American word for *scrimmage*, I'd say we're up for it."

"Sure!" Allison said. "Let's show Turner House who's boss."

The Turner captain, a skinny guy in a little Speedo, brought his people down to our end. "We've only got six tonight. Shall we play six on six, or do you want to send us a guy? Or a gal?"

"I'll go!" I raised my hand.

The Turner guy nodded. "Great. Who's keeping time?"

I paddled over to the Turner side, toward the faces of people I didn't recognize. When the whistle blew, I put myself right into the center of the action. It only took a minute until one of my new Turner teammates saw me open and lobbed me the ball. I caught it — thank God — and passed. A couple of minutes later I caught a pass even closer to the goal.

Our Beaumont Goalie was a big, bearded guy called "bear." He'd obviously been chosen for his girth rather than his skills. I faked to the left, and he totally went for it. While I had the ball, nobody on the Beaumont team made a move to dump me. I could have held onto that thing all day long. But I didn't. With speed and authority, I nailed the ball into the right hand corner of the net.

My adopted teammates cheered, and I began to enjoy myself.

I passed the ball several more times after that, playing it safe. But when another window presented itself, I tried the same thing again. The only one who had learned his lesson was the goalie — he was a bit harder to decoy the second time. But I managed. The rest of the Beaumonters hung back again while I held the ball.

Fools. I scored twice more before they got tired of it.

On my next possession, Alison wised up. While I was lining up my shot, she sailed into my tube, levering me towards the water. I managed to pass the ball over her head before she upended me. I flopped into the pool with a splash. We were both laughing when I came back to the surface.

After that, the gloves were off. The Beaumonters stopped being afraid of me, and so I had to pass more often than I shot. Then, just before the whistle, the Turner captain flipped me the ball when I was right in front of the net. My hope fairy, dressed in a bikini, did a quick little cheer with silver pom poms. And I slipped the ball into the corner before the oaf knew what hit him.

Game over. Advantage Turner.

By the time it was done, I was waterlogged and panting. I heaved myself onto the side of the pool deck, twisting around to sit up. The Turner captain pushed out of the water right next to me. "Hey, thanks for playing on our side. I don't like our chances half so well for the real game."

I smiled. "That's nice of you to say, but I was working an odd kind of advantage there at the beginning."

He raised an eyebrow. "I noticed that. How come?"

I cocked my head toward the other end of the pool. "Actually, I could use a favor. That wheelchair down there belongs to me. Do you mind kicking it over here?"

He looked across the room and then back at me. Then he laughed. "Okay, I think I understand."

I nodded. "People mean well. But sometimes they have to be taught a lesson. Sorry if I was a ball hog."

He stood up, shaking water off his head. "Honestly, it was fun to watch." He went off to retrieve my chair.

After I'd toweled myself off, and dried my hair against the January wind, I zipped up my fleece and wheeled myself out of the ladies' locker room. Beside the elevators, captain Daniel leaned against the wall, arms crossed. When he saw me approaching, he straightened up. "Corey," he said, his accent making my name sound more weighty. "I'm terribly sorry."

Shrugging, I pressed the elevator button. "It's okay. That sort of thing happens to me a lot."

He shook his head. "Really, I feel like an ass." The way he pronounced "ass," was very British. It came out *ahs*. We boarded the elevator together.

"I hope you'll come back for our game on Friday," he said. "We need you."

I gave him a sneaky grin. "What's it worth to you?" I was actually *flirting* with him, and I had no idea why. But it was sort of fun.

"Well," he scratched his chin. "Let me buy you an ice cream on the way home. I have a little addiction to Chunky Monkey which needs feeding."

Surprising myself, I said yes.

"Philosophy? That sounds complicated." I ate the last bite of my cone.

"Oh, it isn't really," Daniel insisted. "You get to argue your way through every seminar. What will you choose for a major?"

"I haven't got that figured out yet," I told him. "That, and a whole lot of other things."

"Well then," he said. "Best to focus on the water sports. Inspiration will strike."

"That's my strategy."

"You got past our goalie pretty well there, Corey. Hopefully you can get past Turner's on Friday."

"Turner's goalie has good reflexes, but he sits too far out of the net."

Daniel had a pleasantly dry laugh. "That's a high level of analysis for inner tube water polo. You're a little scary, Corey. Scary for the other team, that is." His eyes crinkled at the edges when he smiled.

"I used to play hockey. Watching the goalie — it's what I do."

"Can't wait until Friday, then." He pushed back his chair.

As we left the ice cream shop, Daniel held the door. There was a bit of a slope to the floor that I did not anticipate. I propelled myself into the dark, and nearly ran over Hartley, who lurched backward.

"Whoops." I said, grabbing my wheels.

"*Jesus*, Callahan," Hartley yelped. "Are you trying to kill me?"

Daniel came to stand beside me. "If she was trying to kill you, you'd be dead already. This is something I've learned about Corey."

I laughed, and Hartley looked from me to Daniel to me again, his mouth tightening. "Right."

"I'm sorry, Hartley. Really."

Just then, Stacia sashayed out of the adjacent door, where the ATM machines were. "Evening, Daniel," she said. Then she took Hartley's hand and steered him toward the library.

Without a word to me, of course.

"Cheers," Daniel called to the two of them, and I followed him back toward the dormitories.

"I'm invisible," I said under my breath.

"Oh, that one snubs most everybody. You're not special."

"Good to know," I sighed. Though if Hartley were in love with a nice person, I might be able to bear it. But she was a monster, and he didn't seem to mind. It drove me half insane.

"She snubs women generally," Daniel added. "With a particular focus on the pretty ones." I wondered if that was a compliment. "Most men aren't good enough for her, either. She's nice to me because I'm European. Her knowledge of British accents is not fine enough for her to hear that I'm from the wrong end of London."

"You are full of interesting theories, Daniel."

"It's what I do," he replied. We came to a stop outside of Beaumont House. "Promise me I'll see you on Friday?"

I held up a hand for a high five. "I'll be there. And thanks for the ice cream."

"My pleasure." He smacked my hand.

An hour later I turned in early, feeling truly victorious. It had been my Bravest Day Ever since coming to Harkness. It wasn't as special as my Weirdest Night Ever, but for the first time, I felt that it was possible to move on.

I closed my eyes. But before I could fall asleep, a tiny fairy voice whispered in my ear. *Hartley didn't like to see that you were hanging out with Daniel.*

In my mind's eye, I took a tiny piece of duct tape and slapped it over her tiny lips. And then I went to sleep.

Chapter Seventeen: *It's Not a Sex Toy*

— *Corey*

The text came in about ten minutes after my first Shakespeare lecture got underway. *Everything OK, Callahan?*

It was rather rude to text during class, but after Hartley sent a second one asking after me, I hid my phone in my lap to answer him.

Fine! Sorry! I owe you a call. Switched classes. See you later?

Directly at noon, just as Dana and I were discussing which dining hall to favor with our business, my phone rang with Hartley's number. "Callahan!" he bellowed into my ear. "What do you mean you switched classes?"

"Sorry, Hartley." I went with a little white lie. "When I went to buy the textbook, it was just like you said. Exchange rates and monetary policy. The book should have come with a semester's supply of espresso drinks. I just couldn't do it."

There was a silence on the other end of the line. "So you just ditched?"

"What, you've never dropped a class?"

Another pause. "So, are you coming to lunch, at least?"

Then I heard the garbled through-the-phone sound of someone calling him in the distance. Someone with a shrill voice. "Hartley!"

"I think you have company for lunch, no?" I said.

"Well, sure, but…" I'd never heard him at a loss for words before.

"I'll see you at dinner, maybe," I said. "Or swing by later. We'll play some hockey."

When I hung up, Dana's eyes danced. "You really

cut him loose, didn't you?"

"I guess so."

"Playing hard to get?" she asked.

I shook my head. "It's just pure survival," I told her. "And it's really not as hard as I thought it would be."

— *Hartley*

Houston, we have a problem.

I lay on my bed, staring at the steadily darkening ceiling. Classes were done for the day, and it was still that blissful early part of the term when only the overachievers had begun to do any homework. So I had plenty of time to overanalyze my friend's behavior.

See, I didn't think it was all that weird that Corey didn't call me over break. Ours was not a phone-based friendship. But when she got back, she didn't stop by. And then the ditched lunch, and the dropped class? It couldn't all be coincidence.

Corey was avoiding me.

Why would you complicate our friendship? She'd asked me that question, and I'd given her some smartass answer. But, hell. If I knew she was going to drop me like a puck, I wouldn't have gone there.

I should never have gone there.

As I lay there worrying about this, the dusk turned to pitch black. My phone lit the bed with a text message from Stacia.

Dinner?

It was five-thirty, and my stomach growled its approval. But I didn't text her back because there was something I had to figure out. I got up and put on a jacket. Then I crossed the hall and opened the door. Dana and Corey were sitting hip to hip on the sofa, a laptop in front of them. So far as I could tell, they were watching cat videos on YouTube. "Dinner time, girls," I said. "Shake a leg, it's pasta bar night."

"Shake a leg?" Corey asked. "Did you really just say that to me?"

"I was being ironical, Callahan. Seriously, now. That line gets long. It's hard on a gimp."

Dana and Corey shared a glance that I could not interpret. Corey shrugged. Then Dana snapped her laptop shut. "Okay. I'm in." She tossed Corey her coat and put on her own.

Together, we headed into the crisp January night. Maybe she wasn't avoiding me after all.

"I heard we're getting snow," Corey said.

"That ought to make the morning commute fun," I complained. It was nice to be out of a cast, but I still wasn't one hundred percent.

"Oh, it will be worth it," Corey said. "I love snow."

"I can't wait," Dana agreed.

"What kind of happy pills are the two of you on?" I asked, dragging my cane between steps. The end of the day still made my leg ache. "You should score me some."

"We're just high on life," Corey said, and Dana shot her an amused look.

When we got to Beaumont, Corey and I took the service elevator together, while Dana nabbed us a spot in line. "You know," Corey said as the ancient lift began to move, "I've missed the comforting sound of these gears grinding."

"Me too." Since she sounded just like old times, I began to relax.

Until Stacia arrived.

We were seated and tucking into our pasta when my girlfriend plunked down next to me. Without a word to

Dana or Corey, she opened with a complaint. "Hartley, you didn't return my text."

I went for the innocent look. "Sorry, hottie. What did you need?"

She tossed her hair. "Well, the hockey team has Friday off, and Fairfax is having a little party. I told him we'd be there."

Dana and Corey exchanged another loaded glance. And I didn't blame them. Stacia wasn't the warmest creature. I wiped my mouth and thought over my answer. I'd rather not argue with her in front of my friends, but Fairfax's party wasn't that high on my list. "I don't know about Friday, Stacia. Maybe not this time."

Her perfectly-styled eyebrows wrinkled in distress. "But we *have* to. You can climb the stairs slowly. I'll wait with you."

Huh. While I was glad that Stacia had finally decided to remember my injury now that it was almost healed, that wasn't really the problem. "I appreciate that. But I told Bridger that I'd go with him to the basketball game. Of course you're welcome to come along. You too, guys," I lifted my soda glass toward Corey and Dana.

Stacia pouted. "A basketball game? What about Fairfax?"

I didn't want to go there, but she wasn't going to let it drop. "What about him? He hasn't been that good a friend this year, if you want to know the truth. Hell, my digital teammates on RealStix have been nicer."

"Oh!" Corey slapped the table, and then turned around to get into the bag on the back of her chair. "Hartley, you just reminded me. I've had this in my book bag since before break." She dug out a small package with Happy Birthday paper on it. "Somehow I didn't get around to giving it to you on your birthday.

I'm not sure how that happened."

She met my eyes then, just in time to see me freeze up. Damn, I wasn't ready for that. My neck got hot as I took the gift from her hand. "Thanks, Callahan. You shouldn't have." I set it down on the table and picked up my drink.

"Aren't you going to open it?" she asked. "It's not, like, a sex toy or anything."

Because I'm suave like that, I actually choked on my soda.

"Good grief, are you okay?" Stacia asked, whacking me on the back. She was the only human alive who could manage to sound pissed off that her boyfriend was struggling for breath.

"Went down the wrong pipe?" Corey asked.

I nodded, coughing.

"I hate that," Dana said. Something in the tone of her voice made it sound like she was enjoying herself.

I was in deep shit. And it was entirely my own fault.

Manning up, I slid my thumb under the edge of the wrapping paper on Corey's present. When I tore it back, I looked up at her again. "Aw, you got me the new RealStix?"

"I *did*." She smiled for real this time. In fact, it was the first smile I'd gotten out of Corey since The Weirdest Night Ever. "It's pretty much the same as the old version — but with all the recent draft picks."

I rubbed my hands together. "I'm going to be unbeatable."

"*Please*," she said. "As if." Her eyes sparkled, just the way they were supposed to.

Stacia scowled at her plate, saying absolutely nothing.

— *Corey*

"Oh my *God*," Dana said once we got home, her voice low enough that we couldn't be heard in the hallway. "That was hysterical!"

I tossed myself from the chair onto the couch. "I'll admit, that was fun."

"You are a fierce competitor. I had no idea."

"That's not even the point," I admitted. If I had it to do over again, I wouldn't have bought the game for Hartley. Inviting him in for more hockey did not fit with Operation Forget About Him.

"Well, then you have perfect comic timing," Dana giggled. "And did you *see* her when he said he wouldn't go to the party? She all but stamped her foot."

"I know," I whispered, but then shook my head. "And yet, he's still with her."

We were both quiet for a minute. Dana came over and sat beside me, tucking her legs up Indian style, the way I used to do. "You know what? I think it's going to be okay either way."

"How so?"

"Well, either Hartley will realize he's a fool to be with her, no matter how attractive she is on the outside. That's what I hope will happen."

"Or?"

"Or, you're going to stop caring. Because, honestly, she makes him less interesting. You two used to gab all the way through dinner. And now you don't, because she's a drag on him. In the meantime, some other guy will catch your eye, someone who knows his own heart."

"That would be nice," I said.

"Which thing?" she asked, cocking an eyebrow.

"The first one, of course."

Chapter Eighteen: *Can't Believe I Even Bothered to Ask*

— *Corey*

I was sitting at my desk in my bedroom a couple of nights later, outlining a paper for my Shakespeare class.

"Callahan?" Hartley appeared in my doorway.

At the sound of his voice, my chin automatically snapped in his direction. "What's up, Hartley?" I heard the cheer in my own voice, and felt my body lean forward.

Hell and damn. How long would it take until he stopped affecting me like this?

Hartley stepped into the room, rubbing his hands together. "Will you go somewhere with me Friday night? It would be just the two of us."

My heart gave a little lurch of joy, before I reeled it back down to reality. I turned to my computer screen. "Sorry — I can't. I have a game."

"A what?" He came all the way into the room, standing between my chair and the bed.

"A game," I repeated. "Inner tube water polo. It's an intramural sport."

Hartley grabbed the back of my chair and spun me around to face him. He sat down on the bed so we were eye level. "You signed up for that?" His face broke into the most beautiful smile. "That's awesome."

I chewed my lip, trying not to fall into that smile. "Actually, it's a bit lame," I said. "But I thought I'd give it a shot."

He wouldn't break our gaze. "Callahan, you are amazing."

"Really?" I rolled my eyes. "I fall out of the tube a lot."

"You…" He looked down, and shook his head. Then

he nailed me with another dimpled smile, and I felt the force of it like a blow to the chest. "You worry a lot about people staring at you, right? And then you're like, 'oh, fuck it. I'll just play a sport that requires me to wear a *bathing suit*, and get dunked every time I have possession of the ball.'" He flopped back on my bed and laughed. "The other team better watch out. They have no *idea* who they're dealing with. You just kill me, Callahan."

"Uh huh," I said.

I started to swivel back to my computer, but Hartley sat up and caught my hand, stopping me. "Hey, what if we could hang out on Saturday instead of Friday, would that work?" His eyes were earnest, waiting. "I'd have to check something first..."

I was suddenly too conscious of our proximity, and of his hand holding mine. The air seemed to thicken between us, and his gaze locked on mine as if we were the only people in the world.

The trouble was, we weren't.

Whatever activity Hartley had planned, I knew it wouldn't be good for my heartache. *Just the two of us*, he'd promised. But that was only an illusion, wasn't it?

Slowly, I withdrew my hand. I shook my head, and the moment was broken.

"What? Callahan, why not?"

With a shaky breath, I opted for the embarrassing truth. "I just can't," I whispered. "Maybe I'm an idiot, but I'm having a really hard time being your friend right now." I swallowed. "So, maybe another time." I leaned back in my chair.

Hartley worked his jaw for a long moment. "Okay," he said eventually. "I see." Then he stood up and walked out of the room.

The sound of the door closing hit me like a punch to

the gut. My eyes filled, and I fought the urge to yell his name, to call him back, to tell him I was willing to go wherever it was he wanted to take me.

The hope fairy flung herself face down on the desk and then proceeded to beat her tiny fists on the surface in frustration.

For a few long minutes, I agreed with her.

Pushing Hartley away felt like a huge mistake. He'd always been a good friend to me, and throwing that away seemed foolish.

Except, it wasn't.

I took a very deep breath. The truth was that following Hartley around like a lovesick puppy was preventing me from making other friends. And as great as Hartley was, I didn't want to spend the whole year lapping up the scraps that were left over when Stacia was busy reapplying her lipstick.

Damn her for coming back.

No, that wasn't really the problem.

Damn him for loving her.

I returned to my homework, but the words blurred together on the page.

On Friday night, I donned my bathing suit again and wheeled over to the swimming pool. This time I remembered to fetch a tube before ejecting from my chair.

A tiny, microscopic part of me wondered if Hartley would show up to watch my game. Intramural sports didn't really have spectators. But hope is tricky. She sneaks up on you even in unpredictable locations.

He didn't come, of course.

The game was tough, because the Turner team showed up with a seventh player who was quite the ringer. Big and fast, he seemed always to be in exactly the right place to intercept our passes. And he had absolutely no qualms about dumping me off my tube when I had possession.

Bastard, I thought to myself the fourth time he'd sunk me. And then I laughed at my own hypocrisy.

Fortunately, the Turner goalie wasn't on his game. With one minute left, I sent a goal into the net from a wide angle, tying up the game 3-3. When the whistle blew, Daniel called it over.

"What? No overtime?" I yelped.

"Someone else needs the pool now," he said. "So we do overtime in our pint glasses. There's a pony keg chilling on my windowsill. Get dressed, everyone."

As I rolled along with the players into the Beaumont courtyard, I realized how long it had been since I had been a member of a team, even one as goofy as this. I'd really missed it.

"This is a great start to our season," Allison said, bouncing along beside me. "Turner is always tough to beat. We lost to them the last two years running."

"Who do we play next?" I asked, as if it mattered.

"Sunday we meet Ashforth House. They'll probably forfeit, because the captain is a pig, and none of the Ashforth women want to get into the pool with him."

"Icky," I said.

"Exactly."

The group stopped in front of an entryway, and I knew exactly what would happen next. Daniel waved his ID in front of the scanner and opened the door. I heard someone say "fourth floor." So my Friday night would end right there. I could always go home to McHerrin and swap my chair for my sticks, and then come back here and make the climb. That would take about half an hour. But I knew myself. Once I got back into my room, I'd find some reason to sit down and watch a movie instead of climbing those tricky stairs.

My teammates began to file into the entryway, and I turned my wheels toward home.

"Aren't you coming, Corey?" Dan called to me.

I looked over my shoulder. "Maybe next time," I said.

"Want a lift?" Bear towered over me. "I think piggyback would work."

I opened my mouth to refuse, and then closed it again. It was exactly the sort of weird attention I was always trying to avoid.

"I know how you feel about overtime," Dan said, opening the door wider. "We'll park your chair inside the entryway door."

"Well, thanks," I said, feeling my neck get hot. "What the hell."

For a while, it seemed like a fine decision.

Our goalkeeper carried me up the three flights of stairs in about sixty seconds flat, depositing me on the sofa in Dan's common room. Allison brought me a beer, and I drank it. It was cold, which helped. And it was served in an actual pint glass. Dan hadn't been joking about that. "A little bit of England right here at Harkness," he said.

I'd done it. I'd surrounded myself with new faces, and found a Friday night activity that did not involve misplaced lust or digital teammates.

The trouble was that I was stuck there on Daniel's couch. I spoke to whoever happened to sit beside me, or stand nearby. But without crutches or my chair, I had all the mobility of a potted plant. Sure, I could have scooted around on the floor, but that would have made me look like a freak.

Daniel swung by frequently, refilling my beer whenever it got low. But he was busy playing host, and didn't linger. Worse, the beer began to take its toll on me. Not only was I tipsy, but I had to pee. Badly.

I had no exit strategy.

Across the room, Bear chatted up Allison with glassy eyes. When I thought of climbing onto his back again for the three flight descent, it seemed about as safe as hopping into a drunk's car. Without a seatbelt.

More time passed, and I considered my dwindling options. I could scoot on my butt out the door and down the stairs. It would take about fifteen minutes. Probably only a dozen people would stop to witness my humiliation.

I looked toward the doorway, measuring the distance.

From the threshold, I was startled to find Hartley looking back at me. "There you are," he said, his face dark. "Why is your chair downstairs?"

"I got a lift," I said, suppressing a burp.

"No sticks?"

I looked down at my hands. "Nope."

"Wait, are you *drunk*, Callahan?" He walked in, bending down to put his face close to mine.

"You say that like it's a bad thing." I whined, my words slurring a little.

"Jesus, I think it's time to go."

"*No.*"

He looked exasperated. "I'm not leaving you here, Callahan. How are you going to get down the stairs?"

"I don't *know*. Someone will help me." *Someone who*

isn't you. Anyone but you.

He scratched his chin. "I could go home and get your sticks. But I don't think you should be practicing stairs right now." Hartley bent down and put his hands on my hips.

"*No*, Hartley."

He let go, but his brown eyes were exasperated. And who was I kidding? I was totally stuck, and he was bent on helping me. "Piggy-back works better," I said in a small voice.

Without a word, he turned around and knelt in front of me on his good knee. I wrapped my arms around his chest, and he reached back to hook his hands under my knees. I rose into the air on his back and he limped for the door. The room spun gently, and I realized I was more drunk than I'd thought.

"Okay," he said. "Leaning on the banister, and going slow, we'll make it."

Going slow. Because of his healing knee. Very slow. *Damn.*

"Hartley?" I quavered as his back pressed into my bladder. "I really need to pee."

"Seriously?"

"Would I lie about a thing like that?"

He stopped walking, poised on the landing between Dan's door and the neighboring room across the hall. Between the two rooms was a shared bathroom. Hartley put a hand on the door.

Before he pushed it open, the neighbor door swung in, revealing Stacia in a sexy silk nightie. No wonder he'd seen my chair downstairs — she was Dan's neighbor. "Hartley? What the hell? You said you were just brushing your teeth. Aren't you coming to bed?"

"Looks like no," he said. "Excuse us."

When he pushed open the bathroom door, the automatic lights blinked on, blinding me.

"Just set me on the toilet." I said in a tiny voice. "Please." *And then kill me. Because this is mortifying.*

He eased me down and then stepped a few feet away, his back to me.

"Um, Hartley? Can you leave?"

"I'm not looking."

"Please."

"Christ, Callahan," he said, the weight of the world in those two words. "Don't fall in."

Someone just kill me already.

I waited until he left the room before fumbling madly with my pants. I yanked at the waistband, hitching myself out, hoping my body would cooperate and hold on for another ten seconds while I wriggled the way a snake sheds its skin. Thank goodness for elastic waistbands.

In the hallway, Stacia and Hartley began arguing. "My friend needs help, Stass. It is what it is."

"I don't see why..." she said.

"You *don't* see why," Hartley cut her off. "Because helping people isn't your style."

"This was supposed to be our night together," she said.

"Was it? I don't know what you want me to say."

"Say you're coming in!"

"Look," he said. "Leave your door open. We need to talk anyway."

"Well, that sounds like fun," she snapped. The door slammed.

I peed for what seemed like ten minutes. Then I inched my clothing back up, hurrying, yet trying not to slip into the toilet. When I flushed, he knocked on the door.

"All clear."

Hartley came in and knelt down in front of the toilet, and then picked me up again. Stacia's door was closed, and he got started on the stairs without comment. But it was slow going. Bracing himself against the banister meant letting go of my right leg. I used all my quad strength to try to tuck it in. But it sagged anyway.

From my perch on his back, my nose was inches from his neck. It was the same neck that I had once stroked with my fingers while we kissed.

Hell and damn it all.

When we made it to the third floor landing, Hartley set me down with a sigh. "Half-time break." He sat down next to me and dug his thumbs into the muscles of his injured leg.

"The extra weight is killing you, isn't it?" I asked. Another night, another disaster. All I'd wanted was to have a beer with the team, but I'd made a mess of things.

"It was already sore," he said.

"Liar." I grabbed my own calf and set it down onto a stair below me. Then I did the same with my other one. Then I pressed myself up with my arms and dropped my butt down onto the next step. Then I started over — move one leg, move the other, scoot down a step. And so on.

I got to the bottom quickly, pausing only once when a group of girls opened the front door and charged up the stairs. "Hi, Hartley!" they sang out as they went by.

"Evening, ladies." His voice was warm and casual, as if there was nowhere else he'd rather be than sitting in a grimy stairwell with his gimpy friend.

After they passed by and out of sight, I descended quickly to the bottom stair.

"You know," he said, stepping around me, fetching my chair and pulling it over to the bottom step. "You made that look easy."

"Great," I said, wiping my dirty hands on my pants. "But I just hate…" I couldn't even finish the sentence for fear that I'd start crying. I *hated* being that girl who crawls away from the party. I *hated* being the girl who needs rescuing. I *hated* being Hartley's little gimpy pal. Watching *The Princess Bride* over and over again was much more palatable than this brand of mortification.

"I know," he said under his breath. He bent over to pick me up, but I pushed him away. I did a transfer maneuver that would have made Pat proud — pulling myself into the chair in one smooth motion.

Hartley turned me around, pushing my chair toward the door.

"We have to do the stoop backwards," I reminded him.

"We do everything backwards, Callahan," he said.

I had no idea what that was supposed to mean, and I didn't ask.

— *Hartley*

When we reached the flagstone path in the Beaumont courtyard, Corey tried to wave me off. "You can go back upstairs," she said.

"You're drunk, Callahan. I'm going to walk you."

"You're babying me," she complained.

"Huh. Well then I've babied every single one of my friends at some point, and most of them puke on me. Bridger does it weekly." We went on in silence for a couple of minutes before I had to ask, "what were you *thinking*, Callahan?"

"I wasn't, okay? I just wanted to go to the party, for

once. Why do I have to plan every minute of my life three hours in advance? Nobody else does." The courtyard was so quiet that her voice echoed off the walls. "Damn it. I'm whining."

"Everyone has their shit to shovel," I mumbled. "How was the game, anyway?"

"Fine. Tie. 3-3."

"Did you score?"

"Of course I did."

I laughed. "Can't believe I even bothered to ask."

"*Seriously*," Corey agreed, slurring the word a little bit.

When I got her to her own room, I hung back in the doorway. She wheeled into the empty common room and the turned her chair around to face me.

The silence between us felt unnatural, and her pretty face was as sad as I've ever seen it. I fought the urge to cross the room and... I don't know what. The urge to take care of her was nearly overwhelming. What I really wanted to do was gather her up and hold her. It didn't seem fair that the best person I knew would be so sad and lonely on a Friday night.

She tipped her head to the side, revealing a span of creamy neck. "I'm sorry I ruined your evening."

"You couldn't ever." Without thinking, I took two steps into the room. Fuck. What I really wanted to do was run my fingers through her hair, and kiss the place just behind her jaw. And then, kiss a few dozen other places.

Fuck. Me.

All I did, though, was to place a single kiss the top of her head. She smelled like strawberries mixed with chlorine. "Goodnight, Callahan," I said, my voice rough. Then I did the necessary thing. I turned around and headed for the door.

"Hartley?"

I turned around only when I was safely at the door. "Yes, beautiful?"

She rested one soft cheek in her hand. "Why do you always call me Callahan?"

The question stopped me cold, because I didn't really want to think about the answer. "Why do you always call me Hartley?" I countered.

"Everyone calls you Hartley. But you're the only one who calls me Callahan."

It was just my luck the she could be drunk and logical at the same time. The reason was simple, but I wasn't going to say it. I called her Callahan because it made her sound more like one of the guys. I'd been trying to set a tone for our friendship. But it was just another lie I'd told myself. I was finding out that there were quite a few of those.

"Because it's your name." I cleared my throat. "If you'll excuse me, I have some of my own shit I need to shovel." At that, I turned around once and for all, and got the fuck out of there.

Chapter Nineteen: *You Deked Me*

— *Corey*

"Oh, my *head*," I complained the next morning, crutching towards the dining hall for brunch.

"You should have taken a couple of Advil before bed," Dana pointed out.

"If there were things I could redo about last night, that wouldn't even be near the top of the list."

"That bad, huh?"

"It was just embarrassing. I had to be rescued. By Hartley."

Dana smiled. "And we know how much you enjoy being rescued."

"And by *him*. Ugh. And then I had to listen to Stacia complain about it. Then I'm pretty sure he went back over to her place afterwards to do the horizontal mambo." I had lain in my bed last night, watching the room spin, and trying not picture his big hands removing her fancy nightgown.

"Look on the bright side," Dana said as we approached the Beaumont gate. "It's waffle day. Shall I meet you inside?"

I shook my head. "Today I'm taking the stairs. I really need the practice."

Ten minutes later things were looking up. I'd climbed the stairs without tripping or panicking. And Dana and I got our favorite table near the door. I was just finishing my waffle when Daniel slid his tray next to mine. "Morning, lovelies," he said. "Can I sit?"

"Of course," I said. "Dana, this is Daniel. He's the captain of our water polo team. Daniel, this is my roommate, Dana."

"It is a pleasure to meet you," Daniel said. "It would be an even greater pleasure if you would join the team."

Dana laughed. "Sports and I do not get along."

"Inner tube water polo is not a sport, it is a calling." He aimed his crinkle-eyed smile at Dana, and I thought I saw her flush. Dana had a thing for British accents. "We have nice parties afterwards." Then he turned to me. "You disappeared last night, Corey."

"I did?" It was funny to think that he hadn't noticed my departure. I always assume that my awkward comings and goings were as vivid as neon.

"Did you leave before or after the fireworks?" Daniel asked.

"What fireworks?"

"Ah..." His expression took on the flavor of conspiracy. He swiveled around to look over both shoulders before continuing. "Your friend Hartley and his ice queen had a spat in the hallway. It was quite the blow out, really. Very theatrical."

Dana leaned forward in her chair. "What happened?"

"Well..."

Just then, Allison set her tray down across from Daniel. "Good morning!"

"Indeed," he agreed. "I was just telling Corey about the neighborhood brawl. She missed it." He leaned in. "It began with Stacia shrieking 'Nobody dumps me, Hartley!' for all the world to hear."

I felt my heart skip a beat, and Dana gasped. "He dumped her?"

Allison clapped her hands with glee. "He did. But not before she whipped out the L word. But then he said that if she loved him she wouldn't be fucking her..." Allison broke off to laugh. "...Her 'Italian Stallion' all over Europe."

I just sat there, dumbfounded, while my hope fairy flew in through the open door, wrestling with the duct tape across her mouth.

"Wow," Dana breathed. "Stacia must be pissed."

"Oh, she is," Allison nodded. "She went right from 'I love you' to 'you were a big mistake.' And he said 'my work here is done,' and then he left."

"And then we all started placing bets," Daniel said, folding a slice of bacon into his mouth.

"Bets on what?" I asked.

"On which of them will pair up first," Allison said. "My money is on Stacia, because she's all about her image. She has to have man candy on her arm. Now, the line of women waiting for Hartley to be single is pretty long. But he won't replace her right away. At least I hope he doesn't. I need time to line up my shot." She mimed throwing a ball into a polo net. "A girl can dream, anyway."

That was the moment Hartley walked into the dining hall, and the four of us looked up just quickly enough to make it clear that we'd been talking about him. My stomach did a little flip flop as I looked up at the newly single Hartley.

Easy, I cautioned myself. *There's no reason to get your hopes up.*

But my hope fairy ripped the tape off her mouth and yelled, *YES THERE IS!*

Daniel wiped his mouth. "You look a little banged up, mate." And it was true. Hartley's eyes were red and tired.

"I may have done a little drinking late last night." He limped around the table, circling behind Daniel and Dana to stand beside me. He dug a little pill bottle out of his pocket and tapped a couple of tablets into his palm. Tossing them in his mouth, he picked up my juice glass and drained it.

"Hey!" I protested, out of habit.

"Bad night?" Daniel asked.

Hartley shook his head. "Pretty good one, actually. But everyone I wanted to talk to was asleep, except for Bridger and his bottle of Bourbon. Hang on." He walked my glass over to the juice dispenser and refilled it. When he came back, I could see that he was limping badly. And that would be my fault, of course.

"Your knee," I said when he got back.

Hartley shrugged. "It's just stiff. I woke up face down on Bridger's floor this morning. Good times." Then he put his fingertips under my chin, tipping my face up, and frowned. He took the bottle back out of his pocket and tapped two more tablets onto my tray. "Shake off that hangover, Callahan. We have plans tonight."

My pulse leaped. "Since when?"

Hartley put two hands on the table and bent down, his eyes level with mine. "Since now." Before I could register my surprise, his lips were on mine. The kiss was gentle, and over much too quickly. He straightened up, leaving me reeling. "Don't make me beg, Callahan. It's hard on the knee." And then he walked away, into the kitchen.

There was a deep silence at our table for a moment, punctuated by a squeal from Dana. I felt myself turning a dark shade of red.

"Already?" Allison gaped.

Daniel snickered. "Looks like Corey lined up her shot before the whistle blew."

It was just like Hartley to plant a kiss on me without filling in the details. I wanted to yell, "WHAT DOES THIS MEAN?" at the top of my lungs. But I'm a coward. So the question I texted him was a small one.

Hartley?

Yes, beautiful?

Where are we going tonight?

You'll find out later, he replied. *Dress is VERY casual. Take your sticks, not your chair. We're riding the van. Meet me @8 at Beaumont gate.*

I spent the day with an entire flock of butterflies in my stomach.

"What do you think it could be?" Dana asked for the tenth time. She was painting my toenails pink.

"I don't KNOW!" I yelped. And that wasn't even the biggest question in my heart.

What did it *mean?*

Dana read my mind, which probably wasn't difficult. "He dumped her for you. It's *true*, Corey. He grew a pair of balls and did it."

My stomach lurched again. I wanted so badly for it to be true. But when was the last time I got exactly what I wanted?

"Why won't you tell me where we're going?" I asked as we waited for the gimpmobile. I was feeling positively giddy, standing next to Hartley, ready to embark on his strange little adventure.

But all he would give me was a maddening grin. And when the van turned up, he asked the driver to take us to the intersection of Sachem and Dixwell. But I didn't know the city map all that well, and couldn't guess what was there.

To my enduring surprise, the van stopped in front of

the hockey arena.

"Really?" I asked as I levered myself off the one low step, onto the sidewalk. "I don't go in there," I said, hearing the sound of dismay in my own voice.

The van pulled away, and I realized how quiet it was. There was no hockey game tonight. There was nobody around except for Hartley and I.

"I know you don't," he said, stepping close to me. "But I want you to come in with me, just this once."

"But *why*?"

He only shook his head. "If you hate it, I'll never ask you to come back." He leaned down. And in the orange glow of the street lamps, he gave me a single soft kiss.

My heart contracted in my chest. There was plenty I would do to get a few more of those kisses. But Hartley didn't know that I hadn't been into a rink since my accident. I wasn't afraid to go in — I just didn't *want* to. Too many happy hours of my life had been lived at rinks. And now that entire part of my life was gone.

"Please?" he asked. He put his arms around me and kissed the top of my head. "Please."

Who could say no to that?

Hartley walked me downhill, around to the side of the building. Taking a set of keys from his pocket, he opened the ice level door.

Inside, the familiar sensations overwhelmed me immediately. Every rink I'd ever visited had the same smell — the crisp scent of ice, mixed with body odor and salty pretzels. I breathed it in, and my stomach did a little twist.

"Just a little further," Hartley said. He walked me right down the chute, where the players step onto the ice before the game.

Ice gleamed a few feet ahead of me, its surface a

recently Zambonied sheen. I stared down at the threshold between the rubber matting and the clean edge of the rink. The memory of how it felt to put one skate over the lip, push off, and fly was so vivid. The lump in my throat swelled.

"Have you seen one of these before?"

I looked down. Hartley knelt in front of two...sleds? Each one had a molded plastic scoop-shaped seat. When Hartley tipped the thing to the side, I could see two blades underneath. A wooden strut stretched forward from the seat, toward a footrest with a metal ball under it.

I shook my head, clearing my throat. "What is that?" I asked, my voice hoarse. "Some kind of adaptive bullshit."

He looked up at me, his expression worried. "They're...it's *fun*, Callahan. I tested it out first. You can go pretty fast." He positioned one of them next to my feet. "Let's just give it a little spin. If you hate it, we'll go home."

Still, I hesitated. How many times had I stood a few feet from the ice, ready to step out onto it, without ever a clue that it was a privilege? A thousand? More? I'd never known that I had so much to lose, that a few bad minutes could end it forever.

Hartley stood up and came around to stand behind me. He put his hands under my arms. "Just bend at the waist, and I can set you down on it."

With a sigh, I gave in. I bent.

It took the usual eternity to remove my braces, strap me in and set me up. Then Hartley handed me not one, but two, short little hockey sticks. "Be careful of the ends," he prompted. When I studied them, I noticed that each stick had three little metal spikes sticking straight out of the top. "That's how you push yourself," he said. "You'll see."

Then he wrestled my sled over the lip and shoved me out onto the rink. I skidded about thirty feet, then came to a stop. Raising my chin, I looked up at the stadium lights several stories above. Harkness had a gorgeous arena. I'd watched my brother play here. And after my Harkness acceptance letter arrived, I thought I'd play hockey here, too.

Hartley slid onto the ice beside me. "Come on, Callahan. Let's move."

I turned to look at him, but his smile did not reach all the way to his eyes. He waited, watching me while I wrestled with invisible demons. "Alright," I said, finally. With one stick in each hand, I reached down, digging the ice picks into the surface. My sled shot forward about three feet. The blades under my backside must have been decently sharp.

"There you go," he said. Hartley dug in too, and went shooting off toward the blue line. I watched him pick up speed. The ice looked enormous from where I sat. I dug in my sticks and pushed. He was right — it was possible to pick up velocity. But when I leaned my body to turn the sled, I quickly lost speed. A real skater tilts on a single blade edge to turn. The sled was less negotiable.

But still, it worked.

I took a few deep, steadying breaths of ice rink air. And then I turned around and skated towards Hartley.

"Getting a feel for it?" he asked, reaching inside his jacket. He pulled out a puck and tossed it onto the ice.

"It's not very maneuverable," I said. "How am I going to get past your fat ass if I can't turn?" I shot forward and smacked the puck with the business end of one stick.

He grinned. "Actually, the blades can be set closer together. But you tip over a lot. It's kind of like kayaking."

I skidded to a stop. "Hartley, are you telling me you have this thing on the baby setting?"

He raised both his sticks defensively. "Simmer down. It was an oversight." He hitched himself closer to me. "Bail out for a second." I tipped myself onto my side, and he reached over to adjust the sled. "Try it now."

I righted myself, and immediately fell onto my other side. "Wait..." I pressed up again and then began sticking like mad. I shot across the ice, leaned, and turned quickly in an arc. When I looked back at Hartley, he was kneeling on the ice, tweaking the blade under his own sled. I fetched the puck while he strapped himself back in. "Face off?"

"Bring it," he said, steering himself toward the dot.

I tossed the puck up into the air, and it came down to his advantage. Hartley hooked it with his stick, keeping it out of my reach. But then he fumbled, trying to use the wrong end of the stick for propulsion. I shot ahead and took possession, stickhandling toward the net. The next thing I saw was Hartley's sled skating past. He spun around, taking a defensive position. With a stick in each hand, his long arms covered quite a bit of the crease. I lined up a wide shot, watching Hartley stretch in preparation for meeting it. At the last second, I flipped my stick around and shot the puck backhand, into the narrow space between his sled and his stick. The puck sailed through into the net.

The look of surprise on his face was priceless. "You deked me?"

I began to giggle, and my sled tipped onto its side. Poised with my forearms on the ice, I shook with laughter. But the joy unhooked something else in my chest, and my eyes got suddenly hot. There were too many ghosts on the ice with me — sweaty little versions of my former self, darting around on sharpened skates, shooting to kill. My chest tightened, and my breath came in heaving sobs. And then tears began running down my face, falling onto the ice beneath me.

Seconds later, Hartley swept into place beside me. With gentle hands he pulled me up off the ice, leaning me against his body. There were sweet words spoken into my ear, but I couldn't hear them. I was too busy shaking, and crying into the collar of his jacket. "Shh," he said. "Shh."

"It's…" I tried. "I was…"

He only held me tighter. "This was a mistake," he whispered.

I shook my head. "No, it's *good*," I bit out. "It is. But *before*…" I shuddered. "It's so hard…to *accept*."

"I'm so sorry," Hartley said, his own voice breaking. "I'm so damned sorry."

"I was *perfect*," I said. "And I didn't even know."

"No," he whispered into my ear. "No, no. Perfect isn't real." I took a deep, shaky breath, and the feel of his strong arms around me began to feel steadying. "There's no more perfect, Callahan. Now there's only really damned good."

Chapter Twenty: *Cry Like a Little Girl*

— Corey

Eventually I stopped crying. When Hartley looked at his watch, he said, "there's twenty minutes until the van comes back for us."

My face was a dribbling mess, and I wiped my eyes on my jacket. "You'd better fish that puck out of the net, then," I said. "I can probably score on you a few more times. In between crying jags."

"We'll just see about that, Callahan."

I managed to put the puck away one more time, to Hartley's three. When we got back on the bus, I was sweating everywhere. "We wore the wrong gear," I said. "Next time I'll lose the jacket. But gloves and elbow pads would be nice."

Hartley winked. "Next time."

I was drained. All day I'd wanted to quiz Hartley about what would happen next. I'd wanted to know where we stood, even if it was difficult to ask. But just then, with the memory of the gleaming white ice dancing before my eyes, it was enough to rest against his shoulder. He put an arm around me, and we barely spoke at all before the bus pulled up on College Street.

"Where did the sleds come from?" I asked as I maneuvered out of the van.

"I saw them in a storage room last year — like a dozen of them. So I asked the facility manager if we could use them."

"And the ice time? That couldn't have been easy."

"That's Bridger's doing. Coach is still pissed at me."

"Will you thank Bridger for me?" I said quietly.

"Sure."

As we approached the front door to McHerrin, Dana

caught up with us. "Hi guys." She squinted at me. I'm sure I looked like a train wreck, with red eyes and a sweaty brow. "Everything okay?"

"Absolutely," I said. "But I need a shower. You're home early."

"My groupies are headed to a bar, but since my fake ID sucks..." She shrugged. "I'm going to make some tea." She swiped her ID to open the front door.

I wanted to thank Hartley again, but his phone rang. He checked the display, and then he answered. "Hey, Mom," he said, trapping the phone beneath his chin. "Yeah, I did call you. There's something I wanted to tell you, and you're going to love it." As he went into his room, I heard him say, "I'm finished with Greenwich, Connecticut."

I left Hartley to his call and headed for the shower.

The reason might sound silly, but I pinned up my hair before stepping into the spray. The icy smell from the rink lingered in my hair, and I wasn't ready to wash it away. I was happily rinsing the sweat off my body when Dana came into the bathroom. "Corey?" she called.

I stuck my head out of the curtain. "You're supposed to knock!" Dana knew I was a psycho about privacy.

"*Sorry*." Her grin was mischievous as she shut the door behind her. "But Hartley just came looking for you. He said, 'tell Callahan that I'm *waiting up for her*.'" She giggled. "I swear I kept a straight face. Almost."

"Wow. Okay."

"So..." she gave me a devilish look. "I came in here to tell you, in case you were on the fence about shaving anything..."

I pulled the curtain closed. "My God. You're giving me a complex."

"Why?"

"I'll bet Stacia has her garden tended professionally."

Dana hooted. "But she's history, Corey. Tidy pubes and all." I heard her leave the bathroom, giggling.

After I'd dried off, I wrapped the towel around myself and transferred to my chair. As I rolled past Dana in the common room, she asked, "what are you going to wear?"

"Excellent question. Let me see." I stared into my dresser drawers far longer than I'd ever done, finally settling on a skimpy camisole top and yoga pants.

"*Perfect*," Dana said when I emerged for her approval. "Sexy, but it doesn't look like you're trying too hard."

"Dana? You're making some high-level assumptions here, I think."

She shook her head. "I saw that boy's face. I think he drooled a little on our rug. Did you put on slinky underwear?"

"I don't own any, so I went without," I said, running a brush through my hair.

She squealed. "I guess you don't need my help."

"Sure I do. Big decision: the sticks or the chair?" This was the real fashion question in my life.

Dana considered. "The chair. Definitely the chair. It will be easier to tear your clothes off that way."

I wheeled toward the door. "Is this the point where I'm supposed to say, 'don't wait up?'"

She arched her eyebrows. "I'll expect a full report."

I gave Hartley's door two knocks, feeling self-conscious. But I could hear the low thump of house music coming from inside his room, so I opened the door. Inside, Hartley was holding a basketball in the middle of the room, wearing jeans and nothing else. My mouth went dry at the sight. Though the light was low, I could see each perfect muscle on his chest, and the trail of fine brown hairs running down the center and into the waistband of his jeans. He shifted, tossing the basketball aside. And then he was coming for me.

For *me*.

It's not easy to get close to someone sitting in a wheelchair. So when he leaned down, I wrapped my arms around his neck. His skin was velvet under my palms. Hartley put his hands on my hips and lifted me right out of the chair, pulling me to his chest. He slung one arm under my bottom and just held me there, nose to nose, studying me with his serious brown eyes.

"Callahan," he whispered.

"What?"

His answer was a kiss, sweet and slow. I wanted this very badly. But even so, my heart beat wildly, and I wondered what it all meant. I pulled just far enough away that I could see his eyes. "Hartley? I...I can't just be a hookup. Maybe some girls can pull that off, but..."

He put two fingers over my lips. "You have me, Callahan." His hand slid to cup my cheek, and I leaned into its warmth. "You're the first person I want to talk to in the morning, and the last thing I want to see at night."

My gasp of happiness was cut off by his lips against mine. Gently, he sat me down on his bed, pushing the hair back from my face with his thumb. He deepened the kiss. As our mouths melded, Hartley groaned from the back of his throat, the sound reverberating down my spine.

When his tongue stroked mine, I felt it everywhere.

Hartley dropped his mouth to my ear, whispering,

"I'm sorry it took me so long." And then his lips brushed my cheek, while his hands reached around my body, pulling me tight against his bare chest. And then we were kissing, and rolling around on his bed like two starving people discovering an unexpected feast. I let my hands skate all over him. There was no longer any reason not to touch him, and suddenly I couldn't touch him in enough places at once. While my fingers explored the hard muscles of his chest, Hartley kissed his way down my neck. He grazed down my body, lifting the base of my camisole to nose across my stomach. When his lips dipped into the waistband of my yoga pants, my breath hitched.

He raised his chin. "Maybe we should go and get our friend Digby."

"No," I shook my head.

Hartley's muscles popped as he crawled back up to me, his face hovering over mine. "You need to tell me what you want," he whispered, tucking a strand of my hair behind my ear. "I don't know what you're ready for."

I thought I already knew all the ways his brown eyes could look back at me. But I'd been wrong. Now they flared with such heat and desire that I could barely believe that I was really in his bed, and that it wasn't just some misunderstanding. "I want you to..." I broke off, because it was so hard to say. "I want everything. I want you to be the same with me that you were with other girls."

His gaze had the intensity of a laser. "But it's *not* the same with you."

My heart faltered. "*Why?*"

"Because, Callahan." The brown eyes came closer. "I never loved anyone the way I love you." The next kiss was long and slow, and full of promise.

When we came up for air, I made a move, reaching for his fly. Watching me, Hartley's face flushed. I unzipped his jeans. And when I reached into his boxers to wrap my hand around him, he groaned.

Fingering my camisole, he slipped it over my head. Then he put his hands on the waistband of my yoga pants. "Is this okay?" he asked, his voice husky. He looked at me the way a man looks at a woman he's undressing — with gravity and longing.

I nodded.

He removed my pants and then shucked off his own. When he lay down on top of me, we were finally skin to skin. The mood was nothing at all like our Weirdest Night Ever. Our kisses were deep and urgent, and our bodies moved against one another with such sweetness and heat that I felt a prickle behind my eyes. "Hartley," I breathed. "Make love to me."

"You sure?" he panted. "You waited for me. I'd wait for you." He hovered just over me, his nose an inch from mine.

But I was finished waiting. I'd never told Hartley straight out that I was a virgin. There was no way I wanted to stop and have that conversation now. I put two fingers over his lips. "Don't baby me, Hartley."

His shoulder muscles flexed as he shook my fingers off his mouth. Then pressed his hips against mine in a way that made both of us gasp. "I'd never baby you, Callahan. You're the toughest person I know." He opened the drawer of his bedside table, emerging with a little foil packet. He tore it with his teeth, and then reached a hand down between our bodies to roll the condom on.

My heart began to pound with nervous anticipation.

But Hartley slowed down, propping himself up on one elbow. He cradled my cheek with his free hand, studying me with such ferocity that it burned me up inside. "I have always wanted you, Callahan." His fingers whispered down my neck and along my shoulder, tracing a shivery line all the way down my arm. He brought my hand to his lips and kissed my palm. "I was just too stupid to say so."

Inconvenient as it was, I felt prickles in my eyes. "I can't believe..." I started, drawing in a breath through my nose, to try to stop my tears.

"What?"

"...That we're finally here," I said. "I tried so hard not to care."

He brought my hand to his chest, pressing it over his heart. "That's my fault. But I can start making it up to you right now." Then his hand left mine, snaking down my body, leaving quivers in its wake. My breath hitched when his fingers first grazed me right where it counts.

Hartley took his time, tempting me with his touch, all the while his kisses drove me wild. I closed my eyes and sank into all the sensation. I had never felt more lucky than at that moment. In spite of all that had gone wrong over the past year, nothing was over for me. Everything was just beginning.

"Look at me," Hartley begged, hovering above.

I opened my eyes to find his brown ones shining down on me.

"I love you, Corinne," he said. And then I felt pressure between my legs, and then a sharp pinch.

"Oh," I sighed, surprised by the unfamiliar sensation of fullness.

"Am I hurting you?" he asked, his lips pursed.

I rubbed my hands along his trim hips. "I can feel

220

you. But I *want* to feel you. Just go slow."

His eyes fell sweetly closed, and his face became serene. Very gently he pulled his body back, and I sighed at the loss of him. But then he crept forward again, and the beautiful feeling of fullness returned. He kissed me as he withdrew again. He moved so slowly that I began to fear he wouldn't be back. But there he was again, pressing on, making me gasp with want.

Hartley lowered himself over me, his lips near my ear. "You don't know how happy you make me," he whispered. Then he began to move in a gentle rhythm, his kisses and his body syncing together. When he gave a twist of his hips, I heard myself moan.

There was no more pain, just a delicious tightening of all my senses. The taste of Hartley's mouth and the heat of his skin were everything to me. I buried my fingers in his thick hair. But it was the sounds he made which really moved me. It began as a hum of pleasure, buzzing in my ear. Then he inhaled very deeply, followed by a groan. As we moved together, his breathing changed, becoming shallow and short.

Everything about it was beautiful.

— *Hartley*
Must. Slow. Down.

Making love to the best girl in the whole world was heady stuff. I'd been lying to myself for a long time about how much I wanted this, and finally letting go of all that tension go really did a number on my self-control. I was a live wire. I was a kite in a thunderstorm. I was a seismograph, the needle quivering in anticipation of the earthquake.

I was probably going to disgrace myself.

Wrapping both arms around Corey, I rolled us over,

flopping my head back onto the pillow. "Time out," I panted. "I'm getting carried away."

She lay on my chest, cheeks flushed, pink lips swollen from my kisses. "That's okay," she breathed. Her hands swept over my pecs, her fingernails scraping my nipples. *Fuuuck.* She was going to kill me.

I caught both her hands in mine, and tried not to look at her boobs, which were very close to my face. "But this...this is okay, too." Smiling up at her, I tugged her arms down, until her elbows were on either side of me. Then I took her hips in my hands and rocked her against me.

That's when her eyes went a little wide. This was all new to her, and I'd never want to scare her. But that's the thing about Corey — she'd speak up if it wasn't right. Even now, the look on her face — one part wonder, one part bravery, with a dash of *oh my God* — it cut me in half. Corey was one hundred percent genuine all the time — there was no artifice, no faking. And when I was with her, I could be just the same. There was no need to hide from her. She wanted all of me, no matter what.

And now I could finally give it to her.

Biting her lip, she began to move, cautiously at first. But after a moment, her body took over, knowing just what it wanted. I watched her face as she found what she was looking for. Her eyes fell closed, and she made that sound again — a sigh so deep and fine that I felt it in my toes. Then she followed it up with a breathy little moan.

Holy hell.

"I like the sound of that," I bit out. And then things began to happen very fast. I knifed upward, claiming her mouth. Her lips pursed with erotic distraction as my hands guided her legs, deepening her motion against me. My vision darkened, and I felt my body pause, like the still air before a storm. Then I growled, and the sound shot through both of us. Corey began to gasp as I jacked my hips up off the bed. Sensation crashed over me, and I lost myself in it. My own release and the happy sounds she made were the only things I knew.

— *Corey*

We lay beside one another, breathing hard. Hartley's strong thighs were tangled in mine. He stroked my breast, his lips brushing my brow.

Wow, I thought. Or I might have said it aloud. I wasn't sure, because my brain had short-circuited.

He pulled me in to lay tight against his chest. "Damn. So much for going slow," he panted. "I've been wanting to do that for a long time." He kissed my forehead, and I grinned like a maniac.

Under my palm, his rapid heartbeat thudded against my hand. This part was wonderful — our clumsy caresses, the gradual slowing of our breathing. Here was an activity — cuddling after sex — for which my disability presented no problem at all. I grinned into his shoulder.

"What's so funny?" he whispered.

"I was just thinking that you don't need two working legs for this. We're just like two normal people."

Hartley tipped his forehead against mine, so he could see into my eyes. "We *are* two normal people, you dope." He gave me a quick kiss. "Only better-looking. And with higher than average SAT scores."

"You forgot humble."

"Right." His brown eyes shone with love, and it made me feel wistful.

"I just wish I could give you the original me. Not the

broken one."

He closed his eyes and gave his head a shake. "There's only one Callahan, the one who removed my head from my ass. I have her already."

"Hartley, you *have* to wish I could always keep up with you. Skating, running. How could you not want that?"

His arms tightened around me. "I want a lot of things. I want a couple million dollars. I want a father who will say my name, and I want the Bruins to win the Stanley Cup. But I'm pretty damned happy right now without any of those things. There'd be no point in moping."

I buried my face in his neck, where I'd willingly leave it forever. "I mope anyway, sometimes."

He smoothed my hair under his hand, and dropped his voice down low. "Don't get me wrong. If I ever see video of you flying down the ice to score on a breakaway, I'm going to cry like a little girl." His lips grazed my face. "But then I'll remove a few pieces of your clothing, and remember that life is good."

Even though that was just about the sweetest thing Hartley had ever said to me, a doubt nagged the back of my mind. "Hartley?"

"Yeah, beautiful?"

"What if I couldn't...be with you? And enjoy it."

His arm came tightened around me. "But you can."

"But what if I couldn't?"

"Okay. What if I'd broken my skull instead of my leg? We can lie here and imagine all the shitty possibilities. Or we can lie here and make out some more."

"I just..." I took a deep breath. "I just love you, Hartley."

"I know, beautiful." Then he kissed me again.

Later, I got up and wheeled myself into Hartley's bathroom to pee, just like the E.R. doctor had told me to do. I borrowed Hartley's toothbrush, because I didn't think he'd mind. And then made my way back to his bed.

He was asleep.

I climbed in beside him, pulling the sheet and blanket up over us. Before closing my eyes, I gave Hartley a little kiss on the shoulder. Just because I could.

Chapter Twenty One: *Those Old Dudes*

— *Corey*

When I opened my eyes the next morning, Hartley was holding my hand, his thumb slowly stroking my palm. I turned my head to look at his handsome face and found it serene, his eyes closed. Since he wasn't looking at me, I left the giant, sloppy grin pasted on my face.

"Nothing better than this," he said sleepily. "Waking up with you in my bed. I must have finally done something right."

We were quiet and lazy for a while. It was Sunday, too. There was no place else I needed to be, except right there next to him. I brought his hand up to kiss it. "Hartley," I whispered. "The other night, when I was drunk, you said you had some shit to shovel."

"Yeah, I shoveled it," he said.

"What was it?"

He turned his head, opening his eyes to look at me. "I don't want to talk about her while I'm lying here with you."

"Her. Really? What does Stacia have to do with it?"

"Plenty," he said. "And she doesn't even know."

What? "Well, now you *have* to tell me."

He rolled onto his stomach and put his chin in the crook of his elbow. "Nobody knows, actually. Not a soul." His long eyelashes flicked up when he looked at me. I moved closer, putting my hand on the back of his neck, and he closed his eyes again. "You probably noticed that there's no father in the picture for me."

"Sure," I breathed, caressing his neck. I could touch him all day long.

"He got my mom pregnant when they were both eighteen. She was a waitress at his country club." He opened his eyes and looked up at me again. "My mom's story has made me very, very careful, by the way. The next time you see a doctor, could you ask about...?"

Birth control. "Okay." It might be tricky, though, because my history with blood clots would probably make me ineligible for the pill. But I would ask.

Hartley closed his eyes before continuing. "When I was little, my father's parents used to send us money every month. But when I was six, they stopped, and he was supposed to start. But he never sent us a dime."

"Classy," I said. "And your mother didn't go after him?"

He shook his head. "She said she wouldn't embarrass him publicly. No matter that she was always embarrassed. No money, no dad to teach me to tie up my hockey skates..." he trailed off. I leaned over and kissed the velvety skin on his shoulder. "Mmm," he smiled. "What was I saying?"

I stopped kissing him. "Your asshole father."

"Right. Well, here I am in the hallowed halls of Harkness, working my tail off. I've learned to forget about him, except when I see his name in the newspaper."

"You do?"

He nodded. "He's a film producer — very successful. Top shelf. And that fucked with me too. I kept thinking that if I was successful, then maybe he'd acknowledge me. I even picked this school because of him."

"But this school is great."

"It's great, unless you have a giant chip on your shoulder about rich people. It would have been more my style to take a hockey scholarship at Michigan or somewhere. But I came here, because he's an alum."

"Please don't say you wish you hadn't come to Harkness." I nuzzled him.

"That's not what I said." He kissed my ear. "It's just that I chose it for the wrong reasons, and it made my pile of shit deeper."

I slid my body onto Hartley's back, spreading out on him as if he were a piece of furniture. "What does your father have to do with Stacia?" I asked.

"Right," he said. And then he took a deep breath. "Callahan, when you're pressing your boobs against my back, it's hard to think."

"Try."

"Okay..." he chuckled. "Stacia was dating Fairfax, and I thought she was the bitchiest, most high-maintenance girl I'd ever met. But one night she happened to mention that their neighbor in Greenwich had been to a dinner party her parents gave. Stacia is a big name-dropper."

"And the neighbor...was your father?"

He nodded.

"Wow. Strange coincidence. So you asked her out because of that? Did you want to meet him?"

He was quiet for a moment. "No, I never tried to meet him. That wasn't it. It was more like...she was inside the gates, and I was on the outside. So she became very attractive to me. If I could get her to love me, then I'd be a member too." He swiveled his head around to look up at me. "This shit sounds even worse out loud than it does in my head."

I sank my thumbs into his shoulder muscles. "Keep shoveling, Hartley." I massaged his neck and he dropped his head in appreciation.

"Last year was great. I thought so at the time, anyway. I won her off of Fairfax."

"Ouch," I said.

He laughed. "That's the only part of this story that isn't awful. Because Fairfax didn't mind that much. There's only so much Stacia a guy can take. Anyway, I worked hard at being with her. It's not like I just phoned it in, to get the invite to her mansion. We went on our little adventures, and she can party with the best of them. I took all the crap she could dish out. And every time I drove past my father's house behind the wheel of Stacia's Mercedes, it felt damned good."

I stilled my hands on his back, thinking.

"You can say it," Hartley said. "Pretty pathetic."

"There is nothing pathetic about you," I said. "I only wish you believed it. Did you ever see him?"

"No, and I didn't expect to. I think he works out of L.A. a lot of the time. But once I saw his kids kicking a ball around on the lawn. It was only for a few seconds, because I had to keep driving. That was hard."

"Oh my God! You have siblings. What did they look like? Did they look like you?"

He shrugged. "Hard to say. They looked like a Ralph Lauren ad. Clean and shiny. Two boys and a girl."

Hartley rolled onto his side, sliding me off of him. We faced each other side by side. Self-conscious, I pulled the sheet up, covering my breasts.

"Don't hide those," Hartley grinned. "It took me months to get my shit together so that I could see them."

"Months?"

"Sure." His smile faded again. "This year has been hard, with the broken leg, no hockey, and no fancy princess around to prop me up. And then I started hanging around with you, Callahan. And that really fucked with my head."

"Why?"

"Because you were so *real*. And you weren't afraid to name all the things that scared you. And I realized I'd never had a single conversation with Stacia like I had with you. I was waiting around for a girl I didn't love. But she said she still wanted me, and I couldn't stop thinking it was important." His eyes were sad. "I was afraid to cut the cord. It made me start hating myself."

"Yikes."

He blew out a breath. "On my birthday, I was sitting in here waiting for her, but the person I really needed was just across the hall. And even when I got off my ass and went to you, I wasn't truthful. I made a game out of it, and it wasn't a game." He reached out, stroking my hair. "I tortured both of us, didn't I? I'm sorry."

That only made me smile. "I'm that transparent, huh?"

"Callahan, you were *honest*. You weren't afraid to tell me to my face the other night, that you couldn't just be friends. That killed me — that you were the one with the balls to say it. So I got ready to make it right." He pulled me toward him, tucking my head onto his chest. I could hear his heart — *glug glug* — under my ear.

My pulse accelerated. I wasn't quite used to the idea that he was holding me, just like I'd always wanted him to. My plan at that moment was to stay in his bed until he kicked me out. And yet I still had questions. "Does your mom know that you were sort of stalking your father?"

"No," he said. "But even without the details, she was on to me. She knew there was something about my relationship with Stacia that wasn't honest, and she loved beating me up about it. 'Adam, why are you with her? She's a stuck-up bitch, you're smarter than that,' and so on. My mom hates everything about Greenwich,

Connecticut. And Stacia didn't do a very good job of winning her over."

"Were you ever tempted to tell Stacia about your father?" I asked.

He shook his head. "You can't show any weakness to Stacia. She'll eat you for breakfast."

"That's not love."

He kissed the top of my head. "I get that now. And here I am, spilling my guts to you first thing on a Sunday morning, like it's no big deal. Because you've always got my back."

"Actually…" I splayed my fingers across his belly. "I have your front."

He pressed his nose into my hair. "Have more of it, baby."

As my fingertips feathered across his waist, Hartley reached for me.

For *me*.

When I opened Hartley's door an hour later, he was still lounging on his bed, half-dressed, flipping through *Sports Illustrated*. He sat up quickly. "Sorry, I didn't realize you'd be ready so soon."

"It was only fifteen minutes, no?"

He grinned, reaching for a T-shirt. "Some women say fifteen minutes when they mean forty-five." He put a baseball cap over his messy hair. "I, on the other hand, need only forty-five seconds." He went into the bathroom where I heard him brush his teeth.

I'd spent my fifteen minutes wisely, pulling myself together for brunch. I made more of an effort than I usually would, changing into new jeans and a top. I'd even added a slick of lip gloss. In other words, I didn't want to walk into that dining hall looking like I'd just rolled out of bed with Hartley.

In spite of my preparations, my face began to burn as I hitched myself toward the top of the Beaumont dining hall stairs. I paused before the doorway, looking up at Hartley. "This is weird for me. I feel like it's tattooed on my face," I whispered.

He only looked amused. "You're cute when you're freaking out. If I didn't know better, I'd think you were embarrassed to be seen with me."

"That must be it," I said, taking a deep breath.

He moved very close to me, his hand resting on the small of my back. "How old is this place? Three hundred years?" He dropped his voice to a hot whisper. "We're not the first people to have a whole lot of sex before Sunday brunch."

His lips brushed my face, heating me everywhere. "The school has only been coed since the seventies," I pointed out, inhaling his warmth.

"What a bummer for all those old dudes." He pulled me even closer to his body.

With his hands on me again, I felt the familiar thrum of desire in my core. For sanity's sake, I pushed him away and took a deep breath. "You're not helping me to appear cool and indifferent." I turned away from his smile and headed for the kitchen.

Now that I was on crutches and he wasn't, Hartley handled our food. "Holding the tray used to be my job," I pointed out. The role reversal stung. He was going back to normal, and I wasn't.

He flinched. "Callahan, are you going to hate me when I go back to hockey in the fall?"

Hmm...*In the fall*. Hartley assumed we'd be together then, too. I loved that. "No," I decided. "I'll finally get to watch you play."

His face broke open with happiness. "Really?" He leaned over to brush his lips against my cheek. "I've been worrying about it."

"Just don't expect me to squeal like a puck bunny when you take the ice. And I'm not wearing a tight-fitting jersey with your number on it."

"C'mon. You have to," he grinned, reaching for the plates on the service counter.

"Good luck with that." My phone buzzed in my pocket. I pulled it out, but it was only my brother calling. I could get back to him later. "I'm going to pour coffee," I told Hartley, and crutched out into the dining room.

Out there, I scanned the tables, considering our options. Bridger was at one of the long, crowded tables, but Stacia was also there. So that was out. At our favorite table by the door, Dana and Daniel were deep in conversation.

"Where to?" Hartley asked, holding out the tray for the mugs.

"Well, they look awfully cozy," I said, pointing to my roommate.

"Interesting," he said. "But they like us, so let's sit."

When I made my way over to Dana, she looked up fast. Then an excited smile broke over her face.

"Not a word," I warned. My face was instantly red.

"O-kayyy..." she said, grinning into her coffee cup.

I sat down beside Daniel. Hartley set our tray onto the table and then slid onto the bench beside Dana. "Morning!"

"A fine day, isn't it?" Daniel asked with a wink.

"A *very* fine day," Hartley began, until I fixed him with a death stare. "If unremarkable."

Dana giggled.

"Miss Corey," Daniel said. "If you don't want

gossip, you should not have let him give you that enormous love bite on your neck."

"*What?*" I looked down, but of course it was impossible to see my own neck without a mirror.

"Made you look!" Daniel said, sending Dana into a fit of giggles.

"With friends like you..." I threatened. But I was starting to relax. Every time I glanced at Hartley's handsome face across the table from me, I felt a little lighter.

"Now Corey," Daniel reminded me. "Don't let a night of passion distract you from your true cause. Ashforth House has promised not to forfeit today's game, but now I'm worried that we'll have to."

"Why?"

"Bear and Allison have a symphonic performance."

"Seriously? Bear is a classical musician?"

"He plays the tuba. And Allison is the first viola. I'll be working the phones after brunch..." he looked at his watch, then at my roommate. "Help a guy out, Dana?"

Dana looked genuinely torn, which is how I knew that she was hot for Daniel. There was no other reason she would even hesitate before saying no. "I just can't," she said after a pause. "I'd duck every time the ball comes near."

"That's not against the rules," I pointed out.

My phone chimed with a text from Damien. *Where R U? Beaumt Dining Hall?* Then my phone buzzed again, and I picked up the call. "Hi? Damien?"

"Please tell me you're at brunch," my brother said. "Because I'm climbing the stairs."

"What — really? Why?"

"What do you mean, *why?* I came to see you. Are you up here?"

Startled, my eyes went straight to the door. A few seconds later, my brother stood there in the archway, peering out from underneath his Harkness baseball cap. I let the phone fall to the table as he met my eyes and then smiled. Then he was standing over me, leaning in for a hug. "Hey! I found you." He grabbed a chair from the empty table next to ours and swung it around. That put him on the end, between Hartley and I.

Hell and damn.

"Um, Dana? I said. "This is my big brother, Damien."

Damien didn't seem to pick up on my discomfort. "So *you're* Dana! Nice to finally meet you, girl."

She beamed at him, shaking hands.

"And maybe you also know Daniel? And of course, Hartley." I could feel my face reddening as I said his name.

"How's it hanging, Hartley? I see you got your cast off. You must be feeling frisky again."

Frisky? I was going to die of embarrassment in the next ten minutes if I couldn't figure out how to extract myself from this situation. I snuck a look across at Hartley. He had the good sense not to look too amused.

Damien looked around the room. "Typical scene for a Sunday. I'm just going to grab a cup of coffee. Feels like I never left this place." He rose again and loped towards the mugs.

"Oh, crap," I whispered.

"Your face is the color of a tomato," Dana whispered.

Hartley reached across the table and gave my hand a quick squeeze. "Be cool, beautiful. We're just having brunch here. Did you know he was coming?"

"No!" I hissed. "He never mentioned visiting."

My brother sat back down, sipping his coffee. "So, how are you holding up?" he asked me.

"Just fine," I said quickly.

His blue eyes were studying me so carefully that it was unnerving. "Well that's good," he said slowly. "Mom and Dad asked me to check in with you."

"That's...nice," I said, feeling as though I'd missed something. "You took the train up?"

"Sure," he said, still eyeing me. Was there some way he could tell that I'd just done the one thing he'd ever told me not to? It wasn't that I cared what he thought about Hartley and me. But my life was evolving at warp speed, and I could have used a day to get used to the idea. I didn't need any push-back from Damien.

Stacia picked that moment to walk by, passing us between the conveyor where trays are deposited and the door. "Hey, Callahan," she said suddenly. I turned my head as a reflex, about a millisecond before realizing that she was speaking to my brother.

My hockey-playing brother. Of course she was.

"Hey, Stacia. Looking good, as always," he winked. "Do you know my sister Corey?"

As her gaze slid from Damien to me, the temperature of it dropped from steamy to subzero immediately. "Oh," she said, frowning. "We've met." And then she stomped out of the room.

"Well, she's still the same," Damien chuckled. Then he glanced at Hartley. "Oh, shit. Weren't you two...?"

Now even Hartley looked rattled. "Yeah...uh...not anymore."

"Sorry, dude." My brother went back to his cup of coffee. My nerves fried, I was just about to declare brunch finished when Bridger trotted up, pausing behind my brother and me.

"What's up, Bridge?" Hartley asked before draining his juice.

Bridger smirked down at him. "I was going to ask you the same thing. Please tell me that somebody had to do the Crutch of Shame this morning. Or do I have to restock the bourbon?"

"Bridger," I gasped.

"Come on, Callahan," he said as he passed behind me, giving my ponytail a flip. "I've been saving up that joke all weekend." He rounded our table toward the door, aiming a lopsided grin at Hartley. And then he did a hard double-take as he recognized my brother. "Whoa, Callahan," he said, pulling up short. "I didn't see you there."

In the silence which followed, Damien looked from Bridger to me, and then slowly to Hartley. "What the fuck?"

Interesting choice of words.

My new boyfriend rubbed his jaw with his hand. If there was a suitable thing to say into the silence that followed, neither Hartley nor I could figure out what it was.

Bridger was still standing frozen over Dana and Daniel, practically in the doorway. "I just, uh…" he said. "Sorry."

Hartley dismissed him with a wave, and then turned back to face my brother's glare.

"My little sister?" Damien bit out. "Out of five thousand undergrads, she's your latest conquest?"

I could see Hartley trying to decide if defending himself was the right strategy or not. "Conquest?" he said, frowning. "It's not like that."

Damien shook his head. "You don't have to sit here and be an asshole about it now. Can't you just get lost now?"

"Actually, Callahan," Hartley said quietly, "*that* would be the asshole thing to do."

Damien turned to me, his face red. "I don't know why I even made the trip up here."

"I don't know why either," I snapped.

My brother's face actually slackened with surprise. "You don't, do you?"

"No, Damien. So why don't you just tell me?"

"Wow." He gave a dark chuckle. "Don't worry. I won't tell Mom and Dad why you forgot what day it was."

"What day is it?" Dana asked. At least I wasn't the only one who was confused.

"It's January fifteenth. I came here to make sure Corey was doing okay."

"Oh," I said, stupidly.

Oh.

My stomach swerved, and memories of last January fifteenth rushed toward me, unbidden. I didn't want to remember. But suddenly it seemed that I had no choice. Lowering my eyes to the table, I was transported back one year.

Last January fifteenth was a Saturday.

I slept through breakfast, and then made myself an egg and bacon sandwich for lunch. My mother had been out jogging, even though it was only ten degrees outside. And by the time she came home, I was tearing the house apart, looking for my hockey shorts. "I washed them," she'd said. "Look on the drying rack."

I ran past her. I *ran*. On two legs. I was full of irritation, worried that I'd be late for my game. I'd had no idea that things were about to change so dramatically

— that running into the laundry room was something I'd never do again.

"Um, Corey?"

My head snapped up. Dana had been trying to get my attention, but I'd been lost — staring with unseeing eyes at my plate. "Yeah?"

She frowned at me. "What's January fifteenth?"

"It's…" I swallowed. She and Daniel were looking at me with confusion in their eyes. Hartley and my brother only looked sad. "Today…" Now I understood why I'd had two text messages from my parents already — messages I hadn't returned. *Call us*, they'd written. *We're thinking about you.*

I didn't feel like explaining. I didn't want to *be* that damaged person, but it seemed that today I had no choice.

Leaning over, I picked up my crutches from the floor. "I was supposed to call my parents this morning, and I just remembered," I stammered. I heaved myself out of the chair and began crutching for the door. Damien got up to follow me.

"The game is at one-thirty!" Daniel called over his shoulder.

Chapter Twenty Two: *January the Fifteenth*

— *Corey*

"The game is at one-thirty," my father had said through clenched teeth.

He was behind the wheel of our car, and I was hurrying to throw my gear into the back. The coach was not supposed to arrive so close to face-off, yet again. As usual, my dad's tardiness would be my fault.

"Sorry," I had said, running around to the passenger seat.

I don't remember the drive. There wouldn't have been any traffic, not in our sleepy little town. What had I been thinking about on the ride to the rink? A homework assignment? The boy I'd just started dating — the one whose face I could barely remember now?

Before my accident, it had been so easy to stare out the car window at the frozen landscape, thinking of nothing at all. I hadn't known that I should love every moment, that every minute of feeling complete and capable was worshipful. I hadn't known.

Back at McHerrin, I retreated into my bedroom.

"Nice room," Damien murmured.

I crawled onto my bed and removed my braces. Scooting up onto the pillow, I set my back against the wall.

A glance at the clock told me that it was almost twelve. I wondered what my parents were doing now, but I was too chicken to call them. Depending on the schedule, my father might have a game. For his sake, I hoped it was an away game. I hoped that one-thirty would not find him standing in exactly the same spot he'd stood last year.

For every one of my games, he had always been right there, in the box with a whistle and a clipboard. It was hard to picture him without those two things. My teammate once asked me in jest if my father wore his whistle to bed at night. Maybe I'd played so hard at hockey because he was always there watching. He was such a good coach, and such a fair man, that I'd never felt hemmed in by being both his kid and his athlete. It was all good, until the day that it wasn't.

My poor father. He had to watch it all go down.

I was skating hard, backwards and fast. The puck shot across the ice in my direction. I leaned in for the pass, but another skater — an opponent — leaned in harder. She flailed her stick in the direction of the speeding puck, but caught my skate blade instead.

My memory of this part is really just a collage of the things people told me later.

Somehow, she tripped me so badly that I went flying backwards. I flew over the other skater in a neat airborne arc. And then I landed on my back. And then I blacked out for a few seconds.

My father was over me when I opened my eyes. "Corey, are you okay?" he asked me.

"Yeah," I said. And I believed it. In fact, I eventually got up and skated off the ice.

"So what else is going on with you?" Damien asked me. "Do you have your new semester sorted out?"

I cleared my throat. "I think so. I'm taking a Shakespeare class with Dana. And that psych class everyone raves about. With Professor Davies."

"That's a fun one," my brother agreed, fingering the bill of his cap. "Want to play some RealStix?"

I shook my head. Today I wanted nothing to do

with hockey. Not even pretend hockey.

"What was that guy Daniel saying about a game?"

I met my brother's eyes, which were warm and clear. I tried to tamp down my irritation, because he was only trying to help. "I joined the coed intramural water polo team. Did you ever play?"

Damien shook his head. "Sounds fun, though."

"It's okay," I said. "It's actually a better workout than I thought it would be. There aren't any extra players. So at the end of an hour, we're all puffing like grannies."

Damien looked at his watch. "I'll come to your game."

I shook my head again. "I'm going to sit this one out."

After my awful crash, I sat the rest of the hockey game out. On the bench, leaning against the wall, my back hurt. But so did my head, and my shoulders. My father wondered if I had a mild concussion. Aside from my intense backache, there weren't any scary symptoms. So we went home. I took a dose of an ordinary pain killer, and went to bed surprisingly early.

That night, I woke up to crushing pain in my lower back. Terrified, I got out of bed and stumbled into my parents' room. I barely made it, sinking down on my mom's side of the mattress. "Corey?" she said, but her voice sounded far away. "What's wrong?"

That's when I passed out.

I woke up in the hospital two days later. I'd had major surgery for a blood clot pressing against my spinal cord. There were beeping machines and tubes and worried faces everywhere. Doctors muttered phrases like "unusual presentation" and "wait and see."

It took everyone a while to realize that the midnight trip I'd made into my parents' room had been the last time I would ever walk unassisted.

At one o'clock, Hartley appeared in the doorway to my room. "Hi there," he said.

"Hi." My voice sounded small and underused.

"It's almost time to go to the pool."

I didn't want to have a big teary talk, or explain. I just looked away.

He came in anyway, and my brother tensed, looking just on the verge of telling him off. "Callahan," Hartley said quietly. "I need a few minutes with Callahan."

With an ornery grunt, Damien got up and went into the common room. I heard the TV come on as Hartley dropped a gym bag on the floor in front of me. "Can I walk you to the gym?"

"I don't think I'm going," I whispered.

"Well, I think you should," Hartley said, sitting down on the bed. He put his arms around me, and I let him pull me in. I buried my nose in his shoulder and inhaled. "The others are waiting for you. Even if it is January fifteenth. It's a shit shoveling kind of day."

"Don't I know it," I murmured into his chest. His arms circled tighter, and we just sat there for a minute holding each other. I could really get used to this.

"There's something I've been working on, and I wonder what you'll think." He leaned over, pulling an envelope out of his gym bag. He unfolded a single piece of paper, handing it to me.

It was a letter, addressed to a Hollywood name I'd known for years.

Dear Mr. Kellers,

I don't have any idea what you'll choose to do with this letter, but I know I had to write it. For too many years I've tried to pretend that it doesn't bother me that we haven't ever met, or that you would rather not say my name out loud. But now I realize how many choices I've made hoping that you'd approve. I'm a junior at Harkness College. I got into this school without listing your name on the legacy part of my application. I'm a hockey player. My grades are decent and I'm majoring in political science.

I've had a tough year, including an injury that kept me away from my sport. With a lot of extra time on my hands, I've had to slow down and figure out what's really important. And I realized that the weight of your rejection is something I've been dragging around for my whole life.

Sir, I think you should meet me. I'm not going to ask you for money or even a public acknowledgment that I'm your son. I can't force you to look me in the eye, but I can raise my hand and let you know that it matters to me. I'm asking now so I can stop wondering whether or not you would have said yes.

Sincerely,
Adam Kellers Hartley

I looked up at him, blowing out a breath. "Wow. Your middle name is his last name?"

He nodded. "Would you send this, if you were me?"

"I would, Hartley. It's a brave thing to do."

"Meeting him wouldn't be easy."

I shook my head. "That's not why it's brave, and I think you know that. The harder thing will be if he doesn't answer. If he lets you just twist in the wind."

Hartley flopped back on my bed. "Yeah. But I'm sick of wondering. I want to make my peace with the question."

I put my hand down on his shapely stomach. "Then mail it. It's a good letter."

He caught my hand, his thumb stroking my palm. "Let's make a deal. I'll mail the letter on the way to water polo."

I squirmed. "See, it was nice there for a minute, talking about your problems instead of mine. Will you think I'm a wimp if I don't go to the game?"

"There is *nothing* you could do to make me think you're a wimp." He sat up and brought my palm to his lips. "But I still want you to go."

"Can't I just wallow? Just once?"

"Wallow tomorrow. Water polo first."

"Why?"

He grinned. "Because I told Daniel I'd play goalie. And I'd really like you to witness my greatness."

"You did? Just because of my funk?" I couldn't help but smile. "Are you sure that's a good idea? What if you jam your leg?"

"Don't baby me, Callahan." His dimple made an appearance.

I kissed him on the nose. "You are a manipulative, evil boy."

"I've been called worse. So where do you keep your bikinis?"

I shook my head. "We're going to have to forfeit anyway. Even if I show up."

"Not true! I convinced Dana and Bridger to play too. I told them you shouldn't be alone today, that you need your friends around you."

My heart skipped a beat. "Really? And they're going? Even Dana?"

"I think she has a thing for Daniel," Hartley's smile grew. "But she *said* she's doing it for you."

I giggled. Suddenly, living my new life seemed more important than mourning my old one. I wanted to watch Hartley's mostly naked body floating around in an inner tube, defending the goal. And I wanted to see Dana try to maintain her bravado with a ball flying at her. "Hartley, get lost for five minutes. I'll change into a suit."

"That's my girl. I'll get your towel," he said, untangling himself from me and walking out.

After he shut the door, I slipped down onto the floor and crawled over to my dresser, because it was a heck of a lot faster than putting the braces on. I crawl better now, thanks to Pat's diligence. But removing my jeans requires me to roll from one hip onto the other, like a flopping fish.

It's very sexy.

Not.

— *Hartley*

Corey's brother was staring at the television, doing his best to ignore me. I sat down beside him anyway.

I understood that he was struggling, but there was no way I was going to feel guilty for being with Corey. Just the opposite — I was pretty damned proud of myself. Also, I felt lighter. Telling Corey my whole freakish family story was such a load off my mind.

"What's she doing in there?" Damien asked without looking at me.

"Changing into her bathing suit."

He turned his head. "Really? You talked her into going?"

"Yeah." I tried not to sound smug, but I might have. Just a little.

He shut the TV off and then turned his body toward

me. There was some aggression in it, but I knew it was just for show.

"My sister, huh?" He scraped his face. "Damn. At least it's not Bridger."

"Dude, please." I had a pang of guilt for throwing my best friend under the bus like that, but Damien had a point. He might not like the idea of me getting naked with his sister, but love 'em and leave 'em wasn't my style.

"You know what, though? She was all kinds of bummed out over the holidays. And I think that's on you."

Okay, *ouch*. But making Corey sad was never my intention. And to be fair, she never said so. Not until later. "We had some things to work through. It took me a while to figure it all out."

"I'm just saying, I know where you live."

And there it was — the threat. Fine. "You know, I don't have a little sister. Actually, that's not right. I have one, but I've never met her." Look at me spilling my guts everywhere today! Next thing you know, I was going to be telling my life story on daytime TV. "So I don't know exactly where you're coming from. But that's okay, because Corey is important to me."

He gave me a blue-eyed glare which reminded me of Corey's. "Just treat her right."

"I plan to. Hey, you know what? I covered for you."

"How do you mean?"

"She asked me if her brother was a total dog, and I told her that you weren't so bad."

His face broke into a very slow smile. "But what does it matter whether I was a total dog? As long as she's not *with* a total dog."

"Double standard, much?"

Damien showed me his middle finger, and then Corey opened her bedroom door. "Um, guys?"

I jumped up off the couch and shoved Corey's towel into my gym bag. Then I brought her ID over, looping it over her neck.

"Hartley?" she put her hands on my chest. "Thank you."

Well, that made me feel like a million bucks. So, Damien be damned, I kissed her right on the lips. Then I tucked my letter back inside its envelope, licked the flap and sealed it shut. "Let's do this thing." I opened Corey's door and waited while Damien put on his jacket to come with us. "You know," I said to him, "I could lend you a suit, if you want to play. You are a Beaumonter, after all."

"He can't play!" Corey protested. "Alums aren't allowed. I don't want our win to be disqualified."

At that, I had to throw my head back and laugh. "Jesus, Callahan. I forgot who I was dealing with." As Corey crutched past me, I leaned down to drop another kiss onto her head.

Even Damien grinned, and I saw his attitude toward me melt by one or two degrees. "The Callahans play to win," he said. "Lead on, you two. Show me how this is done."

So we did.

Chapter Twenty Three: *Later is Better Than Never*

— *Corey, Three Months Later*

Hartley and I sat together on the couch. It was a Saturday afternoon in April, just after brunch. I was trying to stay absorbed in my copy of Shakespeare's *Julius Caesar*, but Hartley pulled me onto his lap, sweeping my hair off my shoulder. He kissed the place where the hair had just been.

"I can't read Shakespeare with your lips on my neck," I complained.

"So don't read it," he mumbled. He leaned me back against his chest, and I felt his firm body shift suggestively beneath me. "That play is 400 years old. It can wait another half an hour. We could just...mmm," he said, his hands sliding down my ribcage and hips, cupping my bottom.

I closed the book, tossed it onto the coffee table and spun around to kiss him.

"Oh, yes please," he said against my lips. His hands fumbled for my shirt.

"Sorry to give you the wrong idea," I said, capturing his hands in mine. "But I have to leave. I have a haircut appointment. And you have errands, too."

He gave a little growl and pulled me closer. "I like your hair long."

"Hartley," I laughed. "I need a trim. Badly. And so you need to wait a few hours, okay? After the Beaumont Ball, I'm all yours."

He flopped his head back against the sofa and sighed. "That sounds like a long few hours. Is this a ploy to skip the ball? Because it won't work."

I reached up to brush my hand against his chin, enjoying the feel of his lazy Saturday whiskers under my fingers. "No way," I promised. "I went to the trouble of shopping for a dress, which is my least favorite activity in the world. You can bet I'll put it on." Sliding off his lap, I retrieved my crutches from the floor and stood up.

He rose to kiss me goodbye. "You are the perfect girl," he said against my lips. "You're hot, but you hate to shop. That dress is gonna look great. *On my floor.*" I laughed, and he smoothed my hair down over my shoulders. "I really do like it long. I wasn't just saying that."

"Me too. But chlorine has burnt the ends, and I'm getting a trim. See you later?" I kissed him one more time.

"Later..." he said, sitting back down on the couch, "is better than never."

"That's the spirit." I put my pocketbook straps over both shoulders, opened the door and crutched out into the hallway.

After pulling the door shut behind me, I turned around. A man stood in front of Hartley's door, as if he had just knocked, and was waiting for a response. "Excuse me," I said. "Are you looking for...?" He turned to face me, and I sucked in my breath.

Because Hartley really did look a lot like his father.

It took me a minute to speak. I was too busy taking in the height of him, and the brown, wavy hair. He had the same full mouth as his son, and the same well-proportioned nose. Only the eyes were truly different. This man's were blue, and not nearly as warm as Hartley's.

"Do you know where he is?" the stranger asked, his voice quiet.

I nodded, finding my voice again. "Just one second. Don't go anywhere."

As I opened the door to my room again, crutching back inside, Hartley said, "Did you miss me already, beautiful?" Then he saw my face. "What's the matter?"

Closing the door behind me, I leaned over the couch, whispering. "Your father is standing in the hallway."

His eyes went wide with shock. "Are you sure?"

"I'm positive."

Hartley jumped off the couch. "Shit. Right now?"

"Did you get a response to your letter?"

He shook his head.

"Wow. So this is it?"

He shrugged, his eyes still wide.

"Maybe it's easier this way, not having to think about it first."

He let out a gust of air. Then he looked down at himself, doing a quick inventory. He was wearing jeans and a Red Sox T-shirt, and bright orange sneakers.

"You are *great*, Hartley," I whispered. "And unless you tell me not to, I'm going to open this door now. You can talk to him in here, okay?"

Hartley glanced around my room as if seeing it for the first time. Then he nodded again. I don't know if he was doing the same math that I was — Hartley's unmade bed would be a more awkward meeting place than my little common room. I watched him take a deep breath. I turned the knob, and Hartley swung it wide open for me. I whispered into his ear, "I love you so much." I turned to walk out, but Hartley grabbed my hand. And even as his father turned to watch us, he pressed a kiss to my forehead before letting me go.

I took one more look at the man who had come to see him. He was staring at Hartley, his face flushed, his body still. "Why don't you come in," I heard Hartley say before I pushed open the outer door and left McHerrin.

— Hartley

For a long minute, neither of us said anything. He sat down on Corey's sofa, and I pulled Dana's desk chair over to sit across from him. I'd seen pictures of him on the Internet many times before, but this was different. I never thought I'd breathe the same air as this man. And it was hard work getting past my shock.

I think it was hard work for him, too.

So we stared at each other for a couple of minutes. "Adam," he said eventually. He cleared his throat. "I'm sorry. I know my apology comes ridiculously late. And I don't really expect you to understand. But I came here to say it anyway."

All I could do at that point was nod. Now that he was here, sitting in front of me, angry questions filled my head. *How could you? Do you know how hard my mother works? Do you know how many kids taunted me? We protected you, and I don't even know why.*

If I opened my mouth, the dam would break. So I sat there, silently, swallowing the bitter taste in my throat. Even so — and I'm ashamed to admit it — a part of me still wanted him to like me. Wasn't that pathetic? After all this time, I was still hoping to make a good impression.

He tapped nervous fingers on the leg of his jeans. They were a dark, expensive color, the sort of thing Stacia would pick out. He had on sleek black shoes, and a jacket which probably cost as much as my mother's car.

"So, I'm getting a divorce," he said suddenly.

"I saw those headlines," I admitted. It's not like I wanted him to know I'd been cyber-stalking him over the years. But his divorce had hit the news right after I'd sent my letter. Anyone could have seen it.

"Well, I didn't lay hands on your letter for a few weeks. You sent it to Connecticut, and I've been staying in the city."

I nodded again, trying to focus on what he was saying. But, seriously, sitting there was like having some kind of out-of-body experience. I couldn't stop staring at him, noticing all the little ways we looked alike. His eyebrows were unruly like mine.

"My wife — my ex-wife — she described the envelope to me, told me who it was from. And that's when I told her about you."

"Told her?" The words came out of my mouth as a squeak.

He nodded. "She never knew about you. I made a lot of mistakes, Adam. But last month I told her anyway, even though she'd already left me. Keeping secrets was never the right strategy. It only took me twenty years to figure that out."

For some reason, that struck me as funny, and I cracked a smile.

"What?" he asked.

"Nothing. It's just...I thought I was slow."

At that, my father smiled too. But his was sad. "Anyway, I waited another month to see you. Because I didn't want your name to end up in the articles about my divorce. I didn't want some reporter deciding that one thing had to do with the other. You don't need that kind of bullshit attention." He leaned back on Corey's couch, crossing one foot over his knee. "And I haven't told my kids about you yet, Adam. Because I've pasted them with so much of my other shit lately."

And that's when I snapped a little bit. It was probably the casual way he'd said *my kids*. The angry response just leaped out of my mouth. "Since I'm already used to being pasted with your shit, what's the rush, right?"

First, my father looked startled. Then his sad grin came back. "That's fair."

But I shook my head. "No, it's just…" I took a deep breath and let it out. "I didn't ask you to meet me so that I could yell at you." But even as I said it, I realized I didn't have any idea what I expected. I'd always wanted a normal father, but when you're twenty-one, maybe the expiration date for having one was long passed.

"Adam, it would be weird if you *weren't* angry at me. I knew that when I drove up here."

"You took me by surprise."

"I know it. But some things just can't be done on the phone." He shifted uncomfortably. "I have three younger children. The boys — Ryan and Daniel — are eleven and nine, and my daughter Elsa is seven."

Ryan. Daniel. Elsa. "That was the hardest part," I blurted out.

"What was?"

"Having brothers who didn't know I exist." I'd seen them that time in Stacia's neighborhood. I'd told Corey that I didn't get a good look at them, and that was true. But it was burned into my brain, anyway. I could see one brother's arm cocked over his head, and the other running across that perfect lawn to receive the pass. I'd never felt more like an outsider than I did right then.

"All right. I'll tell them when I see them next weekend."

I shook my head, because it occurred to me that I was being selfish. "You know, none of this is their fault. So don't worry about it."

My father leaned forward. "No, you were right the first time. Keeping secrets hasn't worked out for me. I'll tell them, and they'll be surprised for about ten minutes. And after that, you'll be like a rock star." He smiled again, and it was one hundred percent genuine. I could see that just thinking about his kids lit him up. "Seriously. An older brother who plays hockey? You'll have a rabid fan club. Be careful what you wish for."

I rubbed my knee, thinking about how long it had been since I was on skates.

"You didn't get to play this year?"

"Nope. I broke my leg in two places."

"That must have sucked."

I shrugged. "Yeah, it did. But I'm okay now. And I met a great girl." It wasn't lost on me that Corey and I might never have crossed paths if it weren't for the injury. I might still be in the middle of the world's most pathological relationship with Stacia.

My shit would not have been shoveled.

"We could go to a Rangers game, all of us," my father said.

I quirked an eyebrow at him. "The Rangers, huh?"

He surprised me by chuckling. "Who's your team?"

"The Bruins, of course. The Rangers are sissy men."

"Good to know," he said, his shoulders relaxing a bit. "Good to know."

— *Corey*

Needless to say, my two hours at the salon and running errands were excruciating.

I spent the whole time trying to imagine how their very first conversation would sound. And I couldn't decide if I was irritated with Hartley's father for just dropping in like that. Was it better to show up unannounced, or never to show up at all?

The day was warm for April, and I worked up a

sweat on the way home. I'd had my new braces for a month already, and I was getting around on them pretty well. Grudgingly, I had to admit that the new technology was pretty amazing. I still had to use forearm crutches, but I was truly walking on my legs now, not just swinging them like stilts. Stairs were so much easier, and I rarely used my wheelchair anymore, except at home in our suite.

When I finally got back to my room, I found a note on our couch.

Callahan — I have so much to tell you. But I've borrowed Stacia's car to drive home to talk to my mom. It had to be done. I will absolutely be back by 8 p.m. — so put on that dress.
Love you, H.

The suspense was killing me, of course. But I would have to be patient. I texted him: *Drive safe, DON'T SPEED. Love you. C.*

I went to dinner in the dining hall with Dana and Daniel, who were pumped up to go to the Beaumont Ball together. It had taken Daniel two months to get up the courage to ask Dana out. Now that they'd been dating a couple of weeks, and I hoped to see Daniel do the walk of shame from our suite tomorrow morning. I'd been stockpiling taunts for tomorrow's brunch, just in case.

But tonight I was so distracted I could barely follow their conversation.

"Is everything okay, Corey?" Dana asked me after the third time I failed to answer a simple question.

"Hmm? Yes. I'm fine."

"Where's Hartley?" she asked. "You two aren't fighting, are you?"

I shook my head. "He went to see his mom for a

couple of hours. His...there's a family thing he's dealing with today. He said he'd be back in time for the ball."

Dana looked at her watch. "Let's go get ready. I can make your nails match your dress."

I made a face. "Sounds fussy."

"Tonight you're not a jock, Corey," she said. "Tonight you're a party girl."

"If you say so," I sighed. Honestly, I didn't care one way or another, as long as my jock made it back to me in one piece.

"You're not going to tell me what's wrong with Hartley, are you?" Dana pried. I couldn't see her, because my eyes were closed. But I could feel her breath on my face as she stroked shadow onto my eyelids.

"I'm sorry," I said. "It's not my story to tell. But nobody is sick or dying, I swear. It's just family drama."

"Well that's good," Dana said, and I wasn't sure if she meant Hartley or her makeup job. "Open your eyes and take a look."

I did. And when she moved out of my view in the mirror, it was almost as if another girl looked back at me. I'd never been a fan of makeup, and after my accident I'd fallen out of the habit of wearing any. The girl — no, the *woman* in the mirror was a more glamorous, stylish one than I usually saw there. Dana had promised not to overdo it, and she'd kept her word. But her artistry seemed to bring my face into sharper focus. The gold-brown color of the eye shadow complimented my hair, which was still sleek and curled under at the ends from my salon visit.

But the dress was my favorite part of the whole ensemble. Dana had picked it out, of course, and she'd outdone herself. It was red, and long. (Dana had called it a maxi dress, whatever that meant.) The design was incredibly simple — it widened gently from a tank-style top to a swirl of silk near my feet. The uninterrupted sweep of fabric hid my braces, giving me back a sleek shape that I hadn't seen in a mirror in over a year.

"Wow," Dana said. "Hartley is going to faint. If he ever turns up."

I couldn't stop looking. When was the last time I'd looked in a mirror without critical thoughts? A long time. An eternity. And I knew in my heart that the dress and the makeup didn't really change me. But it did give me a reason to pause and study myself, to celebrate all the visible parts of me that were whole and well — the flush of my healthy skin, my grown-out hair. The mirror was really very friendly to me, yet I'd been holding it in such contempt.

"Do you like it?" Dana whispered.

I knew she was referring to her makeup job, but she might as well have been asking about my whole life. "I do," I told her. "I really do."

Just after eight, my phone chirped with a text from Hartley. *On my way. So sorry.*

I replied, *Don't text and drive! Take all the time U need. I'm heading over there with D&D.*

During the two hours since we'd left it, the Beaumont dining hall had been transformed. The largest tables had been removed, making space for a five-piece band and a dance floor. Candlelight flickered on the remaining tables. Couples danced in the center of the room, or stood talking in clusters around the edges.

I couldn't help but watch the door, so I didn't see Bridger sneak up on me. Before I could protest, he grabbed me around the waist and whirled me around in a circle before setting me down again. "Who are you, and what have you done with Callahan?" he asked, handing back my crutches which had slid to the floor.

"Um, thanks?" I'd gotten versions of that compliment about a dozen times in half an hour. It was all very flattering, but I was starting to wonder if it didn't mean that I should make a little more effort on a regular basis.

"Seriously, you look amazing," he said. "Where the hell is Hartley? If he stood you up, I'll break his balls."

"No need," I said. "He's on his way. He'll be here any minute." Bridger frowned, but I didn't offer any more details. "Aren't you going to introduce me to your date?" An unfamiliar buxom blond hovered behind him. I'd never seen Bridger with any girl more than one night in a row. He seemed to go through them like tissues.

"Of course! This is…" he cleared his throat.

"Tina," she said.

"Hi Tina!" I offered my hand quickly, trying to cover Bridger's gaffe. "Nice to meet you."

"A pleasure," she said stiffly.

"Don't let me keep you two from dancing," I said.

Tina tugged on Bridger's hand, and he raised his eyebrows to me. I think he felt rude walking off to dance when I couldn't really follow them. "Go on," I whispered.

Bridger kissed me on the cheek before leading his date onto the dance floor. I watched them for a few minutes. Bridger was a good dancer, and it made me guess that Hartley probably was too. Neither one of them had many inhibitions, that was for sure.

I smiled to myself when Hartley finally skated through the door, his head swiveling left and right, looking for me. I could see that he'd run home to change, but hadn't spent much time there. He'd donned khakis and a button-down shirt, but both could have used either an iron or at least a little of the old hang-in-the-steamy-bathroom-while-you-shower treatment. And his tie had been hastily tied.

No lie, he was still the most handsome guy in the room. By a long mile.

My smile grew as I watched him. Standing up a little straighter, I waited for him to find me in the crowded room. Unfortunately, Stacia found him first. I saw her sashay over to him. From his pocket he withdrew something that must have been her car keys. I watched him thank her, and then kiss her on the cheek quickly.

The whole time, his eyes never stopped sweeping the room. Looking for me.

Over here, I mentally coached him. Then his eyes flicked towards me, drifting past. Then he did a small double-take before his gaze landed on me. Even as his face lit with the most beautiful smile, he was weaving past bodies and chairs, rushing in my direction.

I expected him to sweep me into his arms, but instead he pulled up short. "*Damn*, Callahan," he said, staring. "I mean...wow." He took a step closer. "I'm so sorry to be late, I..."

"Shh," I said, putting my fingers on his lips. "You're not even very late." I straightened his collar.

"Sure, but," he looked down at himself and chuckled. "I talked you into coming to this thing, and I meant to do it right. I was supposed to pick up my suit at the dry cleaner's. But they're closed now." He stepped closer to me, slipping his hands over the silk on my ribcage. "Damn, you're beautiful," he said. Then he kissed me on the lips, in front of God and everybody.

I let him.

The band began to play a slow song, and Hartley pulled back, smiling. "Here we go! Lose the crutches." Hartley put his hands on my hips. I leaned forward on both feet, locking the knees of my new braces. Stashing the crutches on a chair behind me, I looked down, stepping carefully onto first one and then the other of Hartley's shoes. "There you go," he whispered in my ear. Taking small steps, he slid backwards into the crowd of dancers, my feet on his. Just like we'd practiced.

And there we were, slow dancing together, our arms around each other. If anyone had been watching us, they might not even have noticed that without Hartley stabilizing me, I couldn't stand on my own.

"Now this is what I sped home for," he said, kissing my hair.

"This is great," I agreed. "But if you don't tell me *right now* what happened with your father, I'm going to burst."

He chuckled. "Yes ma'am. But it will take me hours to tell you everything."

"I have the time."

His nose tickled my ear. "I'm going to tell you every last thing, I swear. But my head is still spinning, and I'm not sure where to start."

"He must have gotten your letter."

Hartley's lips brushed my cheek. "He did. But it came right in the middle of his divorce."

I looked up at Hartley. "I read about that. He was married for fifteen years?"

"Yeah," he said. "When I read that article, it made me wonder if he got the letter at all."

"But he did."

Hartley nodded. "His wife...ex-wife, whatever, she told him over the phone —'you got an envelope from someone named Adam Hartley, it's marked personal and confidential.' And that's when he told her about me."

My head jerked back as I looked up at him, and it destabilized us for a second. My foot slipped off Hartley's shoe and onto the floor. "She never knew?"

He shook his head. "But he said that when she told him about the envelope, he didn't even hesitate. He said that if he'd always been straight-up with her about that and a lot of other things, maybe he wouldn't have gotten a divorce at all."

"Ouch," I said. "Sounds like he has quite a bit of shit to shovel."

Hartley's hands skimmed my back. "I got the impression today that he needs a bulldozer and a back-loader for all his shit. But it sounds like he's working on it."

"What did you talk about?"

"A little of everything. We spent about an hour and a half, I think. And I'm going to see him again next month."

"Wow."

"I couldn't stop staring at him, honestly. It was like looking in a funhouse mirror — he looked just like me, but different."

"Hartley, I'm sure he couldn't stop looking at you, either. You're yummy."

He snorted. "You've got it bad, Callahan."

The slow dance ended, and the band began to play something faster, a swing dance. We needed to leave the dance floor. Hartley held out both his hands and walked backwards, and I pushed down on them, using Hartley for my crutches. My gait on the new braces would never be graceful. But it was a hell of a lot more natural than it had been before.

"Whoa, sorry!" Hartley said suddenly. He had bumped into Dean Darling while walking me backward.

The dean looked at us and then did a double take. "Miss Corey Callahan!" he exclaimed. "I did not expect to find you on the dance floor — which is yet another ridiculous error on my part."

"I didn't expect me there either," I admitted. "But I was told the Beaumont Ball was nonnegotiable."

"As it should be," the dean smiled at us. "Carry on."

Hartley tucked me to his side, lining up his hip against mine. He wrapped one hand around my waist, and the other he brought across his own body and in front of mine, where I leaned on it. We had a few new tricks, he and I. It was more fun to go to parties than it ever had been before, with my personal spotter to lean against. And nibble on.

Bridger gestured to us from a doorway that I'd never seen open before. "What's over there?"

"A terrace," Hartley said. "Want to walk out there for a minute?"

"Sure," I reached for my crutches, but Hartley stopped me. "Walk with me. I won't abandon you." He stood up in front of me, his hands by his sides, bent back to reach for me. I took both of them in my own hands, pressing down on him for support. It was only about fifteen feet to the door. I had a little trouble with the threshold, which was a stone ridge in the floor. So Hartley picked me up by the hips, made a half-turn and set me down on the other side. Then he grasped me around the waist, giving me his other hand for support, and we inched forward towards our friends in the darkness.

When I looked up, there was an unfamiliar guy

watching me, a quizzical expression on his face. "I'm not wasted," I said to him. "This is a permanent condition."

"Uh, sorry," he said, breaking his stare.

I shook my head. "I'm just having a little fun with you." Then I heard the telltale sound of a popping cork, and caught a flash of Stacia's blond tresses as she turned around, a bottle in her hand. "Colin, the glasses?"

The guy who'd been staring at me held up a stack of little clear plastic cups, and Stacia began pouring a small serving into each glass. Hartley held me to his side, and I sniffed the April evening. Spring was coming. It seemed impossible to believe, but my first year at Harkness would be over in six weeks.

Colin passed cups around, but when he offered them to Hartley and I, Hartley declined. There weren't any chairs outside, and it took all our free hands to keep me standing.

"Hang on," Bridger said. He disappeared behind us, then reappeared a moment later with a dining hall chair, which he set down behind me.

"Thanks, Bridge," I said, sitting.

Stacia came over then, with two cups for us. "You look great tonight," she said.

When I realized she was talking to me, I was almost too stunned to respond. "Thanks," I stammered. "So do you. But that goes without saying."

It was dark. But I swear she winked at me.

Bridger raised his glass in the air. "To contraband," he said. Drinking wasn't allowed at the college-sponsored ball.

"To contraband," everyone agreed.

The champagne hit my tongue with a smooth bubbly tang. It was spectacular. I tugged on Hartley's hand, and he leaned down to me. I whispered in his ear.

"Stacia complimented me, and your father showed up all on the same day. I fear we've reached The End of Days."

He kissed my neck. "Did you notice? This is really good hooch."

"I did. Remember what happened the last time we drank expensive champagne?"

"I was just thinking the same thing," Hartley whispered, his mouth ghosting over my ear.

"Where've you been all day, Hartley?" Bridger asked, putting a hand on Hartley's shoulder.

"If I gave you a thousand chances, you wouldn't guess right," he said.

"Well now I have to know."

"Bridge, I'm not ready to tell the whole story. But I will say this — I drove a check out to my mom today, for twelve years of back child support."

"What?" I yelped. "You didn't mention that."

"Patience. I told you it would take me hours."

"Whoa, dude." Bridger drained his wine. "You're right. I was never guessing that. So who is he?"

Hartley shook his head. "It's messy for him. We're taking baby steps, here."

"That doesn't sound like a baby step," I said the next time Hartley leaned down to me.

He scooped me up and sat on the chair, with me in his lap. I wrapped my bare arms around him, and he rubbed them. "You feel cold."

"I'm okay."

Hartley whispered into my ear. "The check was for a quarter of a million dollars."

"My God! He just showed up with it?"

Hartley nodded, his nose skimming my face. "He had his lawyer calculate how much he owed. There's a formula the state uses."

"And he just said…here? This belongs to you?"

"Yup. I told you he was shoveling his shit with a bulldozer. So I took it to my mom, and of course she said, 'I won't take the money.'"

"What?" I yelped. "She *has* to take it. Then she can quit that awful job."

"It took me two hours to convince her. That's why I was late. But now she can go back to school. She's thinking about becoming a nurse."

The idea made me bounce with happiness. "She'll be amazing. Hey — I'll show her how to remove an IV."

"God, I love you," he chuckled, holding me close. "You crazy, brave, sexy thing. I thought about you all day today. Because if it weren't for you, I wouldn't have met him."

I snuggled closer. "That's not true. You might have gotten there a different way."

Instead of arguing the point, he kissed me. "Come on," he said. "We have to dance again."

"Why?"

"Because I dragged you to a dance. And so we'll dance, at least once more. Before I take this dress off of you."

"That sounds like fun," I whispered.

His breath was hot in my ear. "Which part?"

"All of it," I answered.

And it was.

The End

Thank you!

Thanks for reading *The Year We Fell Down*. I hope you enjoyed it!

Would you like to know when my next book is available? You can sign up for my new release e-mail list at **www.sarinabowen.com**, follow me on twitter at **@sarinabowen**, or like my Facebook page at **http://facebook.com/authorsarinabowen**

Reviews help other readers find books. I appreciate all reviews, whether positive or negative.

Ready for More?

You've just read the first full-length book in the *Ivy Years* series. The next book is *The Year We Hid Away*, and it's Bridger's story. Hint: his family troubles will only get more complicated. His junior year at Harkness will be the hardest of his life. The only bright spot is meeting Scarlet, who understands all too well how family can derail your life.

While Scarlet is hiding something big, Bridger is hiding *someone* small.

To be kept abreast of the publication of *The Ivy Years* series, sign up for my mailing list at www.sarinabowen.com/contact

About the Author

Sarina Bowen is a Vermonter whose ancestors cut timber and farmed the north country since the 1760s. Sarina is grateful for the invention of indoor plumbing, espresso products and wi-fi during the intervening 250 years. On a few wooded acres, she lives with her husband, two boys, and an ungodly amount of ski and hockey gear.

Sarina is the author of *Coming in From the Cold*, published by Harlequin.

CPSIA information can be obtained at www.ICGtesting.com
Printed in the USA
LVOW05s1508250914

405880LV00023B/1398/P